STRAWBERRY KISSES

CHARLIE NOVAK

For Ceri and the Thursday night pole crew. Thanks for the laughs, the bruises, and the confidence.

CHAPTER ONE

Patrick

THERE WAS something calming about the chaos of a kitchen in the middle of service.

It sounded like madness with Aaron shouting somewhere and the hustle and bustle of chefs and servers moving in a calculated dance. The sizzle of pans on the burners, the continuous hum of the ovens, the clatter of crockery, and Antoni and Oli's arguing and off-pitch singing from the pot-wash room. It was all familiar and comforting.

The pastry kitchen was, for the moment, a tiny bit quieter, but that was because we were only thirty minutes into service, and nobody had ordered pudding yet. Not that there wasn't plenty to do. I'd been chopping fruit and whipping cream for miniature pavlovas for the past hour. Deseeding twenty passion fruit and another ten pomegranates was a pain in the ass and had taken a ton of time.

One day I'd get a sous-chef on service with me who I'd be able to ask to do it. Even though we'd been open for four years, The Pear Tree was still a growing restaurant, and I wasn't sure adding additional pastry staff would happen anytime soon. When we'd first opened, I'd done everything myself, and on my days off, it had been up to Aaron to assign someone to cover puddings. Now we were lucky enough to have two pastry chefs, so I didn't have to work every weekend, even if Ben and Aaron had had to pry me out of the kitchen at first.

We'd even refitted one of the small, side spaces into a dedicated pastry kitchen. It was barely bigger than a cupboard and hotter than the sun because of the oven, but that didn't matter because it was mine.

Even if I couldn't swing a cat in here without hitting something.

"Patrick," said a cheerful voice from behind me. I turned to see Lucy, one of the waitstaff, grinning at me from the edge of the pastry kitchen. The waitstaff all knew not to set foot in here without my permission, but unlike Aaron, our head chef and one of my best friends, I didn't enforce the rule with violent swearing.

"Hi, Lucy. Busy service?" I kept chopping strawberries as I talked. These days, the task was as natural as breathing.

"Packed, same as normal for a Sunday." She sighed. "I just wanted to warn you that we've got a birthday they didn't warn us about. Someone from the party just asked if we could do a special dessert plate. Any chance?"

I glanced at the little piping bags of chocolate I kept on a plate on top of the oven, which kept them at the perfect temperature. They were full, and I had enough bits to put a birthday plate together—especially since I'd had some warning. The worse thing was trying to do one while also trying to fill ten other pudding orders.

"Sure, just let me know when you want it. I'll do it now and put it to the side. Any allergies?"

"Not that they told me. You're a star, Chef."

"It's fine," I said, scooping the diced strawberries into a tub and tipping the stalks into the nearby compost bin. "Just go grab me a couple of the rectangular glass plates from the storage rack. I don't have any in here."

Lucy disappeared, and I began looking in my two little under-the-counter fridges to see what I could easily put on the plate, hoping I wasn't going to have to make the trip down the corridor to my walk-in fridge. I tried to get everything in here before service so I didn't have to go back and forth all the time, but it didn't always happen the way I'd planned. There was nothing that spelt a recipe for disaster like a busy, narrow corridor and a large tray of desserts.

Luckily, I had enough cream and fruit to make an extra miniature pavlova as well as a slice of lemon tart I could cut in half, a couple of macaroons, and a couple of small brownie bars. Add a little decoration and it would be good to go.

When I looked up, I noticed Lucy had left me a stack of plates on the silver service rack that formed half the wall onto the corridor between the kitchens. I grabbed one and plated up the desserts. I'd add the final touches, including 'Happy Birthday' piped in chocolate, when Lucy came to collect it. Then the front of house staff could add one of the sparkler candles to it before it went out.

As soon as I finished the dessert plate, I looked up to see my first ticket of the day sitting on the service rack, tucked into a little holder. Two crème brûlée—nice and simple to kick things off. I grabbed my blow torch and the golden caster sugar, plus two vanilla and raspberry brûlées out of the fridge, carefully caramelising the sugar into a perfect crispy shell. I added a little fruit to each plate and popped them onto the pass. Two seconds later, Callum appeared to collect them, giving me a half-smile before calling, "Thanks, Chef" as he bustled out of the kitchen.

After that, things settled into the regular rhythm of a Sunday lunch service.

It was a busy one, as Lucy had said, but nothing unusual happened. We had a lot of puddings ordered, and at one point I thought I was going to run out of lemon tart, but that was about it. It gave me a chance to start thinking about the week ahead, and what I wanted to make.

I was lucky because, as the head pastry chef, I got the final say in what we made, and Aaron, who was also co-owner with Ben as well as head chef, pretty much gave me free rein to do what I wanted. Not that Darcie, the other pastry chef, really minded. She wasn't long out of culinary college and was still eager to learn. She had a great palette and a creative mind though, and we already worked well together.

My mind ticked back to thinking about next week and next weekend, the first weekend in July. I had a nagging

feeling there was something important happening, but I couldn't remember what it was.

In a quiet moment towards the end of service, I grabbed the huge diary I used to keep notes about what we were serving, and Darcie and I used to leave each other messages, off the windowsill. It was a bit old fashioned, but I still hadn't found anything as useful for keeping track of things like a good old diary the size of a brick. I flicked through until I found the following Saturday and saw neatly printed capitals across the top of the page.

PATRICK OFF. FAMILY PARTY - TAKE CAKE.

Feck. I'd forgotten about the party.

Or rather, I'd shoved it far into the recesses of my mind and pretended it wasn't happening.

It was my parents' fiftieth wedding anniversary and my dad's seventieth birthday, and my family was throwing a giant party to celebrate with the whole of my extended family and a load of friends. They were having the party catered, but they'd made me promise to bring a cake. I wasn't a professional cake decorator by any stretch of the imagination, but I could do a good enough job. My mum had insisted, and because I was a good son and a complete pushover, I'd agreed.

Well, that was one thing to add to my list for the week: find time to make a giant cake. Then find a way to get it all the way to Devon. Maybe Aaron had some sort of cool box I could borrow. Or maybe I could just take it in pieces and finish assembling it in mum's kitchen. That would probably be easiest. I knew my mum wouldn't object.

If I was honest, the cake was the least of my worries about the party.

In the back of my mind, I knew the party meant I would finally have to tell my family I was gay. I was dreading it, which meant I'd put it off for ages. If I didn't tell them before the party, I knew my mum, in the most well-meaning way, would spend the whole weekend dropping hints about having a girlfriend and why I shouldn't use work as an excuse not to meet someone. All of my sisters, except one, were married with kids, and Mum seemed to have given up on Mary. I knew she just wanted me to be happy, but her comments weren't helpful.

I sighed. I really should have told them years ago. Now I had no choice but to do it over Skype… a week before the biggest family event in years.

A crash and the sound of shouting distracted me.

"What the fuck is this fucking bowl doing here?"

I sighed, shaking my head at the sound of Aaron's raised voice.

"Maybe if you hadn't fucking left it there, you wouldn't have fucking knocked it, dickhead!" That was Josh, Aaron's sous-chef.

"I didn't fucking leave it there! Why the fuck would I leave it there? We're on fucking clean down."

"Don't be a wanker, Aaron."

"Fuck off!"

I shook my head because those two idiots had been at each other's throats for four years, and nothing seemed to change. It was like putting two volatile chemicals in a room and expecting them not to explode.

Ben described it as too much ego in one space. I had to agree. Their fighting had put a few new staff members off until they realised that their anger was very rarely aimed at anyone except each other.

There was silence for a moment, but it was loaded. I knew exactly what was coming.

"Fucking wanker. I can't fucking cope with him. I fucking swear, Pads, I'm gonna fucking quit." I looked up from my diary to see Josh leaning on the wall that made up the other side of the kitchen door, bristling with anger. His chef's whites were covered in stains, and his dark eyes glittered. Josh came into my kitchen threatening to quit at least once a week, so this wasn't exactly a surprise.

"No, you're not," I said, putting my knives and boards in a pile to take down to the pot-wash. "You're just letting him get to you again. You like working here."

"No, I fucking don't."

"Then why are you still here? It's been four years. You're good enough to go somewhere else." Josh grumbled under his breath, and I gave him a half-smile. "It's because you like working here, and you don't actually hate Aaron. If you did, you'd have decked him by now."

"I might fucking do that. It would make me feel better," he said, but he looked slightly less angry now. Like the wind had gone out of his sails. I grabbed a plate off the side that had a few bits of brownie on them.

"No, it won't." I held out the plate. "Have some brownie and go calm down. Aaron'll clean up."

"Can you do that?" Josh grinned.

"What? Send you home?" I smiled knowingly.

"Yeah. You know he'll be fucking pissed at you."

"Aaron has never raised his voice at me in four and a half years, and he's not going to start now." I was the only person Aaron had never yelled at. I'd known him too long. It was the same with Ben. Aaron had tried it once, and I'd made it absolutely clear that if he tried it again, he would be without a pastry chef. I may have been quiet and reserved, but that didn't mean I was going to let him walk all over me, especially not in my own kitchen. After that, Aaron had apologised, and he'd never raised his voice at me again. Instead, I'd become the person he vented to and his voice of reason. If I told Aaron he was wrong, he usually accepted it. *Usually*.

"Cheers, Patrick. You're a star." Josh took the plate and wandered off towards the kitchen door, probably to go smoke and calm down. I gave it ten minutes before Aaron was in here grumbling, but in all honesty, I didn't actually mind. Besides, it was nice to have someone to talk to while I cleaned the kitchen. I shook my head, trying to turn my thoughts back to the week ahead and grabbed a pen. I wanted to get a head start on my planning before Aaron's inevitable arrival.

Since it was Sunday, there was no evening service, which meant movie night with my favourite person in the whole world: Connor.

We'd been best friends since we'd first met three years ago, and now I couldn't imagine my life without him. Connor was one of those people who lit up every room he entered with his exuberant energy and radiant smile. Sometimes I wondered why he wanted to be my friend, since we

were the exact opposite in so many ways, and yet, we just seemed to work together. We'd fallen into an odd friend-ship and had gotten closer over the years.

Now we spent every Sunday evening, at the *very* least, together—making dinner, watching films, and chatting for hours. It was always the best part of my week.

Six o'clock couldn't come soon enough.

CHAPTER TWO

Connor

PATRICK'S HOUSE was empty when I got there, so I assumed he was stuck at the restaurant. Probably trying to stop Aaron and Josh from murdering each other. Again. One day, I was going to suggest he let them duke it out with pugil sticks like in that nineties show, *Gladiators.* If nothing else, it would be highly entertaining.

I stepped out of my car, grabbed my bag and the supermarket bag for life beside it, and headed for the back door, locking my little car behind me. Since Patrick had always been a little unreliable about getting back to his house on time, he'd given me a key for the back door, insisting it was easier for me to just go in rather than waiting in the car.

Patrick had handed me the key after a memorable evening when he'd been nearly an hour late and had arrived to find me loudly singing along to Beyonce on his front doorstep. He'd been utterly distraught at leaving me so long, but I hadn't minded. I never minded when it was Patrick. His neighbours had given me slightly funny looks though.

I flicked on the lights, set the bags on the kitchen side, and waited for the customary yowling to greet me. It took all of twenty seconds for Patrick's monster of a cat, President Whiskers, aka Whiskey or sometimes The President, to stalk around the kitchen door and meow pitifully at my feet as if trying to convince me he'd never been fed in his entire life. I knew this was an obvious lie because I'd known Whiskey since Patrick had brought him home as a tiny, straggly kitten. The President had been pulling this shit since day one.

Neither of us had quite expected him to get so big though. I was convinced there was definitely Maine Coon somewhere in his parentage, but since Patrick had rescued him from the local Cats Protection who'd found him and his litter mates dumped in a box, nobody was quite sure of his breed.

The President yowled at my feet again, stretching his enormous paws up and resting them on my hips.

"I can't pick you up, Whisks. You're almost as big as me," I said, affectionately scratching his ears and listening to him purr. It was pretty much the same noise as a jet engine. "Come on. I'll feed you." Mostly so I could make dinner without fear of tripping over Whiskey.

I tipped some biscuits and a pouch of wet food into his bowls, watching with a warm feeling in my chest as he began eating. Technically, The President was Patrick's cat, but since I spent so much time here, I couldn't help thinking he was a little bit mine as well. He was the one I came and cuddled when I was having a shitty day and needed a little bit of non-human comfort. Patrick always said I was his friend for his cat more than anything else, and while that wasn't really the case, there was a grain of truth to it. I'd always loved animals, but my landlord was strictly anti-pet no matter how much money I offered or how nicely I asked. I had claimed Whiskey as my step-pet so I could spoil him rotten.

With the cat distracted, I unpacked the shopping bag and flicked the oven on. I wasn't on par with Patrick when it came to cooking, but I could knock up a mean baked mac and cheese, which was exactly what I needed today. And since it was a Sunday and Patrick wasn't back yet, I assumed he'd need it too.

I'd spent most of my day at the dance studio where I taught, supervising an open-practice pole session and doing some training of my own. Pole competition season was upon us, and this year I'd set my goals higher than ever before. Not only did I want to win—that was a given— but there were several competitions I wanted to enter at the highest level, and for that I needed the best routines I could put together. Especially because only the top five to ten entries were invited to compete in the live final. I usually did very well when I competed, not to brag or anything, but I couldn't afford to get complacent. That wouldn't earn me any prizes.

I'd been dancing for as long as I could remember. Mostly ballet with some jazz, tap, ballroom, and modern thrown in for good measure. My mum had thought it would be good for me, so I'd started baby ballet as soon as I could walk. I'd grown up doing nothing but dancing, and I'd wanted to join a ballet corps. But considering the ideal height for a male ballet dancer was six foot, and I'd barely cracked five-three, I'd quickly put that dream aside.

I'd discovered pole dancing while browsing YouTube at seventeen and had been immediately transfixed. The tiny Essex town I'd grown up in didn't have a pole studio, but the nearest city, an hour away, did. So every week, I'd gotten on the train and taken myself to a class, then gotten the train back home afterwards. As soon as I'd passed my driver's test and could borrow my mum's battered little car, I'd started taking myself up to the city two or three times a week. I'd done my degree in ballet education at the Royal Academy of Dance in London because I hadn't been quite ready to give it up, but I'd kept taking pole classes around my other coursework. They were actually very complementary, which sounded strange when you said it out loud, but the strength, grace, and flexibility flowed easily from one to the other.

Pole just allowed me to embrace my sexuality and queerness in a way ballet never had.

I flicked on Patrick's Bluetooth sound system and connected my phone, throwing on Lady Gaga's *Chromatica* and dancing my way around the kitchen as I put the pasta on to boil and began making a roux for the white sauce. Baked mac and cheese deserved more than just packet mix. I also put some little bits of pancetta on a tray to crisp up because I felt like being a fancy bitch. Patrick and I deserved it.

I wiggled my hips and swayed to the music, humming lyrics to myself while half wondering if any of the songs had the perfect tempo for the routine of my dreams. I'd already picked my music for this year's routines, but I was always on the hunt for the perfect pole song. So far, it had alluded me, but my insane pickiness might also have had something to do with it.

I was so distracted I didn't hear Patrick's keys in the door or him coming into the kitchen until I looked up to see him standing in the doorway, his customary soft half-smile on his face. My chest twinged because he always looked gorgeous. Even like this when he looked like he was about to drop dead from exhaustion.

"God, you look knackered, babe. Rough day?"

Patrick chuckled. "No. Well, not until the end. The service went fine. How was your day?"

I gave him a little smile and shook my head. That was the thing about Patrick, he always thought about everyone except himself. He was the sort of person who'd give you anything you asked for and never complain. He was utterly sweet and selfless, and I loved that about him.

"Mine was fine. Just open practice to supervise, and nobody managed to injure themselves, which is always a bonus." I drained the pasta, mixing it into the thick, rich cheese sauce I'd made, throwing the pancetta in alongside it. "What happened at the end of the day? I'm guessing something major since it's already half seven and you were supposed to be done at six."

Patrick perched on the edge of one of the kitchen chairs looking simultaneously distracted and dead on his feet. He was wearing black jogging bottoms and a dark hoodie over a white T-shirt. The restaurant laundered his chef's uniforms, and while I adored the way he looked in them, there was something extra soft about Patrick dressed like this. His honey-blond curls sticking out slightly, his cheek smeared with something he clearly hadn't realised was there, his grey eyes warm and tired.

"Well, I'd have been done quicker if Aaron and Josh hadn't kept trying to kill each other." He let out a small laugh and shook his head. "I swear, one day I'm going to end up breaking up a fistfight."

"Just let them fuck it out." I fished in the drawer for the grater so I could add more cheese to the top of the mac and cheese. I knew my way around Patrick's kitchen almost better than I knew my own. I looked over my shoulder at Patrick's stunned face. It was like he'd never considered the possibility before. Knowing Patrick, he hadn't. He was so adorably naive sometimes.

"Fuck it out?"

"Yep. Hate sex is a great stress reliever, and they'd probably feel better afterwards." I picked up the nearby block of cheese, which was about two-thirds of the size it had been twenty minutes ago. "Orgasms make everything better."

"Well," Patrick said with a dry chuckle, "as long as they don't do it in the kitchen, I don't mind what they do." He gave a little sigh, and I could see something lingering on his face. There was something else bothering him, but knowing Patrick, he didn't want to worry me.

He'd been exactly the same for the three years I'd known him. Of course, by this point, he should also know that I wasn't going to let it go until I got an answer. He couldn't hide anything from me.

"What's up, babe? Something wrong?"

"It's my parents' wedding anniversary next weekend… and my dad's seventieth birthday," he said slowly, chewing his lip. The soft, lilting Irish note in his voice was suddenly more noticeable. I knew his mum was Irish, and I assumed he'd picked it up from her. "I have to go down to Devon for it and take a cake."

"Oh. Do you need me to watch Whiskey for the weekend?"

"Yeah, but…" Patrick sounded distracted. He looked up at me through his long lashes. "I think I need to tell them I'm gay."

Patrick's words landed, but I didn't actually hear them. Not at first. And when I did, it took me a while to process them. I must have looked like a complete tit standing there staring.

I'd known Patrick for three years, and in the three years I'd known him, he'd never had a boyfriend… or a girl-friend… or any form of romantic partner as far as I was aware. He didn't do hook-ups, and he didn't do casual flings. He was quite private, so I figured he hadn't wanted to share or that he wasn't the sort of person who wanted or needed a relationship. And that had been fine.

It *had* to be fine.

Because there was one teeny tiny sticking point in my friendship with Patrick that I'd been trying to bury for the past three years.

I was hopelessly and irretrievably in love with him.

And when I'd thought he wasn't gay or wasn't interested in dating or sex or anything, that had been fine because I could put my feelings for Patrick into a box, label it "disaster crush", and never, ever look at it again.

But now? Now I was threatening to vomit my feelings all over Patrick's kitchen in rainbow glitter. And once you spilt glitter, that shit was never going back in the box.

I was well aware Patrick was still staring at me and that I was still holding the cheese grater in mid-air.

"Oh..." I said, beating the glitter rainbow back so I could try to find words. "Thank you for telling me and for trusting me. Is, um, is there a reason you want to tell them now? Or that you haven't before?"

"Well, I guess... my mum used to talk about me getting married and finding a nice girl, and I kept putting it off with the restaurant starting up and everything, but I can't use that as an excuse anymore. I've always worried because mum's family is Catholic, and I was never sure how she'd take it. She says she just wants me to be happy, which is sweet, but I still wasn't sure." He paused, and I rapidly shoved dinner into the oven so I could forget about it for thirty minutes and focus on Patrick, who looked about two seconds away from passing out. He'd gone the colour of sour milk. "But then a couple of months ago she was talking about something she'd been watching, a film I think, and how the leads had been a gay couple and how nice it was to see that." He looked up at me and chuckled. "I think she might already know, but, um, I think I want to tell her and Da before the party. Just so they know. And my sisters too... Feck, that's a lot of people all at once."

I walked over and took his hand, squeezing it gently. "It's going to be okay. You don't have to say anything if you're not ready, honey."

"No, I want to. We've got a family Skype tomorrow to sort out the last few details for the party, so I thought I'd do it then. At least... at least then if they don't want me to come down, they can tell me."

A flicker of pain caught in my chest. "Do you think they would?"

"I don't think so. I mean, I'm pretty sure Mary's best friend is a drag queen from the pictures I've seen on Twitter. But it's hard." He smiled up at me, and I squeezed his hand tighter. I'd never really met Patrick's family, but he talked to me about them all the time, and honestly, they sounded slightly insane but in the best way. I knew he loved them fiercely, even if he didn't see them that often.

"Was it hard for you to tell your mum?" he asked quietly.

"A little," I said, then I grinned. "But I think she already knew. I mean, I threw a temper tantrum at four because I couldn't wear a tutu like the girls in my class for the dance school showcase. And I was wearing eyeshadow at seven. I mean, that all sounds horribly stereotypical, but look at me." I gestured to the flowing, pink off-the-shoulder top I'd found in the River Island women's section and my skin-tight ripped jeans. "So honestly, I don't think my mum even blinked when I finally told her when I was thirteen. She just told me she loved me, asked me to stop wiping fake tan on her nice white towels, and helped me put posters of the Jonas Brothers up in my bedroom."

"Fake tan?" Patrick asked with a wry grin and raised eyebrow.

"It was Essex in the early noughties. Everyone had bad fake tans, glittery lip-gloss, and the thinnest eyebrows known to humankind."

Patrick snorted. "Well, I'm glad your eyebrows grew back in."

"So am I. It was touch-and-go for a while. I know at least one person who now has to draw them on because she over plucked them so much." I squeezed his hand again. "I'm sure it's going to be fine. Your family sounds a little crazy from what you've told me, but they obviously love you."

"Thanks. You're the best."

"I know." I leant down and pressed a kiss to his cheek. "Why don't you go grab a quick shower while this cooks, and then we can watch a movie? Mr. President and I can take up our positions on the sofa until then."

Whiskey yowled in confirmation, appearing to rub his head up and down Patrick's leg in a gesture that was a combination of love and a demand for food.

"No, you've been fed," I said. "Don't tell lies."

Whiskey meowed grumpily and stalked off towards the living room. I'd never met such a vocal and emotional cat before, but then again, Whiskey was a unique being.

"A shower sounds great, and dinner smells amazing. Baked mac and cheese?"

"With pancetta. And at least three-quarters of a block of cheese."

"Thanks, Connor," Patrick said, giving me the same

warm smile that always made my insides melt. It was the smile I'd do anything for.

I watched him head towards the stairs before I scrubbed my face with my hands, very, very glad I wasn't wearing make-up for once. I couldn't tell Patrick he'd just utterly upended my entire universe with one simple sentence, especially because it had clearly been a huge deal for him to share, and I wasn't such a self-centred asshole that I was going to make this all about me.

Even if all I wanted to do was suddenly pour my heart out and tell him how perfect he was.

Not that he'd want a relationship with me, of course. I'd never managed to be very good at them, but maybe it was my choice of man that was the problem. None of my exes had turned out to be relationship material. Fucking, yes. Dating, not so much. Not that I'd minded since they'd all been somewhere on the scale of self-absorbed dickhead to complete wanker, even the ones who'd initially shown some promise. Heartbreak and I were old friends by this point. I should know better than to get too attached to fuckbois.

But this was Patrick… I sighed. No, I was not going there. Patrick did not need this. Especially not now. He had more than enough shit to deal with. I would just keep my mouth closed for once. With superglue if necessary.

CHAPTER THREE

Patrick

"IT'S GOING to be fine. It's going to be fine," I whispered to myself over and over, repeating it like some sort of mantra. Maybe if I told myself enough, I'd start to believe it.

I stared at the laptop on my kitchen table like it was about to bite me. There was still time for me to back out of this call and the party. I could tell everyone I'd gotten food poisoning from bad takeaway. That would work. Or I could just not tell them I was gay. I'd been putting it off for twenty-nine years; it could wait a little longer.

Except, I didn't really want to wait any longer. I'd been wanting to tell them for years now, but I'd never had the right words and it never seemed like the right time. But now I was getting to the point where I wanted to find someone, or at least try. Maybe it was selfish of me to want to tell them now purely because I wanted to find a boyfriend. I'd just thought it would be easier to do it before I actually found someone, but maybe that was the wrong decision. Maybe I should have told them years ago when I'd finally figured it out for myself, rather than waiting another five years to tell anyone.

But before I could linger any more on when or where I might have told my family, the familiar digital ringtone of Skype started echoing through my kitchen, and soon my screen was filled with familiar faces.

I was the youngest of five children, so I had four incredibly lovely but incredibly nosy older sisters. I'd been what you'd call a "surprise", arriving nine years after my sister Mary, by which time my oldest sister, Cara, was already sixteen. My sisters had always viewed me as a combination of baby brother and communal pet project, so despite the fact that I was nearly thirty, they often treated me like I was seven. It was never meant to be mean-spirited though. I just think they forgot their baby brother was a fully grown man sometimes. But since my oldest nephew was already in his early twenties, I got where it came from.

It didn't help that I was soft spoken and a bit of a pushover around them just like my Da. My sisters were largely extroverted. I loved them though, and that was what mattered.

"Patrick!" my second sister, Imogen, cried as soon as my Skype connected. "How're you doing?"

"I'm good, Im. How're all of you?"

"We're good. I can't wait to see you next week. It's been too long since I got a Patrick hug."

"Get in line," said Orla, sister number three. "We all miss our baby brother."

A pang of guilt set in because I hadn't seen them for ages. I'd missed last Christmas because we'd decided to open the restaurant for the first time to do Christmas bookings, since so many people had asked for them. I'd used the excuse that I was the senior pastry chef and it was my job to cover the service. I hadn't wanted Darcie to have to give up her family Christmas since her sister had just had a baby. Secretly, I was happy to work because I wanted to avoid my family while I tried to work out how to tell them the whole *surprise I'm gay* thing.

"How was your weekend?" my mum asked, finally getting a word in edgeways. She still had her Irish brogue, even though she'd lived in Devon for nearly fifty years. It had stubbornly refused to shift into a Devon burr, and as a result, most of my sisters and I had a lilting Irish note to our voices too.

"Fine. We had a busy service yesterday, and I made some plans for the cake," I said. "I think I'm going to bring it down in pieces and assemble it in your kitchen if that's okay?"

"Of course! Just let me know if you need me to get anything."

"Thanks, but I think it will be fine. I was chatting it over with Connor yesterday, and I've made a plan."

"Oh? I thought Connor wasn't working at The Pear Tree anymore?" Mary asked, and I saw her raise an eyebrow in her tiny onscreen picture.

"No, he doesn't. But he came round last night and made dinner, then we watched a movie." We'd ended up curled up on the sofa, his head resting on my chest while we watched some ridiculous romcom that was supposed to be really popular. Connor and I loved watching cheesy movies together, the more ridiculous the better, but this one had really pushed the boundary of possibility. I think that had made me enjoy it even more. It had been a nice way to end the weekend, and the fact that Connor had been so supportive about me telling my family had made many of my worries melt away.

We'd been friends for three years, and even though I'd known Connor was gay, I was still worried he wouldn't accept me or that things would change once I'd told him. I'd felt a slight pang of guilt that I should have told him ages ago because he'd always been open with me, but, again, I'd never been able to find the words. I'd always been afraid that if I said something, it would change everything between us, and that was the last thing I'd wanted. But considering we'd ended up curled up together, the same way we always did, I didn't think things would change at all. Which made my chest lurch for two different reasons I wasn't ready to examine.

Mary hummed, and the conversation moved on to other things—mostly a general catch up and then details about the party. It was taking place in one of the barns on my parents racing yard, and apparently Da and some of the guys he worked with had already spent three days clearing it out. There was going to be a band, a bar, a catering company providing canapes and a huge buffet, plus a wood-fired pizza oven because my mum didn't want people going hungry. Apparently, mum thought she was feeding a thousand people instead of just the couple of hundred or so guests.

Half my brain turned back to the cake, wondering whether I should do something tiered to make sure there was enough or if I should just make a couple of extra cakes that could be cut up to serve. That would certainly be easier than moving several tiers, and I had some large, rectangular cake tins at work I could use. I usually made brownies or large traybakes in them, but they'd do fine. I could probably even borrow them for the weekend. Aaron wouldn't care, and I could give Darcie a heads-up so she knew where they were. We were closed on Mondays, and I'd have them back for Tuesday morning when I needed to start baking for the week.

"Patrick? Did you get that?" Cara's voice pulled me from my thoughts.

"Sorry, I missed that."

"Are you okay?" Imogen asked gently. "You're distracted today. Is something wrong?"

"No, not really." I took a deep breath. Now was as good a time as any, I guessed. "I need to tell you all something." There was a pause, and I looked at my hands rather than the camera. The last thing I needed was to see their faces right now. My heart was racing, and the lump in my throat made it so I could barely get the words out. "I… I'm gay."

My laptop speakers exploded with chatter, and when I finally glanced at the screen, all I saw was a gaggle of smiling faces. I'd sort of tuned out their reactions, mostly because they were so loud, I'd been half-deafened. From what I could pick up, there seemed to be non-stop words of love and support. Relief flooded my system, and I let out a breath that I felt like I'd been holding for years. I'd imagined having this conversation a thousand times with my family, but I'd never quite pictured it happening like this. Everything was going to be okay.

Just like Connor had said it would be.

Until I heard Connor's name and all my thoughts came to a screeching, grinding halt.

"Sorry, repeat that," I said, staring blankly at my screen. This time, I knew I'd missed something important.

"So we're finally going to get to meet Connor then?" my mum asked, a beaming smile on her face.

"I… I…" I couldn't figure out how the two connected. What mental maths had my mother done to connect those points?

"You have to bring Connor," Mary said. "We've heard so much about him! I always wondered if he was your boyfriend, but Orla told me I shouldn't ask."

"Well, I was right," Orla added. "I told you he'd tell us when he was ready. And he obviously is."

"I… I… What?"

"It's okay," Imogen said softly. She'd always been the gentle voice of reason, and out of all my sisters, she was the quietest. "We're so happy you felt like you could finally tell us. We've all thought Connor sounded amazing from the moment you first mentioned him."

Da nodded and spoke for the first time. "Imogen's right. He sounds like a good man"

"We all want to meet him," Mum said. "He's your boyfriend, and he's important to you."

"You have to bring him with you!" Mary added, and the sentiment was echoed around the little screen bubbles.

I stared at them, their words finally sinking into my brain.

Somehow, we'd gone from me telling them I was gay… to them thinking Connor was my boyfriend and demanding that I bring him to the party. How the hell had we gotten there?

"Er, I… I…" was all I could say, but somehow everyone seemed to take it as my agreement. My mum started muttering about changing the sleeping arrangements around while my sisters made a variety of happy noises before the conversation suddenly moved on again.

Shit. How on earth was I going to get out of this?

I was now expected to turn up, not just with a cake, but with a boyfriend. Heck, the cake was the least of my problems right now. I could do that in my sleep. Figuring out how to convince Connor to pretend to me my boyfriend for a whole weekend with my family was going to be a lot harder. I got the feeling that my family thought we'd been dating for a while—which could be anything from a couple of months to a couple of years. But, of course, I couldn't ask that question without opening myself up as the target for a ton of questions, none of which I wanted to deal with right now.

I racked my brain trying to think of the first time I'd mentioned Connor to them. It was probably not too long after we'd first met at the restaurant, nearly three years ago. Connor had picked up a second job as a waiter around his dance teaching where he'd just been part-time, and we'd met on an evening service. He'd been sweet and funny, immediately blowing through all my shy barriers and utterly enchanting me.

There was a reason I'd never had a boyfriend in those three years, and it wasn't just work related. Even though that was the reason I kept telling myself. But it wasn't the truth.

The truth was I'd been hopelessly in love with Connor since about thirty minutes after I'd met him.

Okay, maybe that was a bit strong. But I'd definitely been stunned by him, and that had grown into the most enormous crush, like a many-headed mythological monster. To me, Connor was perfect. Sure, he was bossy and mouthy, and I knew he annoyed people—he'd ranted to me enough times about stupid exes and hook-ups over the years—but that was why I loved him. He knew exactly what he wanted, and he would never change who he was for anyone. Connor never let anything dull his sparkle, and to me, he shined brighter than any star in the sky.

But Connor was never going to want a guy like me.

Maybe that was why I'd never told Connor I was gay. I was just holding onto the stupid idea that maybe one day we'd be together. I'd been putting off him rejecting me for as long as possible, and although he'd accepted that I was gay and had been nothing but supportive, that didn't mean he'd want to date me. I didn't think I was his type. I'd met some of Connor's ex-boyfriends, and they were all the complete opposite of me. I was quiet and soft and round— just a normal bloke, nothing special at all.

I wasn't some chiselled hero who could sweep Connor

off his feet. All I could do was give him hugs when he was sad, watch endless romcoms with him, bake him pastries to make him smile, and be prepared for the day when he met the man of his dreams. I was never going to be the hero of the story. I was just the sidekick, waiting to be forgotten. The Skype call finally wrapped up with a reminder that Mum and Da were expecting Connor and me on Friday afternoon and to let her know if I needed anything. I nodded and smiled because I was too stunned to say anything else.

Afterwards I sat there, staring into space, my thoughts swirling in a nebula of chaos.

CHAPTER FOUR

Connor

"Remember, face down, ass up! You need plenty of tasteful side ass for this spin," I said, a wicked grin on my face as I patted my ass and demonstrated my back-angel spin to my Tuesday night improvers pole class. My class giggled, well used to my comments by now. It was pole; there was always going to be innuendo involved.

At least there was when I was teaching it.

I spun gracefully to the floor, then demonstrated it a couple more times before setting my class loose. I had ten students in total, which I'd found was the maximum number I wanted in a class. It was busy enough that they could cheer each other on, and it covered the cost of my teaching, but it was small enough that I could give everyone some personal attention.

"Point those toes, Ali," I said as I walked past. The class was a mix of genders, ages, and sizes. That was something I loved about pole; it was so inclusive. Everyone could do it, no matter who they were. You didn't even have to be that fit when you started either, although pole would soon help with that. Most people didn't seem to realise just how much strength was involved in throwing yourself around a metal pole, especially when you wanted to get off the floor.

Most people also didn't realise how painful it was either. There was a reason I had very little feeling in my inner thighs these days, and I was always covered in bruises.

We practised the back angel for a few more minutes before I showed them the next part of the flow combo I'd developed for tonight—some gentle floor work with a simple swing onto the pole afterwards.

"No floor humping today?" asked Ianto with a cheeky grin.

"No, we're saving that for the heels workshop next week. Are you signed up?"

"Yeah," Ianto said, wiping down his pole with a nearby cloth. "But you can't laugh. I've never really worn heels before, and I've had to borrow Rhys's to practice in."

Rhys and Ianto were twins who'd started coming to the studio a year ago. They were both complete naturals, but Rhys was a little further along in his pole journey because Ianto had broken his wrist in a motorbike crash nine months ago, which had put his practice on hold. They were both incredibly sexy with mussed dark hair and a variety of tattoos and piercings across their rippling muscles. But I made it a policy *never* to date students. It made things too messy.

Plus, as sexy as they were, they weren't really my type.

I'd done the whole muscled thing before, and it never ended well. I wanted someone who wasn't going to give me intense lectures on his leg-day routine or the protein powder he was using or who tried to get me to go to the gym at five in the morning for two or three hours. Ugh, no thank you!

For one, no matter how early a riser I was, nothing on earth would make me want to get up and go straight into cardio and lifting weights. I was much more of an early morning stretch or yoga person.

And two, I'd rather do the gym my way—with cute patterned vest tops, my rainbow trainers, and Lady Gaga blasting through my headphones. I was definitely not one of those gym gays whose exercise routine was their whole personality, and I didn't want to fuck a guy like that either.

Besides, ninety percent of those guys were alpha tops who wouldn't even consider putting a dick in their ass. And I was not about to give up being vers. From my experience, none of them were *that* good in bed.

"Don't worry," I said. "You don't have to be able to walk in them. You just need to look pretty! The routine is simple, and we'll be using 'No Diggity' if you wanna listen to it beforehand."

"Cheers." Ianto still looked nervous, but I knew he'd be fine. He just needed to let loose and be sexy. It was amazing what a good booty shaking could do for your mood.

"Now, show me your flow," I said, stepping back to watch him. Ianto smiled, taking a deep breath before reaching for the pole.

The rest of the class went smoothly, and when everyone

had stretched and headed home, I finally checked my phone. There were a couple of notifications from Patrick, which wasn't totally unusual because we were always messaging, but the tone of the messages worried me.

PATRICK *I know you're teaching right now, but can you call me when you get home?*
PATRICK *Or when you've finished, whichever is easiest*
PATRICK *I need to ask you something. It's nothing bad though*

The fact that he'd had to say "it's nothing bad" meant it probably was. Although he hadn't tried to call me, so it obviously wasn't a complete emergency. Still, it worried me because Patrick was the furthest thing from overdramatic that I could imagine. We were at opposite ends of the spectrum in that respect. Patrick kept my ass grounded with his reason and logic, and he just laughed when I got dramatic, like I was the most adorable thing in the world.

I pulled my tiny pole shorts off, adjusting my equally tiny underwear before sliding my leggings on and pulling a pale-blue hoodie over my vest top. Then I sank onto the wooden studio floor to pull on my socks and trainers, hitting the Call button as I did so. I'd been debating staying for another hour to do some additional practice, but that wasn't going to happen now. I put my phone on the floor next to me, making sure it was on speaker.

"Hey," Patrick said, sounding both nervous and drained as soon as he spoke. I suddenly remembered he'd been planning to Skype with his family yesterday, and I wondered if something had happened after that. He'd said in his messages the night before that everything had been fine, but that didn't mean something hadn't kicked off since then.

If it had, I'd be getting in my car and driving all the way to Devon to sort this shit out because there was no fucking way I was going to let anyone upset Patrick. Not on my watch. I was small, but my wrath was mighty. As several people had found out in the past.

"Hey, babe." I tried to keep my voice neutral as I answered. "Everything okay?"

"Sort of." He paused, and I heard the clattering of pans.

"Are you at work? I thought you were off tonight?"

"I am… technically. I'm just stress baking." He sighed. "It's fine, honestly."

"It doesn't sound fine, babe." Patrick only stress baked when things were bad. Really bad. "Did something happen with your family? Did they get upset?"

"No, no, it's all fine… more than fine, actually. They were great about it, and it was like I thought. They pretty much all knew. They'd just been waiting for me to bring it up."

"That's fabulous!"

"Mmm." Patrick hummed in a non-committal fashion that was highly suspicious. "Yeah, it's great. It's all great."

That was the most obvious lie I'd heard since fourteen-year-old me had tried to convince my mother my new white bedsheets were orange because something had gotten mixed up with them in the wash.

"Do you want me to come down?" I slipped on my trainers and picked up my phone, flicking it off speaker before I tucked it under my ear. I just had to clean the poles and tidy up, but that wouldn't take me long. Then I'd stick my head in the other studio to tell Levi, who owned Above the Barre, that I was heading off. I could be at The Pear Tree in thirty minutes, and if Patrick was stress baking, he'd be there a while.

"Maybe. Ugh, this is all wrong," he muttered to himself. I just wasn't sure if he was talking about the cake or whatever was going on with him. There was definitely something going on, and I wasn't going home until I'd found out what it was. If Patrick wouldn't tell me over the phone, I was going to make him tell me in person.

The back door to the kitchen of The Pear Tree was still unlocked, despite the fact that evening service was pretty much finished and Tuesday nights were always quiet. I made my way down the cool corridors towards the pastry kitchen. The restaurant was built in an L-shaped building that had once been a coaching inn. One part was a maze of little corridors and tight rooms that had been converted into the kitchens. There was a separate office, staff toilets, and a teeny tiny break room where people could sit between services if they were doing a double and due a break. At the back of the building was a space with three giant walk-in fridges and a freezer. Behind the dining room, the large main kitchen stood on one side of the corridor, and on the opposite side was a separate pot-wash room and the pastry kitchen, plus a small space for crockery and cutlery storage.

Oli was washing the last of some pots, whistling to

himself as he jet-washed a large mixing bowl. It was one of the ones that came from Patrick's stand mixer—the industrial-sized one that sat on the floor just inside the pastry kitchen.

As I reached Patrick's domain, I paused to watch him. He hadn't noticed me as he was too busy laminating pastry —carefully folding rolled out rectangles of butter between layers of pastry dough. Patrick's puff pastry was to die for, and the desserts he made with it were even better. My mouth watered at the thought.

I glanced at the counter beside him, noting a fresh tray of brownies and another of lemon drizzle tray bake he made for afternoon tea. It was something the restaurant offered on Wednesday through Saturday afternoons, and although it was popular, I knew what a pain in the ass it was to prep for. Especially because they still only had two pastry chefs who had to do the whole thing between them. Patrick never complained though, even though I knew it stressed him out. It just wasn't in his nature to make a fuss.

"You know, I think you've got enough cake here to feed the whole of Nottingham, not just the customers."

Patrick jumped, his face frozen in shock as he spun on the spot. "Jesus Christ, Connor," he said, letting out a weak, breathy chuckle. "You scared the hell out of me."

"I'm sorry, babe."

"It's fine. I just hadn't realised you were coming." He turned back to the pastry, turning it to make another neat fold. I'd always loved the way Patrick worked with his hands. I'd never thought of myself as a hand person, but Patrick's were just so beautiful. They were delicate and forceful in equal measure with strong fingers that I *would not* imagine doing fabulously filthy things to me. That was a place we did not go, brain. Not now. Not ever. Those were the rules. Patrick was stunning in my eyes, both physically and as a person, but I wasn't going to hit on him, especially as he'd just come out. That was just rude.

"What's going on?" I leant against the wall and watched him carefully. There was tension in his shoulders I hadn't seen before. "Please, Patrick. You know you can tell me anything."

Patrick let out a long breath but didn't look at me. That was fine. I didn't care where he looked as long as he finally told me what the ever-loving fuck was going on. "So… when I spoke to my family yesterday, there may have been a bit of a mix-up."

"Oh? What sort of mix-up?"

"They, um, well… they think you're my boyfriend, and they want me to bring you to the party this weekend."

CHAPTER FIVE

Patrick

I STARED at my carefully folded puff pastry, waiting for the fallout from my admission.

I was sure this was going to be the end of my friendship with Connor, which was why I'd spent the last twenty-four hours agonising over it. I had no idea what I was supposed to do. Was I supposed to keep it a secret, never tell Connor what had happened, and hope he never found out? Or should I admit it and laugh about it with him and hope we could pass it off as a joke? Or did I tell him what had happened and ask him to pretend, just for the weekend, that we were together?

I'd been up half the night worrying about it, and then I'd ended up going for a long walk in the hope of clearing my mind. When that hadn't helped, I'd headed for the kitchen. Tuesday morning was usually the day Darcie and I did most of our planning, and I started baking and prepping for the week ahead, so it worked. I just hadn't gone home when I was supposed to.

Part of me had been tempted to ask Darcie for her advice, but I hadn't wanted to burden her or put her in an awkward situation. If Aaron had been around, I might have asked him about it, as we'd been friends since our culinary school days, but it was his day off, and I hadn't wanted to bother him.

In a moment of recklessness, I'd ended up texting Connor. I'd regretted it afterwards because I'd known he'd ask questions, and I still had no idea what to say.

Out of all my options, I had to admit that deep down my favourite was the third. Would it be so terrible to pretend, just for a few days, that all my dreams had come true? I knew it was never going to happen, but I wanted to live that fantasy just once. Then I could get on with the rest of my life. Maybe I'd even be able to find a real boyfriend.

There was still silence from the other side of the tiny kitchen. I looked up to see Connor staring at me, mouth wide open. Crap. I'd known texting him had been a bad idea. I should never have opened my mouth.

"I'm sorry," I said. "Can we just forget I ever said anything?"

"I'm not mad," Connor said quickly as he suddenly sprung to life again. "I'm just… Why do they think we're dating?"

"I don't know. I mean, I've mentioned you before and told them we spend time together. You know, that we make dinner and watch movies and you come round to mine. I guess…" my voice trailed off, and Connor nodded.

"They put two and two together and made five." He smiled wryly and shook his head. "Well, I guess it makes sense in a way. I mean, you talk about me making you dinner and then you suddenly announce you're gay. Not that you did anything wrong," he added hastily. "But I can see how they came to that conclusion."

"I suppose." I looked down at my pastry again and realised it needed to go back into the fridge. I grabbed the cling film dispenser and began to wrap it. It was too big to go in one of my under-counter fridges without getting squashed, so I'd have to take it down to the chiller.

"So, what are you going to do?"

"Honestly, I hadn't gotten that far," I admitted. I gave him a small smile, trying to keep the worry out of my voice. "Would… would you consider being my boyfriend for the weekend?" I looked at him, taking in his fine features. Even dressed in leggings and a loose hoodie, he was still the most elegant and beautiful man I'd ever seen. Connor could probably wear a bin bag and I'd still think he was gorgeous. He was only wearing a little make-up, just a swipe of eyeliner and soft, smoky eyeshadow that made his blue eyes pop. His full lips had a touch of colour to them, and it made me want things I knew I couldn't have.

"I… maybe…" Connor pouted then chewed his lip. "Do you have any cake? I feel like I need cake right now. And some tea. Then we can talk about it."

It wasn't an outright no, so that was a start. I nodded. "Yeah, just let me stick this pastry in the freezer. Then maybe we can test that lemon cake." Connor nodded. "And if you want to make tea, nothing's moved since you left. I think we've got some chamomile too if you want some. We can sit in the break room since everyone else has pretty much finished."

"Sounds good. Do you want some tea too?"

"Please," I said, hefting the pastry carefully in my hands. "I'll be right back."

I made my way through the corridors to the fridges, leaving the pastry on the low, chest freezer while I opened the fridge door. I found a tray for the pastry to sit on, checked how my cheesecake was setting, and did a quick reconnaissance of what we still had and what I needed to order for later in the week. I'd already ordered some extra bits for the party cake since it was cheaper to buy them in bulk. I'd tried to tell Aaron he could take the extra cost out of my paycheck, but he'd just waved me away saying he wasn't going to charge me for a little bit of flour and some cream.

I'd tried arguing it would be more than that, but it was pointless to argue with Aaron, so I'd just given up.

When I went back to the kitchen, I heard the gentle sounds of crockery being moved and the hiss of the water heater, so I assumed Connor was making tea. I cut two pieces of lemon cake out of the tray, taking two edge pieces that we never used for afternoon tea and made my way to the break room. I collapsed into a chair and scrubbed my fingers over my face. What the fuck was I doing? I was never going to be able to pull this off. And even if, by some miracle, Connor agreed, I wasn't sure our relationship would ever be the same again.

"I can see your brain working," Connor said as he put a

tray with a large teapot and two cups down on the table. "Careful, that much thought is dangerous."

"True." I grinned, taking the proffered cup of tea and sliding a piece of cake over to him in return. "I might hurt myself."

"Exactly, and we wouldn't want that." Connor picked up his square of cake and sighed happily as he took a large bite. "God, I've missed your cake, babe. It's so fucking good."

I felt my face heat, but for once it wasn't the oven making my skin the colour of a strawberry. "You know, you can ask me to bring you some any time. There are always bits going spare. I can put some in a box for you before it goes into the break room."

I always put edge pieces, spare bits of desserts, things that hadn't quite turned out the way I'd planned or weren't good enough to serve, in the break room for the staff to help themselves or take home. It was better than throwing it in the bin. When I'd been on one of my placements during college, I'd seen a chef throw a whole tray of scones into the bin because they hadn't quite risen the way he'd wanted. I'd been horrified, and one thing I'd been very clear to Aaron and Ben about when they'd started this place was that I wanted a plan for food waste. I was not going to work in a restaurant that casually dumped a whole tray of food because it wasn't quite good enough. Aaron and Ben had agreed, and now we worked with several local food kitchens to distribute things that were leftover or that we had too much of. And we'd always had an open policy about feeding our staff and letting them take home extra.

"I may have to take you up on that," Connor said. "The only thing I really miss about working here is the free cake. And you, obviously, but now I get to see you whenever I want without getting grumbled at by Aaron, so I think things work better now."

I chuckled. We were skirting around the elephant in the room, but the room was small, and we couldn't avoid it for long. It was like a crushing pressure weighing down on us. I took a sip of my tea, hoping it would calm my rising nausea.

We sat in silence for a few minutes longer as if we were waiting for the other person to speak first.

"So…" Connor said finally, "this weekend."

"Yeah…" I swallowed and pushed my uneaten cake away from me. I'd vaguely told Connor about the party in the past, but I hadn't shared many of the details, mostly because I'd been trying to forget it was happening until it had snuck up on me.

"So, my, um, my parents are having a big party this weekend because my Da is turning seventy, and it's their fiftieth wedding anniversary."

"They got married young then."

"Yeah, they got married on Da's twentieth birthday, about six months after my mum turned eighteen. I think they'd have gotten married before that if they could have, but my nana put her foot down." Connor snorted. "Anyway, they're throwing this big party and loads of mum's family are coming over from Ireland. Mum's literally catering for about five hundred, even though I think there'll be two hundred people max since some of them are getting a bit old to travel."

"That's still a lot of people."

"Yeah, Mum and Da have a lot of friends, and Mum's family is pretty big." Mum was one of six, and each of her siblings had at least three children. Plus, each of her parents had large families, so there were always various aunties and uncles around. I didn't see most of my Irish family that often—mostly just weddings, funerals, and large parties like this—and to be honest, I didn't know many of them that well.

"Anyway, Mum and Da, and my sisters too, I guess, want me to bring you because they think you're my boyfriend. It would just be for three, maybe four days? I've got to go down on Friday afternoon. The party is on Saturday, and I was supposed to be staying until Monday, but I could easily come back Sunday instead. I know it's a lot to ask, and it's really short notice, especially because I know you have classes, and if you don't want to I totally understand. I can just tell them that we broke up or that you couldn't make it. I'm sure they'd understand…" I trailed off again as Connor raised a finger.

"First of all, I am not having a family I've never met think so ill of me as to dump their son just after he came out. That's just plain rude, and I'd never do something like that, so the breakup excuse will never work. Besides we both know we'll keep spending time together, and they're bound to find out, so that's another reason against that." He looked pensive, a little frown wrinkling the smooth skin between his brows as he drummed his fingers on the table.

"Okay, no breakup. But I could just tell them you couldn't make it. I mean, they sprung it on me yesterday, and that's pretty short notice. They'll understand." At least I thought they would. I didn't think any of them were crazy enough to stalk Connor on social media and bombard him with messages. They did have some boundaries. Maybe.

"I suppose," Connor said. He took a deep breath. "But I don't want to put you in that position. And I don't want you to have to go through the whole weekend explaining yourself."

"So, what are you saying?" A flicker of hope and excitement bubbled up in my chest, and I tried desperately to tamp it down.

"I'm saying I'll do it. I'll be your boyfriend for the weekend." Connor grinned and reached for my cake. "But we're going to need to set some ground rules, and you're going to need to tell me all about your family."

CHAPTER SIX

Connor

THIS WAS MADNESS. Sheer, irrevocable madness.

What the actual fuck had possessed me to say yes to this insane idea?

Oh, yes, maybe it was because I was head-over-fucking-heels for Patrick, and the idea of being his boyfriend, even if it was just for three days, was better than nothing. I had tried really, really fucking hard over the past twenty-four hours to forget that Patrick was gay. Honestly, I'd actually tried. Well, at least for the first couple of hours anyway.

After the initial shock had worn off, I'd tried to tell myself that just because Patrick was gay didn't mean he suddenly had a neon sign floating about his head that said he was available. But I was still thinking about it two days later.

Maybe Patrick didn't want to date. Maybe he wasn't sexually or romantically inclined, although I had to admit that the non-romantic thing felt like a bit of a stretch given what I knew about Patrick. Then again, I knew better than to make assumptions about people. Enough people made them about me, and I knew how much they hurt.

Part of me wanted to be hurt that Patrick hadn't told me before, but then I sagely remembered the advice of my other best friend, Taylor, who'd always reminded me that just because I was happy to be my own Pride parade and shout my gayness from the rooftops with a megaphone while throwing glitter at people, it didn't mean that everyone else felt the same way. I realised I would never hold it against my beloved chef because that just wasn't who I was as a person.

Still, a teeny-weeny part of me was still holding out hope that it might mean *something*.

Even if I didn't ever see myself being Patrick's type.

I would be the first one to admit I wasn't everyone's cup of tea. I was short, mouthy, and could kick most guys' asses while wearing heels and not putting a hair out of place. I liked women's jeans and pink T-shirts and sparkly Converse. I wore eight-inch heels, thigh-high boots, and tiny shorts while regularly throwing myself around a stripper pole. I had a better make-up collection than a lot of the women I knew. And I liked topping.

I *knew* I wasn't most people's thing. My entire twenty-eight years of life had shown me that. And if people didn't want to date me because of it? Well, fuck that.

I was never going to be anyone else, and I refused to change who I was as a person just to make some dickhead happy. I'd tried it once, and I'd been fucking miserable for two weeks until I'd finally seen sense and kicked him to the curb. No cock was worth not wearing lipstick. Men could take me as they found me, or they could leave. Unfortunately, they always ended up choosing the second option. Sometimes it hurt more than others, but I always told myself that if they didn't like who I was then they weren't worth my time in the first place. My mum had always taught me that.

Patrick was the absolute opposite of me in so many ways. Where he was quiet and thoughtful, I was loud and had a tendency to look before I leapt. Patrick was organised, whereas I had the organisational skills of a headless chicken. Honestly, sometimes it surprised me that we were friends, not in a bad way, just in a how-on-earth-did-we-make-this-work way.

I couldn't see Patrick wanting to date someone like me full-time. I was a handful, and I didn't think that would be his style. If he even had one.

And yet, here I was, agreeing to pretend to be his boyfriend in front of his entire family because they'd decided we were together, and Patrick, being the adorable sausage that he was, hadn't been able to tell them no. Although, from the sound of the conversation he'd described, I wondered how he'd managed to get a word in edgeways. Then again, my entire family consisted of exactly two people—me and my mum—so I didn't really have any experience with big family conversations.

There was a knock on the front door of my flat that jolted me from my internal pacing. I hopped up from my place on the sofa. I knew exactly who it was, and I wanted to laugh.

"I've told you a million times to just come in," I said, throwing the door open to reveal Patrick on the landing. "You have a key to the building. I don't get why you don't just let yourself in."

"Well, it feels rude," Patrick said with a little smile and a shrug. He followed me into the narrow hallway, slipping off his battered old trainers. "Thanks again for doing this."

"It's fine. Honestly." I waved my hand dismissively, trying to pretend everything was, indeed, fine.

We flopped onto the sofa, and I grabbed the panda notebook and biro I'd left on the coffee table. We'd agreed there needed to be ground rules for the weekend and that we needed to lay out our expectations. I wasn't sure if I was insisting on this to protect my heart or to encourage my feelings. After all, there was a chance I'd get to kiss Patrick, and I couldn't resist that.

It might be the only chance I'd get.

"Did you want a drink or anything before we start?" I asked, tucking my feet under me.

"No, it's fine. I had a cup of tea at home."

"Good, good… okay… so." I was stalling, and we both knew it. One of us had to take the first step. Time to pull on my Pleasers and stride out into the world. "Ground rules, I guess."

"Yeah. That sounds good."

"So… first rule? It's just for this weekend, Friday to Monday, then we go back to being friends again."

Patrick nodded. "Yeah, just for the weekend."

It almost hurt to write that on the page, but this was for my protection as much as anything else. I had to remember this was just temporary, otherwise I was going to end up getting hurt, and I'd had enough of that shit.

"Okay, um, rule two. We need to be honest with each other this weekend. Talk about things. Like if things make us uncomfortable." Patrick looked confused, so I elaborated. "For example, let's say we decide we're okay with some minor PDA, but then one of us realises we're not actually happy with it. We should tell the other person and agree there will be no hard feelings."

"That sounds fair." He paused, his skin starting to flush adorably from under his honey-blond curls. "What, um, what do you want to do about PDA?"

"Well, I think that comes under general expectations. How long does your family think we've been dating?"

"Er, I don't know. Probably somewhere between a couple of months and a couple of years."

"But you've only just come out, so I don't think they'll be expecting much, and every couple is different." I gave him an encouraging smile. "How does hand-holding, hugging, and maybe some kissing sound? It can just be cheeks if you really want, although they may expect lips. You don't have to use tongue though." I winked at him, and Patrick's face went from pastel to neon. Fucking hell, he was so cute like this.

"That, er, that sounds good."

I had a sudden thought—one I knew I needed to bring up because I'd been around straight people and they *always* asked the most inappropriate questions about my sex life.

I'd taken to asking about their own genitals and preference of positions, just to watch them squirm, but I wasn't going to inflict than on Patrick. Not unless he wanted me to.

"Are you a top or bottom, babe?"

"What?" Patrick stared at me in horror like I'd just asked him if he preferred to eat cats or dogs.

I decided to elaborate because I had to assume Patrick didn't understand the perils of navigating conversations about gay relationships with straight people and because I was desperately nosy, which I was well aware wasn't always a good thing. But I'd asked now, and there was no taking it back.

"Well, virtually every time I've been at a gathering with straight people, they inevitably decide to ask how I like to fuck. I'm not saying you have to tell them—you can just politely tell them to fuck off—but I have to say I'm curious."

"Er, I… I…"

"I mean, you don't have to tell me if you don't want. But since we're sharing… I'm vers, but I prefer to top. Not that I won't say no to a good dicking from the right man. Sometimes you just need to get pounded."

"I, um, I…" Patrick looked down at his hands, then at the floor. Anywhere, it seemed, that wasn't me. I had a sinking feeling in my stomach that I'd accidentally stumbled onto something I shouldn't have, like I'd opened my mouth and put both feet straight into it like the idiot I was. But… Patrick had to have had sex, right? I mean I knew he'd finally come out to his parents and me, but he must have had boyfriends before? Even if that thought made me want to vomit with jealousy. Green was not a colour that suited me.

"Babe, are you okay? You don't have to tell me if you don't want," I said as gently as I could, treating Patrick like he was a spooked horse. He looked about ready to bolt.

"What if I don't know?" There was an anxious look on his face and an earnest note in his voice that made me want to pull him into my arms. "I, um, I've never had sex before."

"Oh…" It took a moment for my brain to catch up and come back online, but there was absolutely no way in hell I was letting Patrick feel bad for never having sex. Society did a good enough job applying that pressure. "That's okay. Don't worry about it. It's not a bad thing." I reached out to take his hand in mine and squeezed it comfortingly.

"I know… I just… It's a bit embarrassing, isn't it? I'll be thirty in August, and I've never had sex."

"No, it's not embarrassing. You don't have to have sex, babe. It's not the end of the world. Plenty of people get on just fine without it. You never have to have sex if you don't want to."

"I know, but I do want to. One day." He sighed. He twisted his hands together, arms resting on his thighs, looking like the weight of the world was on his shoulders. A deep sadness seemed etched on his face, and I would have given anything to wipe it away. "I just… I didn't figure out I was gay until I was twenty-three, and by then I was really busy with work. I always thought I'd meet some-one, but it hasn't happened." A weak chuckle slipped from his lips, and my heart sank. I hated the way he was trying to play it off like it was no big deal when I could see that Patrick wanted nothing more than someone to love. "People don't really like dating chefs. They find the schedule a bit unpredictable. So I just... stopped looking after a while."

My mind was made up. After this weekend and this whole fake boyfriend thing was behind us, I was going to find Patrick someone. Someone who'd appreciate him, who'd cherish him, who'd give him everything he needed.

Someone who'd love him as much as I did.

"Don't worry, sweetie. If you want someone, you'll find someone. I'll help you if you want. Let's just get this weekend done first, then we can find you a boyfriend."

Patrick let out a little noise, which almost sounded sad. "That sounds nice. Thank you."

There was an awkward pause, and I looked down at my list. "So, um, are there any other rules or guidelines you want to add? Do I need to write down that you'll always eat my olives and whole bits of cold tomato if there are any?"

"No, I'll remember that. You could just pick them out you know."

"I know, but that looks odd if I'm standing at a buffet. I'd much rather just give them to you." I smiled at him, hoping the change of subject would bring a little sparkle back to his eyes. Patrick grinned, which was a start.

"Well, it's mostly a buffet and a pizza van so I'm sure you can avoid any olives."

"But what if everything else on the pizza is tasty?"

"Then I'll eat your olives."

"See? We're the perfect pair. Now, how did we start

dating? We should probably think on that since we're bound to get asked a bajillion times. And if anything is going to trip us up, it'll be plot holes in that story. I've heard nosy relatives are better at sniffing out relationship problems than drug dogs."

Patrick laughed, his whole body shaking. I loved him like this—carefree and laughing, his grey eyes twinkling and the dimples evident around his mouth. I didn't want a lean, muscled gym rat. I wanted a man like this, soft and warm with wide shoulders and a thick chest and a bit of a belly. Someone who, when they wrapped me up in their arms, made me feel totally and utterly safe and wanted.

"Yep. Wait until you meet my aunts. They're all in their seventies, and they're Irish, so they'll have absolutely no issue asking you a million questions. And they'll spot any inconsistencies a mile out."

"We'd better get it right then. I'm not getting thrown out before I've eaten cake because we got a date wrong!"

"No dates, got it," Patrick said with a grin. "So, who asked who out?"

"Clearly, I asked you, and you were utterly charmed by my stunning personality, wit, and charm."

"Oh, is that what that is?" Patrick asked cheekily, his Irish brogue thickening and making me melt from the inside out.

This weekend was going to be a fucking disaster.

CHAPTER SEVEN

Patrick

THE STAND MIXER clattered loudly as the large K-shaped beater clanged against the sides of the metal bowl. That was the only problem with industrial mixers: the noise. Still, it was a lot easier than making the mix for four giant cakes individually. I didn't think any of my other mixing bowls could accommodate a thirty-egg cake mix.

Perhaps I'd gone overboard on the amount of cake, but it was better to over-cater than under. And I knew Connor wouldn't complain about eating leftover cake for breakfast. Connor seemed to think cake was suitable for every meal, no matter the time of day.

I chuckled to myself as I watched the creaming mixture of butter and sugar. At least he'd be happy, and that was all that mattered. I didn't want to admit that I'd chosen the cake flavours because I knew Connor would love them, even though the cake wasn't even for him.

I resisted the urge to scrub my face with my hands. What the fuck was I doing? Connor and I weren't dating. This was all fake. I could pretend as much as I wanted, but the number one rule of our arrangement was that this was just for the weekend.

Four days. That was it. Then it was back to reality.

Something squeezed in my chest as I thought about Connor writing the terms on the list. It had been the first thing he'd mentioned, and he'd been very clear in his expectations. This was not going to be a long-term thing, and no matter how much I secretly wanted it to magically transform into a real relationship, that wasn't going to happen.

Connor was never going to want to date me. If the four-day rule hadn't made that clear, his insistence on finding me a boyfriend after this was all over had. I had zero relationship experience, zero sexual experience, and zero points in my favour, unless you considered being able to make a cake a plus, which nobody had in the past. I was not the sort of person Connor wanted, and I needed to stop thinking about it.

There was absolutely no use in me mooning over Connor when nothing was going to happen between us. I just had to get through the next few days without screwing this up and giving myself away. At least when I inevitably had to tell my parents that we'd broken up, I wouldn't have to fake the emotion.

The mixer continued clanking away, and I looked down to check its progress, slowly losing myself in the process of cake making—hefting in scoopfuls of flour and cracking in several trays of eggs, along with tablespoons of baking powder. This really was baking on an industrial scale. When the mixture was finally done, I poured it into four large cake tins and slid them into the oven, double-checking the temperature before I left them to bake.

Looking around the kitchen, I began thinking about everything I needed to prep for the lunch and dinner service I was working. I also wanted to get as much prepped for Darcie as possible since she was going to be on her own until I got back to work on Tuesday. It wasn't that I didn't trust her or think that she could cope, but I was a worrier by nature, and I didn't want Darcie to feel like I'd left her in the lurch. I opened the under-the-counter fridges, taking stock of everything.

We were doing pretty well since my Tuesday night stress baking had helped us get ahead. But I wasn't sure it would quite be enough. I'd have to check how many covers were booked in for the weekend. That would either ease my mind or send me into rapid production.

"Fucking hell. What the actual bloody fuck is this?" I heard Aaron grumbling loudly. Clearly he was working lunch service today and had arrived to prep. I had no idea what bee was in his bonnet, but I was sure I'd find out in the next few minutes. I'd become the unofficial mediator between Aaron, Josh, and several other members of the kitchen staff over the years because I didn't have the hot temper some of them did. I really should have asked Ben for a raise at this point, considering how much I'd done to keep the peace.

"Pads, did you have something to do with this?" Aaron

asked. I looked up to see his grumpy head sticking around the corner of the kitchen. His dark-red hair was pulled back into a bun, and his heavily tattooed hands were clutching a large Kilner jar with a label stuck to the front. The label had the words Aaron's Fucking Swear Jar written across it in neat printed letters.

I laughed. "Nope, that's not me."

"Who the fuck thinks I swear too much?" he muttered, turning the jar around in his hands. "What the fuck? It's even got a bloody price list on it! I bet this is all that bastard Josh's fault."

"Don't you blame Josh," I said, raising an eyebrow and giving him a hard stare. "You deliberately antagonise him, and you know it."

"But, Paaads," Aaron whined, trying to pout and failing. "He deserves it."

"You're lucky you still have a sous-chef. Don't you think you could be a little nicer to him?"

"I knew you'd take his side."

"I'm not taking anyone's side. And you know if he was here I'd be saying the exact same thing. You're both in your thirties for God's sake. Grow the hell up and stop acting like toddlers." It came out sharper than I'd intended, but I'd been putting up with their arguments for years, and I did not have time for it right now. Aaron stared at me.

"Okay…"

"And another thing. Would it kill you to shout and swear less? No, it wouldn't, and you'd probably make everyone a lot happier. You're not Gordon bloody Ramsay."

"But, Pads—"

"Don't you 'but, Pads' me. Head chef or not, you are not God here, so stop bloody acting like it."

"Yes, Chef," Aaron said. For a minute he looked pensive, then he gave me a wry smile. "See? I always know when I've gone too far when I get a Patrick lecture."

"Hmmm. I shouldn't need to give you them in the first place."

"I suppose." The oven timer dinged, surprising me. Aaron was nearest, and without prompting, he grabbed some gloves and opened the oven. "Jesus, you looking to start your own cake shop?"

"I wish," I said, shaking my head as Aaron pulled one of the tins out, holding it outstretched for me to inspect. I tested it quickly, watching the cake spring back into place where I'd touched it. The top was a perfect golden brown and nearly level. I nodded at Aaron, and he put the tin carefully on the counter before reaching for the next one. There wasn't a lot of counter space, and we had to do some creative placement, but eventually we got all the cakes out to cool.

"So, Oli said Connor popped in the other night." Aaron leant casually against the wall that made up the open door frame. Clearly, he wasn't in a rush to go back to his own kitchen. "Is there something you want to tell me?"

"No, there's nothing." I reached into the fridge for some fruit to prep, including my nemesis, pomegranates.

"Really?"

"Nope."

"I overheard Levi telling Ben that Connor had asked him to cover open practice this weekend as he's going away." Aaron's voice was casual, but I could tell he was digging. Why was everyone I knew so insufferably nosy?

"Oh, and how did you hear that?"

"Just casually when Levi was in yesterday. They were in the office when I went in to talk to Ben about staffing." It was just my luck that Connor's boss, Levi, and my boss, Ben, happened to be brothers. And it was just my luck that Aaron had a habit of sticking his nose into things whether he was wanted or not.

"What Connor does with his weekends isn't up to me."

"You're being really bloody obstinate about this."

"Careful," I said, shooting him a grin. "Doesn't that count for the swear jar?"

"Bloody is an adjective, Pads. It doesn't count."

"Doesn't it?"

"No." Aaron picked up the jar from where he'd set it down on the service rack, scanning the list of fines. Then he grabbed a sharpie out of my pen pot and crossed something out. "Not any more it doesn't. I can't get by without at least one good descriptor."

I smiled to myself and shook my head. I wasn't going to argue with him. Ben was the one who'd probably made the swear jar, and Aaron could take it up with him if he wanted. They'd known each other since they were five, and if anyone was going to call Aaron out on his colourful use of language, it would be Ben. Maybe he'd gotten just as sick of the fighting as the rest of us. Not that I was convinced a swear jar was the best solution. I was pretty sure Aaron would just come up with more inventive ways to insult Josh instead, but I wasn't going to say that.

"Hey, Pads," Aaron said, lowering the jar, sharpie still in hand. "Can I ask you something?"

"Er, sure?"

"Are you happy?"

I stared at him, my fingers stilling in their chopping of strawberries for an Eaton Mess. "Yes. Why?"

"I just wanted to make sure." He shrugged. "You spend a lot of time here, and as your friend, I just wanted to make sure you were happy. I mean, I know being a chef is tough as shit, especially with the hours, but I want to make sure you have a life outside this fucking place. Like, I know we all put our hearts and souls into it, but there's more to life than fucking work."

"Thanks, but I'm fine. I like my job, and I like being here. Besides, I have things outside work." Mostly President Whiskers and hanging out with Connor, but I wasn't going to say that. I didn't want Aaron to suddenly get the idea that I was sad or pitiful. I liked my life. Truly, I did. Sure, it would be nice to have a boyfriend to come home to in the evenings or someone to curl up in bed next to when I finally dragged myself home at midnight after a long dinner service, but I wasn't going to complain. I was perfectly content.

The last thing I needed was Aaron trying to find me a boyfriend as well. He and I had vastly different ideas about what made for a good relationship. I didn't think Aaron had ever had one that lasted more than three months.

"Like Connor?"

"Don't you have work to do?" I asked, raising an eyebrow. "And you need to put money in that jar now."

"Nope, it doesn't apply to your kitchen. Only mine."

"So this is my kitchen now?" I gestured at the small space that now smelt strongly of sponge cake.

"It's always been your kitchen, Pads. Everyone knows that." Aaron grabbed his jar and turned to go. "Have a good weekend if I don't see you before you leave. And have some fucking fun. You fucking deserve it."

Yes, I could definitely see the swear jar working. If it didn't end up in the bin before I came back on Tuesday, it would be a bloody miracle.

CHAPTER EIGHT

Connor

I STARED at the large suitcase and bag on my bedroom floor, wondering for the first time if I was taking too much stuff with me for three nights. I mean, some of it was essential—like my toiletries and my make-up—but I was starting to wonder if I needed six pairs of shoes, three different pairs of jeans, and two suits.

I wasn't even sure what I was supposed to wear to this party. Was it formal suit, or was it cute top and a nice pair of jeans? I probably should have double-checked with Patrick before I packed half my wardrobe. He'd said something about the party being in a barn, but that didn't mean anything these days. People got married in barns!

Sighing, I glanced at my phone, double-checking how long it was until Patrick was due to pick me up. I had an hour, which was plenty of time to totally repack everything if I needed to. Ugh, I was probably horribly overthinking this, but it was preferable to worrying about this whole fake boyfriend thing, which was what I'd been doing for the past two days. I was a complete and utter mess. I just couldn't show it. I needed this thing to be a success for Patrick, I needed to keep my own feelings sufficiently under wraps so I didn't ruin our friendship, and on top of that, I couldn't stop worrying about what Patrick's family might think of me. I'd never met any of my boyfriends' families before, so I had no idea what to expect, and even though we weren't in a real relationship, I still wanted to make a good impression. Hence trying to fit an entire wardrobe into two bags.

Fuck it. I needed to repack.

CONNOR *Just exactly what should I wear for this party? Do I need a suit?*
PATRICK *It's not that posh! Just a shirt and jeans will do*
PATRICK *Or whatever the you version of that is*
CONNOR *Full-length ballgown it is then ;P*

Okay, so I probably didn't need both suits. I could probably take one… and maybe a nice waistcoat if I wanted to be posh. Although I wasn't sure if I fancied it. I left it in the bag, just in case.

I thought trousers were probably more appropriate than jeans. I did have a couple of nice skirts for the days when I really felt like it, but I didn't want to totally shock Patrick's family. I wasn't even sure how they'd react to the make-up, and I suddenly realised I probably should have asked Patrick about it.

I'd been wearing make-up for so long that it was just part of who I was now. The first time I remembered wanting to try it was watching my mum put it on before she went to work and thinking how pretty she looked and how I wanted to look pretty too. I think I'd been about six at the time. High school had been an ongoing battle between my teachers, the school rules, and my own defiance. I'd worn pancake foundation, bright eyeshadow, and sticky lip-gloss as much as the girls. I mean, it had been Essex before the invention of make-up tutorials on YouTube, so by today's standards we looked a mess, but we'd thought we looked good. I'd certainly felt good. Mum had never been against it, although she had suggested laying off the orange fake tan and heavy foundation because it wasn't good for my skin.

When I was sixteen, my mum had bought me an expensive set of make-up brushes and a couple of eyeshadow palettes, then asked a friend of hers who did wedding make-up to show me how to use them. Steph had been amazing, and I'd utterly adored her. She'd taught me how to enhance my features and do soft, smoky eyes and helped me choose colours that made my skin pop. She'd also taught me the meaning of the word subtle, which was a totally new word for me in terms of make-up.

After that, I'd been off with a bang, and I'd never looked back.

These days, my make-up collection resembled a professional's, and it was what I spent the most money on, apart from pole shoes, but I managed to justify it somehow... like telling myself that two good palettes were the same as one pair of Pleasers and both were necessary purchases.

My make-up was part of who I was. It was my armour for my bad days or for when, heaven forbid, I was nervous. With a full face on, I felt like I could do anything. And I wasn't going to be ashamed for liking something that wasn't traditionally masculine.

The haters could fuck off as far as I was concerned. I just hoped Patrick's family wasn't among them.

I grabbed another couple of pairs of shoes out of the bag, realising I didn't need them, and began condensing everything down to one bag. I'd just about managed to get it closed by the time I heard a knock at the door and the squeaking of hinges.

"Connor? I'm here. Are you ready to go?" Patrick said. I stuck my head out of the bedroom.

"Yes! I actually am, and I managed to get everything into one bag. Aren't you proud of me?"

"Depends on the size of the bag. You do realise it has to go on the back seat since the cake is in the boot, and I don't have a people carrier, right?" He gave me a cheeky grin, and I couldn't stop myself from beaming at him.

"So rude to your poor boyfriend," I joked.

"Am I your boyfriend now?"

"Well, it's Friday, so yes."

"Poor me. I'm clearly being punished for something." He rolled his eyes, and I laughed. I loved this sharp, funny side of Patrick. It was something people only saw when he was comfortable around them, but sometimes I thought he kept it all for me.

"So fucking sassy today! Be nice to me. I only packed two pairs of shoes, and I'm suffering."

"Is that including the ones you're wearing now?" He raised an eyebrow, giving me the knowing Patrick smile that told me he'd seen straight through me.

"Fine, three then."

"I appreciate your sacrifice and so does my poor car."

I rolled my eyes, gripped the handle of my suitcase, and tapped my ass to double-check my phone was in the back pocket of my jeans. I grabbed my keys off the little table by the door and my pink, faux-leather jacket—which was one of my favourites for the summer—before running through a quick mental checklist.

"Okay, I've got everything. We can go now," I said, giving Patrick my most charming smile. Patrick was staring at me, a faraway look in his eyes. "You okay?"

"Yeah… I was thinking. You look very nice by the way." He leant down and gently pressed a kiss to my cheek. "And I like your perfume."

My skin burned under his lips, his touch sending a million electric shocks through my nerves. He'd never done that before.

"Sorry," he said gently. "I just… I thought I ought to get used to doing that. You know, so people don't suspect we're faking."

The electricity turned to ice in my veins, pain lancing through me.

"Y-yeah, no, I get it." I swallowed and nodded, trying not to let it show how much his words had crushed me. This was just fake, and I fucking well needed to remember that, or it was gonna hurt a *lot* more on Monday. "Let's go then."

Patrick picked up my suitcase, because of fucking course he was a gentleman like that, leaving me to lock my flat door before we made our way down the three flights of stairs to the little car park behind my building. Patrick's little blue Fiesta was parked in one of the visitor's bays, and he carefully placed my case on the back seat without even so much as a tiny swear when it needed a push to slide onto the seat. He seemed genuinely unfazed while I felt like I'd just ridden The Smiler at Alton Towers twice in a row. I wasn't sure whether I wanted to laugh, cry, or vomit into a bag.

At this rate, I was going to be a complete mess by Monday. And by that I meant an even bigger mess than I already was.

"Are you ready?" Patrick asked, looking at me from the driver's side door.

"Yeah, all ready." I pulled open the door and slid onto the seat, noticing the shopping bag tucked in by my feet. A quick glance showed me bottles of water, some of my favourite Pepsi Max Cherry, and some snacks, including my all-time favourite, wine gums. Damn, Patrick knew me well. My stomach clenched again. Patrick being adorably caring and automatically bringing me my favourite sweets and some drinks was not going to help the situation.

Instead, I looked around, trying to find something else to focus on. Anything to take my mind off the fact that I could still feel Patrick's lips against my cheek. I glanced at the old TomTom SatNav stuck onto the windscreen, noting the driving time was currently sitting at four hours, twenty-three minutes. I was going to have to find something to talk to Patrick about, otherwise it was going to be a very long trip.

"So," I said as we turned out of the car park and onto the leafy street where my flat was located. "How're you feeling about this? You doing okay?"

"Er, I think so. I mean, it'll be nice to see everyone again I suppose. I haven't actually seen them since before Christmas last year."

"Been avoiding them?"

"Maybe a little."

"I get that. I mean, your family sounds lovely but ever so slightly overbearing." Patrick had spent an hour the other night telling me about his sisters and his parents, and they all sounded completely bonkers. Even if it was in a loving way. "How long do you think it'll be until someone asks if we're going to get married?"

Patrick laughed weakly as we stopped at some traffic lights. "I mean, do you want an honest guess?"

"Oh, definitely." I kicked off my Converse, wondering if it was too early to start the wine gums.

"Well, if anyone's going to ask, it'll be Mary or Cara because they're both nosy as hell. But I don't know if they'd ask me when you're around." I made a mental note and rummaged in the shopping bag, giving in to my desire for sweets. I'd been trying to hold out until we got to the motorway, but since it always took forever to get out of Nottingham, I'd decided I couldn't wait.

"Anyone else?" I asked, opening the bag.

"Probably a couple of aunts since they all love a good wedding, and they wouldn't want us 'living in sin' together. Mum doesn't think they'll be fussed about the gay thing at all. It might just be the whole 'having sex before I've made an honest man of you' thing."

I snorted. "Well you could always be honest and tell them we haven't had sex."

Patrick's face turned a beautiful shade of beetroot. "No thanks. I'd rather they keep thinking the opposite."

Oh… that was interesting. Very interesting…

Unprompted, because it clearly hated me, my brain started to wonder just what Patrick would be like in bed and what he might look like naked. I'd never seen him in less than a T-shirt and shorts, but my brain was happy to fill in the picture, reminding me that if we had to share a room, there might be a chance I'd get to see Patrick shirtless. Or even in his boxers…

My cock twitched in my jeans.

Shit. No. Bad dick. Very bad. We were not allowed to imagine Patrick naked, and we were not allowed to try to sneak peeks at him over the weekend either.

I shoved two wine gums into my mouth.

This was going to be a long, long four days.

CHAPTER NINE

Patrick

CONNOR'S MUSIC played softly through the stereo as we made our way along the motorway. He was singing along, attempting to find the perfect music for his dream pole routine. He'd already eaten his first bag of wine gums. It was a good thing I'd bought several, considering we were only an hour into the trip.

"So, what are you looking for in music?" I asked, watching Connor do a little chair dance and conduct an invisible band while singing about how much he liked boys.

"Ideally something slow-ish with a strong beat. Too fast and it throws you off and you try to catch up. You need something that you can move to the tempo of and that accentuates your movements. It can be sweet or sad or sexy or anything really. It depends on you as a performer and the things that work for you. I know someone who does more slow, acrobatic routines because they suit her, and I know a guy who uses seventies psychedelic rock. I saw one doubles team do a routine to a mash up of the Baywatch theme song and 'Baby Shark'."

"That sounds… interesting." I tried to imagine how that might work. I couldn't picture it at all.

"Honestly, best thing I've ever fucking seen. It's on YouTube. I'll have to show you one day." Connor grinned and tucked his foot up onto the seat.

"What about you? What do you like?"

"I like sexy songs. I like to feel sexy when I perform." He shrugged, and I swallowed. "It suits me, and it makes me feel amazing. I've tried other styles, and I can do them, but I'm at my best when I'm sexy. I put on my boots, knee pads, and tiny pole shorts, and maybe just a little bit of glitter, plus a full face of make-up, and I feel like I can do anything. I feel… powerful." I glanced across the dashboard at him, and he smiled softly. "Some people think it's slutty and inappropriate, but I love it. I've never felt more welcome than I have in the pole community. It's full of lovely people of all ages, genders, sexualities, and sizes, and none of that matters. It's your passion and your drive that's important. Everyone just supports each other. I honestly couldn't think of anything else I'd want to do. Don't get me wrong, I love ballet, and I love doing ballet-inspired routines, but… ballet was just never as welcoming to me."

I tried to think of something to say, but I couldn't seem to find the right words. Mostly because my brain had started remembering all the videos I'd seen of Connor on Instagram, dancing in the studio in his knee-high boots and little black shorts. I'd always wondered if it was wrong of me to watch them. I wanted to watch them to support him because he was my best friend and he was incredibly talented, but on the other hand, the last time I'd tried to watch one of his videos I'd nearly passed out from blood loss to my brain.

I'd had to go and take a very long, very cold shower while reminding myself it was totally inappropriate to think about my friend like that. Even if Connor probably would have been flattered instead of upset.

Ever since then, I'd liked his videos without watching them. I thought that was a fair compromise.

I must have been quiet for a moment too long because Connor suddenly said, "You don't have a problem with me being sexy, do you?"

"No! Of course not." Well, technically I did. Just not the sort of problem Connor was thinking. "I love that you're passionate about pole, and you're an amazing dancer. You're gonna do great when you compete this year." I hoped I sounded sincere, but I was worried there was a telltale crack in my voice.

"Thanks, babe. Hey, the East Midlands Championships are in Nottingham this year. You should come watch."

"That sounds great." I meant it. If Connor wanted me there, I'd be there. There wasn't anything I wouldn't do for him.

"I already submitted a routine. They had a really early submission date, so I put something in. It was a good warm-up for when I have to submit the routine for Chrome Stars in August."

"What music did you use?" I knew Connor was obsessed with finding the perfect songs for his routines, and I was curious to see what he'd chosen.

"'I Like Boys' by Todrick Hall. It's really fun and sexy, and Levi thinks I'm a shoo-in to get selected for the final."

"Then I'll definitely come and watch. I'm sure you'll be incredible."

"You're the sweetest."

"It's you, Connor, of course I'd come." Without thinking, I reached my hand out and rested it on Connor's leg, squeezing his thigh gently. I'd meant it as a friendly gesture, but now it felt like so much more than that. Silence hung heavy in the air between us. "Sorry," I muttered, putting my hand back on the steering wheel.

"It's, um… it's fine."

I looked at the SatNav, noticing we were just over halfway there, and, as if by fate, we passed a sign that said the next services were in two miles. "Do you want to stop for a break? Get a drink? Stretch your legs?"

"Sounds great."

We pulled into the service station, and I let Connor go on ahead, feigning the need to call my mum to let her know how we were getting on. As soon as he'd disappeared out of sight, I ran my fingers through my hair, buried my face in my hands, and exhaled loudly.

Jesus fucking Christ, Patrick. Get it together. Connor did not need me drooling over him. That was so far beyond appropriate that I couldn't even see the line I'd crossed. We were friends, nothing more. And friends did not want to jerk off to videos of their friends dancing. Even if it was the sexiest thing I'd ever seen.

That was it. I needed to draw the line and get a fucking grip. Just because Connor was my "boyfriend" this weekend didn't mean I had an excuse to act like a total creep.

Nodding to myself, I fired off a text to my mum and headed into the services.

After a quick trip to the toilets, I found Connor in the queue for Costa. He beckoned me over as soon as he saw me, and five minutes later, we both left with some sort of creamy, iced caramel coffee monstrosity. I hadn't been convinced, but Connor had insisted I try one because they were supposedly incredible. Even though I was a pastry chef, I didn't have the biggest sweet tooth, and one sip of the drink convinced me they'd basically just poured sugar and cream into a blender.

At least the coffee gave it a bit of balance.

We headed back to the car, and Connor bounced ahead, clutching the bag of sweets he'd bought from WHSmith. I chuckled and shook my head as I realised I was going to be in the car for another two hours with a highly caffeinated and over-sugared Connor. I wondered how long it would be before he started asking me questions. Inappropriate or otherwise. Although after he'd dropped the "top or bottom" question on me, I didn't think it would be possible to surprise me anymore. I'd been absolutely mortified at the time, but at least Connor hadn't laughed at me, which was the reaction I'd almost expected when I'd admitted I was still a virgin at almost thirty.

"Hey, can I ask you a question?" Connor asked as I pulled the car back onto the motorway, attempting not to get squashed by several lorries.

I smiled. He hadn't even lasted five minutes. "Er, sure."

"Do you think your family will mind that I wear make-up?" There was a slight catch at the end of his voice, and when I glanced over at him, it wasn't hard to spot the worry behind his eyes. I thought for a second. I didn't just want to blithely tell him it would all be fine when it might not be, but on the other hand, I was genuinely struggling to think of who might cause problems.

"I don't think so. I mean, Mum, Da, and the girls won't mind, and they all know already."

"Oh?"

"Well, I mean, um, I'm guessing they do anyway. There's a lot of photos of us together on Facebook and Instagram." I felt my face heating and quickly ploughed on before Connor could start poking at why my face was pink. "So I doubt they'll say anything except how pretty you look. Most of my sisters have kids, and the oldest is in his twenties, so I don't think any of them will mind. Maybe a couple of the younger ones might ask about it, but I think that'll just be curiosity more than anything."

"That's okay. I can handle kids."

"And as for the older lot? I don't know. I mean, some of my uncles might." I sighed. The last thing I wanted was to make Connor feel uncomfortable. I should have thought of this earlier, but I didn't want Connor to even consider changing who he was or how he dressed just because one of my uncles might be a twat about it. "I'm sorry. I should have thought of this, but honestly, if they say anything, I'll just tell them to fuck off."

"You, Patrick Evans, the sweetest and nicest man in the universe, would tell someone to fuck off?"

"For you I would. Yes. Fuck 'em. I'm not having some old gasbag making you feel inferior. And if that fails, I'll set my mum on them." I grinned. "Everyone's a little bit scared of her."

"Really?"

"Yep. When I was growing up and Da was training race-horses with my uncle, all the stable lads and jockeys were terrified of my mum. Don't get me wrong, she's not mean or anything, and she'd have done anything for them, but heaven forbid they put a toe out of line. My mum is like a hippie with a steel core."

"I'll have to remember that," Connor said, and out of the corner of my eye I saw him smile. Some of the worry in my chest eased. "She sounds like an interesting woman."

"Something like that. But seriously, Connor, wear your make-up. You always look amazing, and I don't want anyone to take that away from you."

"Thanks, babe. I have no plans to look anything less than absolutely fucking fabulous, and if I get any looks, then I shall just put on brighter lipstick and more glitter."

"I wouldn't expect anything less."

"And don't worry," he said, his tone turning teasing, "I brought my best liquid lips with me. The ones that don't leave a mark or transfer when you kiss someone.

Although... I bet you'd look super cute with lipstick kisses all over you. And that would definitely do something to silence the haters."

Connor giggled, and I tried not to think about how much I wanted to see his lipstick kisses all down my chest.

CHAPTER TEN

Patrick

IT WAS NEARLY five by the time we reached my parents' house, having spent an hour queueing on the M5 near Bristol because there'd been some sort of accident.

My parents lived on an old farm between the rolling wilds of Dartmoor and the south coast. Once upon a time, it had been a dairy farm, then my father and my uncle had started training racehorses together, turning the whole thing into a small but well-oiled racing yard. They did a lot less of the training now since they were both in their seventies. Or about to be. These days, Cara and her husband ran most of the operation, and they'd had quite a lot of success over recent years.

The farm also had several holiday cottages of varying size dotted across it, from little two-bedroom hideaways to sprawling old barns that slept about twenty. They were always fully booked, and they were all far enough away from the yard not to cause problems for the horses or for the grooms to disturb the guests when they all turned up at seven each morning.

I'd grown up having free run of the place. It was a loving childhood but a bit of a lonely one. My sisters had all been too old to play with me when I'd wanted someone to play with, and I was expected to entertain myself when I wasn't helping out.

My father had wanted me to become a jockey, but even though I loved horses and enjoyed riding, it had never been for me. Besides, I didn't exactly have the body type for it. I'd preferred to spend my days in the farmhouse kitchen with my mum while she taught me to make soda bread and barmbrack. By the time I was nine, I was happily making cakes, unsupervised. Everything I made got put in the tack room in a tin by the kettle, and it was always empty at the end of the day.

When I was sixteen, I'd gotten my first job in the village pub and spent as much time as possible with Jean and Val, the old ladies who ran the kitchen a couple of nights a week and made all the puddings. They'd given me their recipes to take home and try on my family and the stable lads, who ate everything I put in front of them. I don't think anyone had been surprised when I'd said I wanted to be a pastry chef.

I think my family had thought I'd stay local and maybe get a job in one of the pubs here, but then I'd met Aaron during one of my placements. He'd introduced me to Ben, and one night over pizza and cider they'd told me about their plans to open an upscale pub-style restaurant.

They'd needed a pastry chef, and I'd jumped at the chance.

Their original plan was to set up somewhere in Yorkshire where Ben and Aaron had grown up, but then a chef friend of a friend of Aaron's had mentioned he was giving up the lease on the pub he ran in a village on the outskirts of Nottingham and wanted someone to take it over. He owned the building and had told Ben and Aaron they could pretty much do what they wanted as long as the food was good. And that had been that. The Pear Tree had opened six months after we'd finished school, and I'd never looked back. And I'd never moved home.

Considering all my sisters still lived either on the farm, in the village, or in Plymouth, and spent pretty much every weekend at my parents', I wondered if that made me a disappointment to my family. They'd never said anything out loud, but sometimes there was a wistful note in my mum's voice that made me think she wished things were different.

I pulled the car into the driveway between the old metal farm gates, past Cara's house at the top of the drive and down the wide strip of tarmac that led towards the farm under the shade of some trees. Ahead, I could see the cottage my parents called home and the stables and barns of the yard. Behind the hedges I saw fields with a couple of horses out grazing in the early July sunshine.

"Wow, it's so pretty," Connor said, peering out the window at the rough, rolling valleys and old stone walls. "You grew up here?"

"Yeah." I drove slowly around the cottage, watching out

for any stray farm cats, and into a space next to a battered Land Rover and a couple of small cars. It didn't look like my whole family was here yet. "Are you ready?"

"I guess so." He reached over the console and squeezed my hand. "Thanks for driving, by the way. And for never complaining about my music choices."

"It could've been worse. You should hear what Oli and Antoni play in the pot wash sometimes."

"Are *you* ready?" Connor asked, squeezing my hand again and giving me a soft smile. Something bubbled in my stomach, and for the first time since we'd concocted this hare-brained scheme, I worried that I was doing the wrong thing. I mean it was one thing to let my family believe Connor and I were dating, but it was another to straight up lie to their faces.

"I think so." I sighed. "It's a bit late now if not."

"No chance to turn back now."

"Let's go say hi then," I said. Not adding *before I lose my nerve*.

I got out of the car and waited for Connor to follow, then I headed for the back door of the house. I was about two steps away from the car when I felt something warm brush against my hand. I froze. Then Connor's fingers slipped into mine, squeezing my hand tightly. I glanced down at him, wondering if he'd meant to do that, but he was looking out across the fields.

"Come on," he said. "They're going to think we're just sitting in the car making out." He turned to look at me and wiggled his eyebrows dramatically. I snorted, shaking my head as I pulled him towards the house.

"Hello," I called out as I opened the door into the little utility room that then opened into the wide, farmhouse kitchen. I smelled something baking, and it warmed me from the inside out and made me feel like a child all over again.

"Patrick? Is that you?" My mum's lilting Irish brogue responded, accompanied by the barking of dogs as three terriers rushed through the door towards us. I chuckled, letting go of Connor's hand for a moment to brush one of them off my knees.

"Yeah, it's me and Connor." I stepped into the kitchen, still fending off dogs. Mum was pulling something out of the oven. Her long, honey curls were streaked through with grey, but she looked exactly the same as the last time I'd seen her.

"I was starting to wonder where you'd gotten to!" She put the cake tin on the side, then swept over to me and pulled me into a fierce hug. Then she stepped back to give me an appraising look. "You look tired, my love."

"It was a long drive." Mum glanced over my shoulder, and I realised I'd pretty much abandoned Connor to the mercy of the dogs. But when I looked around, he stood by the door, trying to scratch all three of them at once, a wide grin on his face. "Mum, this is Connor. Connor, this is my mum."

Connor straightened and shot Mum one of his beautiful smiles. "Nice to meet you, Mrs. Evans."

"Oh please, call me Aoife. Everyone does." She swept him up into a hug. "We're so pleased you could make it. I can't believe Patrick waited this long to tell us." She released Connor and looked at me again, her grey eyes twinkling. "Why didn't you tell me he was so gorgeous, Patrick? None of the photographs do him justice at all."

I flushed because that was not what I'd expected her to say. I opened my mouth, but nothing came out.

Connor grinned impishly, then winked at me. "It's because he wanted to keep me all for himself since the dating thing is kind of new."

"Really?" Mum asked, and I heard a note of amusement in her voice. "How new?"

"Nearly seven months," Connor said as he flawlessly recounted the lie we'd concocted. We tried to think of what would make it most believable. In the end we'd gone for the whole friends-to-lovers thing and kept it fairly new so none of my family would start asking questions about houses and weddings. "At the end of January. But we've been friends for years."

There was a sudden ache in my chest, and not for the first time, I wished this was real.

"Isn't that perfect." Mum stepped towards the stove, carefully removing what I now realised was a loaf of banana and fruit bread from a tin to cool. "Cara, Mary, and your Da are all in the barn setting up for tomorrow. I thought you'd probably want a moment to breathe before they set on you." Mum grinned and looked over at Connor. "Don't worry. They're all lovely, but it's a little bit like being surrounded by a pack of wolves. I hope you're prepared for it. Luckily the rest of the family isn't coming until tomorrow."

"I'll be fine," Connor said. "Although maybe I should

have brought a spray bottle. Then again, I think that's only for cats. Maybe we should do that hold-the-teddy-bear thing they make you do in primary school where you can only talk when you're holding the bear."

Mum threw back her head and laughed. "Well, now there's an idea. I think I'll get one for dinner time. It'd get me some peace and quiet sometimes." She wiped her hands on a nearby tea towel. "Do you two want to bring your stuff inside now? I can show you what room you're in."

"That'd be great," I said, finally finding my tongue. "I should bring the cake and the rest of the ingredients in too. I had them in a cool bag, but they'll need to go in a fridge."

"There's room in the big one out there." Mum gestured towards the utility room. "I cleared most of it out for you. Have you got a lot left to do?"

"Not really. It should only take me a couple of hours at most. I can do it tonight, so it has a chance to set before tomorrow. If you're okay with me taking over your kitchen?"

"Of course, and I'll keep everyone out of your way. Lord knows you don't need six people trying to help." Mum followed us out of the kitchen and across the yard towards the car, asking about the drive and chatting about the weekend as we walked. She asked Connor a few questions, but they were the kind, gentle small talk variety rather than the pointy, questioning kind.

It took us a while to work out how to carry everything back to the house. In the end we gave up trying to do it in one trip and settled for two. By the time we had the cake and decorating ingredients in the fridge and our bags in the hallway to go upstairs, I heard voices approaching outside the window. I was surprised that Mum had said it was just Cara, Mary, and Da today since I'd thought the whole family would've descended upon us. Maybe they'd decided to come tomorrow to give Connor and me a bit of space. Although whether that was their choice or not was another matter entirely.

I had a sneaking suspicion that Mum had put her foot down so we weren't overwhelmed, and for that I was infinitely grateful.

"You're in Orla's old room," said Mum. "Why don't you two take the bags upstairs and come down when you're ready? We can all have some tea and a piece of cake." She smiled, the twinkle back in her eye. "Don't be too long though, or I'll send Mary up to get you. So that means nothing fun until tonight."

"Mum!"

"What? I had four kids at your age Patrick, you think your Da and I didn't have any fun?" She laughed at the look on my face, which was probably a mixture of shock, horror, and dismay. "Go on. If you don't go now, they'll be in before you've moved."

"Orla's room," I muttered under my breath. I grabbed my bag off the floor, not quite sure I could get out of the situation fast enough. I heard Connor following me, his footsteps light on the old carpet runner that ran up the wooden stairs. When we reached the landing, I turned left and followed it to the end, opening a white wooden door on the right of the house. I'd always loved Orla's room because it looked out over the farm and the wild hills, but when she'd moved out, it had been designated as a guest room, and I hadn't been allowed to have it.

Mum had repainted it at some point since I'd last seen it, and now it was pastel blue with floral wallpaper decorating the wall behind the bed. There was a similar coloured quilt spread across the duvet that was piled high with cream and blue cushions. There was an armchair tucked into the corner, and various pieces of white, wooden furniture dotted around that were obviously from the same place as the bed. There was even a dressing table with a large mirror.

"This is gorgeous," Connor said, flopping onto the bed. We'd kicked off our shoes downstairs, and I noticed the glittery threads running through his pink trainer socks. "Your mum is a hoot. I love her already."

"I still can't believe she said that. She's sixty-eight. I don't want to think about her doing that." I moved Connor's suitcase into the corner.

"I don't think anyone wants to think of their parents like that." Connor sighed happily, wiggling into the middle of the bed and stretching. It lifted his T-shirt and revealed an expanse of perfect, toned skin that I wanted to run my fingers over. It was so different than my own rounded stomach.

I'd never minded my body that much. It got the job done. While once upon a time I might have wanted the lean lines some of the other guys I saw had, I'd learnt to accept that was never going to be me. Where some men were firm and chiselled, I was soft. I might walk thousands of steps a day around a kitchen, and I could heft a twenty-kilogram sack of flour like it was a pillow, but I was never going to have gym-honed muscles or Connor's dancer's figure.

When I'd first really accepted I was gay, I'd wondered if anyone would ever find me attractive. All I ever saw were pretty men with honed abs, and I didn't know if anyone would want me the way I was. Now, thanks to a little bit of porn surfing, I thought I had just as good a chance as anyone else. I didn't think I was unattractive. I just wasn't anything special.

"Are you okay?" Connor asked, tilting his head back to look at me. His T-shirt slid a little farther up, and I swallowed.

"Er, yeah fine. Just spaced out for a second." I flicked my eyes away from Connor and looked at the bed. It was a sturdy double with a solid wood frame. Connor and I had fallen asleep on the sofa plenty of times together, but that was different from sharing a bed. Very different.

For one thing, we were always fully clothed when we fell asleep on the sofa.

"Which, um, which side of the bed do you want?" I asked.

"Either, babe. I usually sleep in the middle of mine."

"So I'm gonna get squashed then?"

"Eh, maybe a little. Or maybe violently snuggled."

"I think I can live with that," I said. "And your snoring."

"I do not snore!" Connor reached out and half-heartedly threw a cushion at me. "You and Taylor are such assholes. He said the exact same thing the last time I stayed with him."

"Was that the night he snuck out to see Simon?"

"Ugh, yes, and I will never get over having to imagine him puking just so I didn't get hard listening to the live porno happening on the other side of the wall." Connor giggled, shaking his head, and I couldn't help chuckling with him. Taylor was Connor's best friend, and the last time Connor had stayed with him in London, he'd still been dancing around things with his roommate, Simon. Apparently, Taylor had snuck out of bed to see Simon in the middle of the night and had come back the next morning to find Connor awake and armed with questions. It had ended in some sort of love confession, and Connor said he took at least sixty percent of the credit for their relationship because he'd forced Taylor to confront his feelings. I could definitely believe Connor had poked poor Taylor with questions until he'd given in. He was good at that.

"I don't think you'll have to worry about that here," I said, then quickly added, "I think we're the only ones staying on this side of the house. At least tonight anyway. I know most of the rest of the family are staying in the cottages."

Connor grinned and opened his mouth to say something, but then I heard a warm, familiar voice calling from the bottom of the stairs, a teasing note in her tone.

"Patrick, are you gonna bring your boyfriend down, or do I have to come and extract you?"

CHAPTER ELEVEN

Connor

PATRICK GROANED, then sighed deeply while I grinned up at him from the incredibly comfortable bed. Seriously, if I didn't have to meet Patrick's family, I'd just stay on the bed and nap. But duty called, and I wanted to find out if the rest of Patrick's family was as fun as his mum.

"Come on," I said, pulling myself into a sitting position and stretching my shoulders out, wiggling my toes before I stood up. All my muscles felt tight from the long car journey, and I wondered if Patrick would mind if I did some stretching at some point. Either tonight or tomorrow morning. I'd brought some leggings with me, so it wasn't like I'd be prancing around in my undies even if I did know that Patrick had seen me in less. He always liked my pole videos on Instagram, even the really sexy ones, so I assumed he'd watched them.

I wondered which was his favourite. Would it be terribly cheeky of me to ask?

"How do I look?" I double-checked my reflection in the dressing table mirror, debating whether I should touch up my lipstick before we went down.

"You, er, you look perfect." Patrick smiled at me softly, and I could have sworn there was a pale blush tinting his cheeks. "Just like usual."

"Thanks, babe. You're too sweet." I reached out my hand and slipped my fingers into his. I loved the way his skin felt against mine, the little burn scars and callouses on his fingers brushing against my own. Pole did not make for pretty hands, but luckily nobody ever looked at mine too closely.

"Let's hope there are no more sex questions," Patrick muttered as he stepped towards the door, leading me back down the landing towards the stairs. I couldn't help laughing. My poor pastry chef.

"There you are," came a sparkling voice, the same one that had called upstairs. It belonged to a tall woman with wild curls that reminded me exactly of Patrick's. She had the same round face and smiling eyes too. "I thought you'd gotten lost on your way down. I was prepared to send out a search party."

"You're just nosy is what you are," Patrick said as we reached the bottom of the stairs. "Mary, this is Connor. Connor, this is Mary. She's the youngest of my older sisters."

"Well, that makes me sound fucking ancient." Mary

beamed at me. "I'm so glad you're here. I thought Patrick was gonna bail on bringing you."

"I-I…" Patrick stammered, looking flustered.

"Don't lie. You were totally thinking about it. I know you," Mary said.

"Don't worry," I said, stepping into rescue Patrick. He clearly didn't know whether to laugh, cry, or run away. "I wouldn't have let him. I'm so excited to meet everyone since Patrick's told me all about you."

"Did he now?"

"Of course, and it was all lovely. Absolutely nothing terrible at all." I grinned. Technically Patrick hadn't said anything bad at all, but I knew that all siblings had some secrets. I'd spent enough time around Ben and Levi to know. They were always at each other's throats over something or other, even if it was just teasing.

"Well, if he did, I'm sure Mum and Da have still got his baby pictures around somewhere. I'm sure there are photos of little Patrick having a bath in the sink."

"Why would you say that, Mary?" Patrick groaned as she led us through a door and into a cosy living room lit by the late-afternoon sun. An older man with white hair and a lean, tanned face sat on a floral sofa with two terriers in his lap and another at his feet, chatting to another woman who had darker blonde hair and a tanned face. The similarity between them made it clear they were related. I assumed the man was Patrick's dad and the woman his sister Cara.

"Patrick!" The man said, a broad smile spreading across his face.

"Hey, Da," Patrick said, giving him a little half wave, still holding my hand.

"I'd get up, but I don't think I'd be very popular," he said, gesturing at the dogs sprawled across him. He turned to me and beamed. "You must be Connor.

"That's me." I suddenly felt oddly tongue-tied. I'd never been in this sort of situation before, and I suddenly felt horribly off-kilter. I wanted nothing more than to ensure Patrick's parents liked me, but all my charm seemed to have vanished. I was *nervous*. What the fuck? I didn't get nervous! Except, apparently, I did. "It's nice to meet you, Mr. Evans." I forced out. "And you must be Cara?"

"Call me John. Everyone does," he said. I smiled because his mannerisms were so like his wife's, but also so like his son's. John pointed at another small floral sofa opposite his. "Don't stand on ceremony. Sit down. Aoife's just getting tea."

"I'm here," Aoife said, bustling into the room carrying a large tray. "Grab a seat."

"Maybe we'd be better off in the dining room," Cara said.

"It's okay. I can grab a couple of chairs," Mary responded from behind me.

I stood awkwardly until Patrick gently pulled my hand and tugged me towards the sofa. I perched on the cushion next to him, not even having to fake wanting to be close to him. It surprised me how out of my depth I suddenly felt. I was always the chatty extrovert, never afraid to throw myself into anything, but suddenly I didn't know what to do or say.

"You okay?" Patrick asked, leaning close to me as his family bustled around. His breath ghosted over my ear and sent a little shiver down my spine.

I nodded. "Yeah, I'm fine." I wondered if he could tell that was a lie.

Patrick's family chatted happily while his mum passed around a plate of cake and offered drinks. Usually I'd be all up for coffee, but since I felt so on the spot, I was terrified of spilling it all down myself, and that wouldn't make a good impression.

"So, Connor," Cara started, "Patrick said you're a dancer?"

"Yeah," I nodded and swallowed. Patrick squeezed my hand. "I'm a qualified ballet teacher, but I also teach a few other things like jazz and modern, and I do a lot of pole dancing too. I compete as well."

"Can you do those things where you hang upside down by, like, your knee?" Mary asked.

"Of course." I smiled and picked at my cake. It was good, but not quite as good as Patrick's.

"That's insane!" Mary turned to Patrick. "You never wanted to try?"

"No, I definitely don't have the strength to do that."

"You'd be good," I said. "And besides, it's not about strength when you start. Pole is for everyone."

"Maybe one day," Patrick said softly and gave me a little smile. It made my chest ache. God, I wanted that smile to be real.

"So you two met at The Pear Tree?" Aoife asked. "Do you still work there?"

I shook my head. "My friend Levi—he's actually Ben's brother—opened a dance studio, and now I teach there full-time."

"You just wanted to escape Aaron before he threw something at you," Patrick teased.

"He's just not used to my charm."

"Yeah, charm… that's what it is."

I laughed and nudged him playfully, the tightness inside me starting to loosen. Things started to feel a little easier, and the awkward, stilted questions slowly dissolved into easy conversation. It was hard to have a single conversation with six people without it feeling like an interview or an interrogation. Soon I found myself chatting to Aoife and Mary about pole. They were both fascinated, and I was pretty sure I'd be able to convince them to give it a try. I knew one incredible poler in her mid-sixties, who'd taken it up in her forties after her divorce. Although I wasn't sure Patrick would forgive me if I introduced his mother to pole dancing, especially after his reaction to her even *suggesting* sex. Patrick's relationship with his mum was very different than my relationship with my own mum, who'd sat me down at fifteen when I'd gotten my first proper boyfriend and given me a very thorough talk on gay sex that included a clip from some gay porn she'd borrowed from a friend.

"How're you doing?" Patrick asked during a lull in the conversation. It was so sweet that he was checking up on me, and it made my stomach squirm in delight. "You okay?"

"Yeah, I am."

"Good." He'd been chatting to John and Cara about

something to do with the yard. I'd heard the words horses and racing and slightly tuned out. "I need to do the cake in a minute. Want to give me a hand?"

"Sure. But I can't guarantee I'll be anything more than a pretty face," I said, giving him a cheeky grin.

"It is a very pretty face though." Patrick's lips brushed against my cheek again. Warmth coursed through me, making my skin prickle and flush.

"Flattery will get you everywhere." My voice was low and hoarse, not quite the teasing I'd been going for. But there was something about Patrick's sweetness that caught me off guard and sent me spinning, like I was riding the Waltzers at Goose Fair.

Patrick's eyed widened and his face turned noticeably pink. He was so cute when he blushed.

"You two okay?" Cara asked, wearing her family's customary wry smile.

"Yeah," Patrick said. He sounded calmer than he looked. "I was just telling Connor that I need to go and get the cake done before dinner. It needs to be iced tonight so it's got time to chill before tomorrow. I can add the final touches then."

"Go ahead." Aoife waved her hands. "I made a giant lasagne for dinner earlier, so if you're okay with me putting the oven on, it can just reheat gently. I've got garlic bread and salad to go with it. Nice and simple and out of your way."

"That's fine. My kitchen's a lot hotter. I keep asking Ben for proper air conditioning, and he keeps telling me it's on the list."

"So until then, pastry in the chiller?" I asked, remembering how I'd often found Patrick working with pastry on the lid of the chest freezer near the chillers, or even in the chiller itself so the butter didn't melt.

"Pastry in the chiller," Patrick said with a nod.

As I looked up, I noticed Mary watching us with a look on her face I couldn't quite place. The word that came to mind was shrewd, but that didn't make sense. I didn't think she'd be able to guess we were faking. In my opinion we were doing a fucking good job. Patrick was more affectionate than some of the guys I'd actually dated.

Fuck, my standards were apparently non-existent.

I needed better boyfriends in the future.

Ugh, the idea of trying to find someone who was better than Patrick was exhausting.

"Come on." Patrick stood, and I realised his fingers were still interlaced with mine. We'd been holding hands the whole time, and I hadn't noticed. My stomach did a little flip.

I followed him out to the kitchen like a puppy and did exactly what I was told—carefully slicing strawberries and weighing ingredients while Patrick mixed and decorated, passing on quiet instructions now and then. I was utterly enraptured in watching him work, and I nearly cut my fingers off twice before I remembered to concentrate.

He was so cutely serious, and I couldn't resist picking up one of the strawberry pieces and offering it to him. "Open wide."

Patrick was still half concentrating, but he opened his lips enough for me to push the strawberry between them.

His lips wrapped around my fingers, and a jolt of electricity shot down my spine. Patrick stared at me wide eyed, as if he couldn't believe what he'd just done. He opened his mouth to say something.

"Wha—"

"Patrick, could you stick the oven on?" Aoife called from outside the kitchen.

The moment snapped, leaving me standing stunned in the middle of the room. My heart racing faster than the speed of light.

CHAPTER TWELVE

Connor

MY HEAD CONTINUED to spin throughout the rest of the evening, replaying the sensation of Patrick's lips wrapped around my fingers on a loop. We'd gone back to decorating the cake in near silence afterwards, but that had only made things worse. I'd just about recovered my senses by the time we got to dinner.

We all took our seats around a wide, wooden table that was obviously old and well loved. It was easy to see from the marks ingrained into the wood and the odd coloured stains across the tabletop. I ran my fingers across a reddish-pink mark, wondering what might have caused it and really hoping it wasn't blood. That would ruin my evening.

"I think that's a Patrick mark," said Cara, who sat next to me. She'd been joined by her husband and her two sons, both of whom weren't actually that much younger than me. I had to admit the eldest, Kyle, was kind of cute—even if that was probably slightly weird of me to admit. "He was helping ice a cake and he spilt a whole bottle of red food colouring on the table."

"Oh God, I remember that," Mary said with a chuckle from her place opposite me. "I was the one trying to clear it up, and I turned all mum's tea towels bright red."

"It looked like you'd massacred something." Aoife laughed as she passed me a huge plate of lasagne. My stomach rumbled noisily, and I saw Patrick's lips twitch as he passed me a bowl of salad.

"I was four. I was doing my best," Patrick said.

"Don't worry. When I was four, I ruined my mum's favourite lipstick by drawing all over myself and her mirror and then I accidentally smeared it into the carpet," I said. "The lipstick was bright pink, and mum's bedroom carpet was cream. I was not popular." I chuckled. "Especially not with the cat, who I'd tried to blame it on."

"Do you remember when you tried to bring in all the farm kittens?" John asked, looking at Patrick as he passed him a plate loaded with thick slices of garlic bread.

"I do," Aoife said with a chuckle. "You tried to put them in your chest of drawers."

"Is this gang up on Patrick night?" Patrick asked, but he was still smiling.

"It's because you're the baby, and we're not used to having you here to tease," added Mary with a wink. "And it's our family duty to embarrass you in front of your boyfriend. We did the same to Kyle when he brought his first girlfriend to dinner."

"And I'm never, ever doing that again," Kyle said.

"Hey, it could've been worse," added Cara's husband, who I think had introduced himself as Steven. "Do you remember when you brought me home?"

"God, I thought you'd never come back after that." Cara shook her head and rolled her eyes. She smiled at me. "Da answered the door covered in blood. He'd been sharpening some knives and cut his fingers."

"He was still holding a knife," Steven said. "He just said 'Oh, you must be Steven', then tried to shake my hand."

"Imogen had to take him to the hospital," Cara added.

John laughed. "I remember that. Your mum said I was never allowed to sharpen knives again without supervision."

"Well, you'd have cut your arm off like a bloody idiot." Aoife rolled her eyes. "It's like the time you tried to light a firework while you were still holding it."

"You thought it was endearing."

"I thought it was bloody stupid."

"But you still married me."

"For my sins, John Evans. For my sins." She leant over and kissed him, and I couldn't stop myself from smiling. I'd never had a family dinner like dinner with the Evanses, and it was oddly charming. I wondered if my family life would've been like this if my mum had still been close with her parents. But considering they were all fuckwits, I somehow doubted it. I was glad they weren't in our lives.

"I can't believe it's been fifty years," Mary said. "I think I'd have killed someone."

"Me either," Aoife said. "Especially since we nearly didn't have a wedding."

"How come?" I asked, suddenly intrigued.

"John's best man decided it would be a great idea to go on an impromptu stag do the night before at the local pub. They all got absolutely wasted with my brothers and my father, and they decided it would be a great idea to tie John to a tree."

John chuckled. "I still don't remember that. I just remember waking up the next morning with a banging headache."

"Thank God they came back for you. I'd have murdered Smiffy if you'd missed the wedding."

"He was very apologetic, and we were only twenty minutes late." He smiled at Aoife fondly. "You were thirty."

"Only because we had to keep circling the village green to wait for everyone to leave the pub to go into the church. They left all the drinks on the wall, came out the church, and went back to the pub to get them."

John reached for her hand over the table and squeezed it. "That was a good day."

"It was."

The conversation moved on to the party and jokes about other family members that were coming and wondering who'd do what. It was warm and cosy in an unfamiliar way, but I liked it. It was almost something I wished I could be a part of more often. Maybe, after all of this, Patrick's family wouldn't hate me enough to ban me from coming back. Somehow I doubted that would be the case though. I'd just have to enjoy it while it lasted.

"Is your family as mad as ours?" Cara asked.

I winced internally because that was one question I

didn't really know how to answer without making her uncomfortable, but it was one I couldn't really avoid either. "I, um, I wouldn't know. It's just me and my mum. We don't speak to the rest of my family, and my dad fucked off before I was born."

"Oh shit. I'm sorry."

"Don't worry about it," I said, waving my hand and giving her a smile. I didn't want her to feel bad because it wasn't as if she'd known. I didn't exactly advertise how shitty my relatives were. "This is nice though. I've never really done the big family dinner before."

"I'm glad we did this before we bring the rest of the family in. Even with just Imogen, Orla, and their families, we get up to seventeen."

"Christmas must be fun for you."

"Yeah, if you want chaos, then you and Patrick should come. If you can drag him away from work." She smiled warmly at me. "Bring your mum too. Mum won't mind. She's a more the merrier kind of person. I think we had thirty for Christmas once. I'm still not sure how Mum cooked all the food."

I felt oddly touched by the gesture, and I didn't know what to say. There was a lump in my throat, and all I could do was force out the word, "Thanks." I couldn't believe how welcoming Patrick's family had been even in the couple of hours we'd been here. I'd never experienced anything like it, and it tugged at my heartstrings, making me feel open and vulnerable. They trusted me with their son and brother, and I felt like a fraud. Would they still like me if they knew this was fake? If I was "just a friend"? Or were they just being nice because I was important to Patrick, and they clearly adored him?

"Did you hear that, Patrick?" Cara said teasingly. "You're coming for Christmas now."

"Oh really? What if I have to work?"

"Then I'll tell Mum to throw a second Christmas on the twenty-seventh, and we'll do it then."

"Sorry," I said weakly, turning to Patrick and giving him a half-smile. I had no idea what to do. Would Patrick be mad at me for getting involved? Then again, I'd never worried about that before. What was it about this whole situation that had me thrown so off balance? It was like I was glued to a spinning pole and couldn't work out how to slow down. "I didn't mean to take sides."

"It's fine." He casually interlaced his fingers with mine, the smile he wore melting my fears away. "There's nothing to forgive."

He tilted his head slightly, and suddenly his lips met mine in a gentle kiss. It was almost uncertain, and for a fraction of a second, my body stilled as it tried to process what the fuck was going on. Except I couldn't process anything. I could barely even breathe because Patrick was kissing me.

Patrick was kissing me.

His lips were warm and soft and more perfect than anything I'd ever felt. I wanted to live in this moment forever or encase it in my memory so I'd never forget it.

My mouth pressed back against his. Time slowed to a crawl.

And then the kiss was over and nothing in the world would ever be the same again.

I stared at him as we broke apart. My heart was racing, my mouth opening and then closing again as no words came out. I couldn't believe he'd kissed me. Especially here, in front of his entire family.

And now I had to pretend my entire universe hadn't just exploded into a billion new star systems and that this was a totally normal and absolutely non-special thing because Patrick and I kissed all the time. I mean, we were dating, why wouldn't we suck face at every possible opportunity?

Except that sounded weird and gross because that was exactly the opposite of what had just happened.

Sure, I wouldn't turn down the opportunity to make out with Patrick. And if that happened to come with a side of groping, grinding, and getting naked, I would be starkers before you could say *go*. But that kiss was different; it was tender and affectionate. The sort of kiss you might give someone you loved…

Which made my head spin even more because that made no flipping sense.

"Are you okay?" Patrick asked. I realised I'd been staring off into space, and both Cara and Mary were watching me.

My face heated, and I grinned wickedly. "Yeah, just thinking about how much I like kissing you."

Patrick's face flamed. I giggled and pressed another kiss to his mouth, letting my tongue brush against his lips for the merest hint of a second. If we were allowed to kiss now, I might have to take a teeny tiny bit of advantage of it as long as Patrick didn't mind. This might be the only opportunity I'd ever have to kiss him, and I was going to make the most of it.

"You two are adorable," Mary said. "And a little gross."

"You're nearly forty!" Patrick grumbled, but he was smiling.

"Still doesn't make it less sickening. You two are so adorable it hurts."

I swallowed the lump in my throat. "Well, what do you expect? Your brother is the handsomest man in the world."

Patrick made a tiny squeaking sound, but he didn't say anything. I grasped his hand under the table.

Slowly, things began to return to normal and dinner continued.

Except, deep down, I knew nothing would ever be normal again.

CHAPTER THIRTEEN

Patrick

THE REST of the evening passed in a blur. I could hardly remember a thing except for the feel of Connor's mouth against mine.

I had no idea what had possessed me to kiss him. He'd just looked so beautiful, but also so worried, like he'd somehow done something wrong, and it was the only thing I could think to do to cheer him up. Which was utterly ridiculous when I thought about it. Kissing someone doesn't fix their problems.

Except it had made Connor smile, so I was struggling to remember why it was a bad idea. And then he'd kissed me, so it couldn't have been the worst thing in the world.

I still didn't know what had upset him. He'd looked a little uncomfortable at various points throughout the evening, and I wondered if my family had been a bit too overbearing. To me, they'd been pretty well behaved. Even if my mum had brought up our supposed sex life. But they were very nosy, and there were a lot of them. Even I got overwhelmed sometimes, and I was related to most of them.

Glancing at myself in the bathroom mirror, I took a deep breath and headed back to the bedroom across the corridor. Connor had offered me the shower first, so I'd left him to relax while I splashed through and brushed my teeth. I'd remembered to pack an old T-shirt and shorts for pyjamas, even though half the time I just crashed out in my boxers or naked. But since we'd be sharing a bed, I'd figured that wasn't appropriate. Even as best friends we weren't *that* close.

Besides, I didn't think I'd be able to see Connor half-undressed without having a very inappropriate reaction, and my shorts weren't going to cover that. I'd die of embarrassment if I somehow got a hard-on in front of Connor.

"Bathroom's free," I said as I stepped into the bedroom and shut the door behind me. I turned towards the bed and promptly dropped the armful of clothes I was carrying. Connor was doing some sort of stretch in a pair of tight, pink briefs, socks, and his T-shirt. His ass was sticking up while his hands and feet rested on the floor.

My dick throbbed, perking up immediately at the sight of Connor's perfect, round ass bobbing in the air. I grabbed my clothes off the floor, holding them at crotch height and praying Connor didn't notice because that was one conversation I wouldn't survive.

"Oh, sorry." Connor tilted his head to the side and looked up at me, smiling. "My legs were super tight after being in the car all afternoon, so I thought I'd do a quick stretch. I thought you'd be longer than you were. If I'd have known you were only going to be ten minutes, I'd have put leggings on." He stood up, his cheeks a little pink, but I didn't know if that was because he was flustered from me catching him or because all the blood had rushed to his head. I was going to go with the second.

"It's fine," I said, looking in his direction but not at him. "I'm sorry for surprising you."

"No, um, it's not a problem."

There was an awkward pause.

"So, Mum left us a couple of towels in the bathroom. I left you the purple one. It's on the rail."

"Oh, awesome. Thanks!" Connor slid past me and opened his suitcase, rummaging in it for his wash bag as I tried desperately not to look at his ass. Even though I'd seen it a hundred times in his pole videos and in those tiny shorts he wore in the summer, seeing him now was different. It was so much more intimate than those situations. And I had absolutely no right to perv on him. I was being a creepy bastard, and I knew it.

I tore my gaze away, looking at the bed and realising Connor had removed the pile of excess cushions, piling them neatly on the floor so we could actually get into the bed.

"Back in a minute," Connor called, closing the door behind him. My breath came out in a rush, and I dropped the clothes I was still holding onto the bed. I needed to get a hold of myself, otherwise tonight was going to be painful. Maybe I should have jerked off in the shower, but that would probably just have made me feel guilty. I almost always managed to avoid thinking about Connor when I masturbated because I knew it was crossing some sort of boundary, even if it was just a fantasy.

I shook my head and tried to clear my thoughts, but that didn't do anything except mix them up further. It was like I was trying to separate a cake mix after it had been beaten— absolutely impossible. Instead, I folded my clothes, separating out the dirty items from the ones I could wear again before climbing into bed with my book and my phone.

Skimming through Facebook didn't particularly hold my interest, and since there were no messages from Darcie or Aaron about any sort of kitchen disaster, I put my phone on the bedside table. I picked up the battered mystery novel I'd packed, hoping it would calm my racing mind. It was an old Agatha Christie Poirot story that I'd read a thousand times before. I probably could have recited it word for word in my sleep, but I loved the warm familiarity of it. There was something wonderfully comforting about reading a book I knew well, like curling up with an old friend or listening to someone I loved tell me the same story I'd heard a million times before but knew they were going to tell me again.

Soon I found myself lost in the cosy pages while Poirot investigated the death of Ruth Kettering aboard Le Train Bleu. I was still reading when Connor appeared again, looking refreshed and cheerful in a pair of shorts and a loose T-shirt that had a colourful cartoon character across the chest.

"Another Poirot?" he asked as he dumped the clothes

and the large wash bag he'd been holding and gave me a wry smile.

"I like Poirot," I said, slightly defensively, as Connor wriggled into bed beside me holding his Kindle.

"I never said it was a bad thing." He grinned. "One day we should swap books and see what happens. You can read one of my romance novels while I read your mysteries." I swallowed. Connor had a thing for very steamy gay romance novels, and although there was nothing wrong with that, I honestly wasn't sure I'd be able to cope with the second-hand embarrassment. I mean, it had taken me three years to be comfortable with even searching for porn. I didn't know if I'd be able to cope knowing that Connor knew what I was reading. My face would probably be bright red the entire time.

"Er, yeah. Maybe." It hadn't quite been the answer I'd wanted to give, but I was terrible at telling Connor no. Hopefully that would be vague enough for me to put it off for the foreseeable future.

"You don't have to if you don't want to, but you might enjoy it. And I promise not to make you read one that opens with fucking or one that has a gangbang. I'll find you something sweet."

I stared at him open-mouthed. I was pretty sure my naivety was written all over my shocked expression.

"You should see your face." Connor giggled. "You're so cute!"

"Thanks. I think." I sighed. Maybe it would be fun to read something different for a change, and maybe it would help me to stop being so embarrassed every time someone mentioned anything to do with sex. And maybe it would even be fun. I'd never read anything like that before. "Fine then. You can read this, and I'll read one of yours."

I took my thumb out of the book, making a mental note of my page and handing it over. Connor's grin was a mixture of pure innocent sweetness and utter wickedness, and it made my insides turn somersaults. He tapped his Kindle's screen a couple of times and presented it to me.

"Try this one," he said. "I think you'll like it. It's ridiculously sweet and fluffy, and it's got like, zero angst and just enough delicious smut without overdoing it. Perfect first-time romance. And it's the first in a series, so if you like it, you can read the rest of them."

"Thanks." I looked down at the screen to see the cover displayed in black and white with the title in pretty, swooping letters and a beautiful, shirtless man smiling up from behind the title. *One Last Kiss* by Ella Fox. Well, here went nothing. I tapped the screen until I reached the first chapter and started to read.

Three hours later, I was still reading.

Connor had curled up and fallen asleep two hours earlier. He'd read a couple of chapters before his yawns had finally gotten too big, then he'd put my book down and curled up beside me. I'd flicked my lamp off, reading by the soft, electric glow of the Kindle so I didn't disturb him. He looked so adorably peaceful when he slept, his little kitten snores filling the quiet room. I almost wanted to snuggle up next to him, watching him sleep and brushing the stray hair off his forehead, but I wasn't quite ready to put the book down yet.

It had surprised me how quickly I'd been sucked into the story and how easy it was to read. It was the story of two guys who'd known each other for years, one of them the best friend of the other's older brother. Now they were in their twenties and had reconnected at college where one of them was doing his PhD and the other was finishing up his undergrad. One of them was also really into sports while the other wasn't, but he still made time to go and watch the other play because... well they were friends even if he wanted it to be something more.

On paper, it sounded slightly cliché and tropey, and maybe it was, but I still couldn't help being drawn into the narrative and the complex feelings they had for each other. It almost felt validating in a strange way. I just couldn't quite put my finger on why.

I flicked the page over, and as the characters kissed, a strange sensation of heat built in my stomach. The characters began to strip off their clothes and explore each other with wandering hands and desperate mouths, and I felt my whole body flush.

Beside me, Connor made a little snuffly sound and snuggled closer into my side, his hand reaching across my stomach as he buried his head in my chest and hooked his leg over mine.

I froze. Heat flooded my face and ran down my body. I flicked the Kindle off and set it down, plunging the room into darkness. I'd survived the solo shower scene, but the idea of reading a sex scene with Connor draped over me was a little too far out of my comfort zone.

I slid down slightly, making myself comfortable and gently tried to nudge Connor free, but it was no use. He clung to me tighter than a koala on a eucalyptus tree, and he was absolute dead weight. For someone so small, he suddenly seemed to have morphed into a mountain, and there was absolutely no way to shift him.

Sighing, I put my arm around him and drifted off to sleep, a contented half-smile curling across my lips.

CHAPTER FOURTEEN

Connor

I'D BEEN a morning person ever since I could remember. I was a naturally early riser no matter how late I stayed up the night before.

When I'd been a student, I'd happily go clubbing until three in the morning then get up at seven for a nine o'clock class looking fresh as a daisy. While I wasn't quite that good anymore, I sometimes worked late shifts at The Pear Tree, got home about midnight or one, and then woke up at six to stretch and be at the studio at eight to open up. I'd never been one of those people who could lounge around in bed all morning. I always needed to be doing something. It had driven more than one ex crazy in the past because they'd always wanted to spend Saturday mornings in bed sleeping, fucking, and then sleeping again. The fucking I had no problem with as long as the sex was good. It was the endless need to sleep that annoyed me. The sex needed to be pretty fucking spectacular to demand sleep afterwards, and so far, I'd never met anyone who lived up to that. It took a lot to wear me out.

So it surprised me when I woke with my arm wrapped around Patrick and my leg thrown across his, that my first reaction wasn't to roll over, stretch, and sit up. Instead, I snuggled in farther, breathing in his sweet scent. He always smelt like icing sugar and something warm, like cinnamon, whether he was in or out of the kitchen. I couldn't explain it. I just wanted to fill my senses with it or bottle it and take it with me wherever I went.

That probably sounded creepy, but I didn't care.

My boundaries with Patrick had gone from a slightly blurred friendship to all kinds of fucked up and weird in the past twenty-four hours, and I'd decided I was just going to lean into it. If Patrick was my boyfriend for the next three days, then I was going to act like it. Although if he really was my boyfriend, I wouldn't have quickly jerked off in the shower last night thinking about him. I'd have walked back into the bedroom, dropped my towel, and crawled into bed with him.

I'd vaguely considered that I should feel guilty for getting off on ideas of fucking Patrick, but I was going to file that under "this weekend's fucked-up boundaries" and keep it there. It was like the whole "what happens in Vegas" mantra, except it was what happened in Devon. The consequences of my actions could all be ignored until Tuesday at the earliest, at which point I'd probably just drown my sorrows in cheese, gin, and terrible Netflix movies.

Besides, there was a good chance if I hadn't gotten off last night that I'd have woken up really horny this morning, and that would not have worked. Especially considering I was sprawled over Patrick with my dick pressed against his thigh.

Patrick shifted underneath me, letting out a sleepy little sigh. I flicked my eyes up towards his face, wondering if he was awake yet or still dreaming. Patrick had always looked hella fucking adorable when he slept, and I wasn't going to miss out on getting my fill now.

I tilted my head slightly, casting my eyes up and across his round face. His grey eyes flickered open behind his long lashes, blinking at me sleepily. He smiled and sighed, his arm wrapping around me to pull me momentarily closer.

"Mornin'," he muttered, voice still thick with sleep.

"Good morning." I knew I sounded perky—the sort of perky that made most men want to turf me out of bed for being too awake or immediately demand a blowjob to help them wake up too. The more I thought about it, the more I realised I'd just dated assholes and fuckbois in the past. Once upon a time, I'd thought I had standards, but apparently not.

Patrick smiled and pressed a kiss to the top of my head. "Do you want to get up?" he asked. "Or can I keep you for another two minutes?"

"Hmm, I'll allow it," I said with mock sincerity. "I might even let you keep me for five."

"So generous." He laughed, his body shaking gently. "What time is it?"

"I have no clue. I haven't actually moved yet. You're too comfortable."

"It's nice to know my purpose in life is to be your pillow."

"It's your secondary purpose." I snuggled into him again. "Your first purpose is to bake me cake."

"So I feed you and let you sleep on me? Have I adopted another cat? You're about the same size as The President so it makes sense."

"Ha, ha. So funny." I lifted his T-shirt and blew a raspberry on his stomach, trying to ignore how his warm, soft skin felt under my lips and the trail of dark-blond hair that ran down to the waistband of his shorts. I wanted to run my tongue through it.

Patrick yelped, and I grinned, flopping back on the bed next to him. I raised an eyebrow in challenge and Patrick rolled over. My legs spread around him as his hands gently gripped my wrists and pinned me to the bed. I wanted nothing more than to wrap my legs around his hips and pull him against me, grinding up against him until we both came in our shorts. Desire burned under my skin, filling me up and scorching me from the inside out. I felt my cock stirring, thickening and pushing against the thin material constraining it.

A moan tried to escape my lips, but I caught it on my tongue.

My hips shifted of their own accord, desperately seeking friction.

Patrick's mouth was inches from mine. It would be so easy to kiss him, to pull him to me and claim his mouth. His eyes were wide, but there was heat burning there. His tongue darted out to lick his lips, and I suddenly realised just how perfect they were.

My hips moved, brushing against his. My cock was hard and aching now, demanding attention and touch. As I moved, I felt my dick brush against Patrick's, which was also hard enough to pound nails. Shit. That made everything so much more real, but it didn't mean I wanted it any less.

Patrick's hips gave an aborted thrust. This time I couldn't keep the moan from sliding past my lips.

"Patrick…" My voice was quiet but so fucking needy. He froze. His mouth was half-open, and I didn't know whether he wanted to speak, groan, or kiss me until I'd forgotten my own name. I honestly didn't mind which option he chose. I just needed him to make a decision.

But apparently the world had decided to take the decision out of our hands entirely.

Two seconds later there was a loud knock on the door, and Aoife's voice sounded from the other side. "I'm sorry to disturb you boys, but if you're up, we could really do with another pair of hands to help set up before the caterers get here."

Patrick cleared his throat. "That's fine. We'll be there in five minutes."

Aoife said something else, but I wasn't listening. I was watching the perfect moment I'd almost had with Patrick disappear over the hills. He released my hands and rolled off me and out of bed with a muttered apology. His face was an interesting shade of deep pink as he reached for his suitcase, grabbing a handful of clothes.

I sat up, reaching out for him. "Babe, wait—"

"I'll get dressed in the bathroom," he said. "You take your time." And then he was gone faster than a bolt of lightning.

I groaned and flopped down onto the mattress, my cock deflating sadly as I melodramatically contemplated the hideousness of my situation.

Twenty minutes later, after I'd pulled myself together and gotten dressed, I padded downstairs and into the kitchen. The large clock on the wall said it was nearly twenty to ten. I couldn't believe Patrick and I had actually slept that late.

I felt a little bad since we were here to help with the party, and we'd ended up sleeping until after nine.

Aoife stood by the oven, pulling out a tray of sausages and crispy bacon, and my mouth watered at the delicious smells wafting through the kitchen. My stomach growled loudly, and I threw a hand over it as if hoping the sound would be somehow muffled, even though I was pretty sure everyone on the planet had just heard it grumbling.

"Morning!" Aoife said cheerfully when she saw me. "Did you sleep well?"

"Like a log. That bed is so comfy. Sorry we slept so late."

"Don't worry about it." She gave me a fond smile. "Years of children and horses and I'm still up at the crack of dawn every day. I used to drive the kids crazy by turfing them out of bed at seven on the weekends."

I chuckled. "I was the other way around. I used to wake my mum up by playing music at half seven so I could practice dancing. She eventually realised I wasn't going to stop, so she bought me a portable CD player and some headphones so I wouldn't disturb her. It made me light on my feet though."

"That was nice she encouraged you."

"It was, although we did have to have ground rules about where it was acceptable to dance. Living room, yes. Middle of Tesco, no."

Aoife laughed as she grabbed a huge bag of bread rolls. "How long have you been dancing then?"

"Since I was three. My mum enrolled me in baby ballet because a friend of hers taught it, and she thought it would be good for me. It stuck." I watched Aoife pull out a tub of Lurpak from the fridge. "Do you want a hand? I feel like I'm being terribly lazy just standing here watching you."

"If you don't mind. I'm just making a load of bacon and sausage baps for everyone. They're just getting the last of the tables and everything all set up. The caterers are arriving at one and the guests about half two." She smiled at me. "We're starting early because most of us aren't good with very late nights these days." She shook her head fondly. "I can't believe John is seventy. I still feel about your age." Aoife sighed and shook her head. "Listen to me blathering on, now I do sound like an old woman. Lord, I've turned into my mother. Grab a knife out of that drawer, and let's get these made. I'm assuming you're okay with bacon and sausages? Patrick didn't mention anything about allergies or you being veggie when I asked him."

"I'm absolutely fine. In fact, I'll probably eat at least one of each. Patrick says I have hollow legs," I said with a laugh, digging a knife out of the drawer and starting to split and butter the rolls that Aoife put in front of me.

"I'm so happy for you and Patrick, you know. For such a long time he seemed so unhappy, and I always wondered if there was something he wasn't telling me... but when he first mentioned you, he was so much brighter, and recently... well, I'm so glad he decided to tell us and let us meet you."

There was an unspoken undercurrent to her words that made me pause. It was if she was worried about putting her foot in it or scaring me off.

"I'm glad too," I said, not looking at her but wondering just how much I could say without dropping Patrick in it or making him uncomfortable. The last thing I wanted to do was betray his trust. "He was so nervous about telling you, but I think it's because he loves you and he was worried. Even if he didn't need to be. That's the way Patrick is though. He cares so deeply, and I wouldn't have it any other way."

"That's my Patrick. Always putting others first," Aoife said as she started to fill the buttered rolls, splitting sausages in half on the chopping board next to me. The smell made my stomach rumble again and she laughed, handing me one. "I think you'd better eat one now. You can test them. There's ketchup and brown sauce on the side if you want."

"Thanks." I took the roll and bit into it, practically squeaking with happiness as I did. There was nothing that beat a sausage or bacon sandwich. Except maybe a bacon *and* sausage sandwich. What could I say? I liked meat. Honestly, I liked food in general. That was one amazing benefit to having a chef as a best-friend-slash-fake-boyfriend; you got lots of free food.

We continued making the rolls, chatting easily together about random little things, until the others came traipsing back into the house. They all made a beeline for the plates we'd piled high, and Aoife flicked on the kettle to start making cups of tea and coffee for everyone. Patrick and John were there as well as Cara and her husband and sons, plus Mary and another couple who Patrick introduced as his sister Imogen and her husband Tom. They had two boys with them, who I'd have guessed were in their early teens, but they took a couple of rolls in each hand and disappeared before I'd been introduced.

Patrick pressed a bacon roll covered in ketchup into my greedy paws and chuckled as I stuffed half of it into my mouth like some sort of giant hamster.

"You laugh, but I'm hungry."

"There's going to be loads of food later," Patrick said, giving me a wry smile. "There's a huge buffet and a pizza oven. And that's without the enormous amount of cake and desserts. I think Da said something about ice cream as well, but he might have been joking."

"That's later though. This is now! I might waste away if I don't eat now."

"How many stomachs do you have?"

"Are you calling me a cow?"

"Of course not, and if I were, you'd be a very cute cow. The prettiest, glitteriest cow ever."

"You know," I said with a laugh, "I'm not sure if that's supposed to be an insult or a compliment."

"Compliment, obviously." Patrick smiled indulgently at me, and I couldn't resist leaning in. Our earlier awkwardness seemed to have dissipated, for which I was eternally fucking grateful. I wasn't sure if I was pushing my luck, but I'd always been good at doing that. I pressed a quick kiss to Patrick's surprised lips and grinned at him.

"Good, I'm glad. Otherwise, I'd have been sad."

"I never want that," Patrick said. "Ever."

CHAPTER FIFTEEN

Patrick

I'D SPENT the whole morning trying to forget about what had happened in bed between Connor and me. Unfortunately, my brain seemed to think that I really wanted to relive every second in excruciating detail instead. I couldn't stop thinking about Connor's wide eyes or wanting smile or the way he'd moaned my name when I'd brushed against him. And the way he'd been hard against me...

Part of me wondered what would have happened if we hadn't been interrupted.

Would we have kissed? I was pretty sure we would have.

Would there have been more? Again, I was pretty sure there would have been. And that was the thought that was killing me. Knowing I could've fooled around with the man I loved. The man I'd give everything to if he asked.

I'd decided to just let this weekend happen, regardless

of the consequences. It was probably the most irresponsible thing I'd ever done, but I couldn't seem to stop myself. If Connor was going to be my boyfriend until we got home, then I wanted to pretend it was real. Then when this was over, at least I'd have some memories to look back on fondly. And while I knew there were a million things that were never going to happen between us, perhaps there were a few things that might. I couldn't deny I wanted them more than I'd ever wanted anything else before. I didn't think I could ask for them because that would be awkward, but if they happened… well, I didn't think I'd stop them.

Currently, I was reclining on the bed while Connor sat at the dressing table in our room carefully applying make-up. There were various bottles, brushes, sponges, and palettes spread across the white, wooden surface. The brushes had iridescent, unicorn horn handles and shimmering bristles, the tips tinted with colour. They were so perfectly Connor I couldn't see him using anything else.

"What do you think?" he asked, turning around to face me and pointing at two different palettes with the handle of a small, fluffy brush. "Do I go more sunset colours, pinks, purples, and oranges, or do I go a little more neutral and toned down?"

I lowered his Kindle, which I'd borrowed to keep reading Connor's book, and looked at him seriously. "Do you want my honest opinion?"

"Of course. I wouldn't have asked otherwise."

"I think you should go with the sunset ones or something pink. I think your make-up should be bright and vibrant. Like you."

"You don't think your family will mind?" He pulled at his lip, and I hated the flash of worry that crossed his face. "I mean, it's one thing to date a boy who wears make-up, but it's another when said boy visibly wears make-up and looks like he stepped out of an Instagram post. I don't want to upset anyone."

"I couldn't give a flying monkey's what anyone else thinks," I said, turning to slide off the bed. I dropped the Kindle onto the mattress and made my way around the bed towards him. Reaching out, I cupped the edge of his jaw in my hand, trying not to smudge his foundation. "You are perfect, Connor, and I want everyone to see you just the way you are. So wear the bright colours. I know you'll look fabulous."

I pressed a kiss to his lips, soft and slow. It was almost a mistake because once I'd started, I didn't want to stop. But I did. Because otherwise I wasn't quite sure where we'd end up, and all we needed was to be interrupted again. "You should finish getting ready."

"Okay…" He swallowed, then grinned slyly. "You're so wicked, you know. You started kissing me, and now you can't stop. If I'd have known you were so sweet, I'd have started kissing you years ago."

"Oh?" I couldn't really think of anything else to say. My brain seemed to have frozen in place, stuck on a reoccurring loop of Connor's last few words. "Maybe I should have done."

"You're so cute. So, what are you going to wear?"

Connor asked as he turned back to the mirror, dipping a make-up brush into the eyeshadow palette in front of him.

"I brought a shirt with me and some smart, dark-blue jeans that I've only worn once. I got them a couple of years ago for best, but it turns out I don't really need best jeans. They still fit though. I checked. I thought that would do. I've got that blazer you got me too if I need it." It had been getting warm outside already, so I wasn't sure I'd wear the jacket even if it did look nice. The idea of getting dressed up was a strange one. I spent my days in loose chef's trousers and whites, wearing chef's Crocs which were ugly but comfortable and practical. When I was chilling at home, I wore jogging bottoms and old T-shirts, and since my social life was largely non-existent, I only owned two pairs of jeans—one for best and one slightly ratty pair I wore for every day.

"Do you think that'll be okay?"

"I think that sounds perfect, babe. You'll look very handsome."

"What about you?" Connor could turn up in a bin-bag and he'd still look breath-taking.

"I'm going… subtle."

I laughed. "What does Connor subtle mean?"

"It means subtle! I've got a pink shirt and a grey suit. I debated the whole shirt and harness combo, a la Adam Rippon at the Oscars, but I thought I'd save that for another time." He winked at me, sending a blush hurtling across my skin. I'd seen harnesses in porn before and the idea of Connor in one was not doing good things for my blood pressure.

I swallowed around my tongue and forced words out. "Sounds good."

Connor grinned at me. I suddenly wondered if he was deliberately winding me up because he loved seeing the reaction from me. It was like he'd worked out which buttons to press to get a reaction and was testing them out to see what happened. It wasn't malicious though. It was more like charming curiosity.

Although maybe charming wasn't the right word since he was likely to kill me if he kept it up.

I turned away from him to the wardrobe where I'd hung up my shirt and jeans last night. I thought I might as well get dressed now, although I wasn't sure the bathroom would be free since some of my other family members were getting changed here too.

"You can get changed in here. I don't mind."

"Are you sure?"

"Of course. Go ahead!" When I glanced across the room, Connor was leaning in close to the mirror, putting on what I assumed was eyeliner. His tongue poked out as he concentrated. It was charming, and I wanted to sit and watch him for some reason, but I also needed to tear my eyes away and get dressed.

I pulled off my faded blue T-shirt and reached for the crisp, white shirt on its hanger. It had survived the journey without getting creased, and I buttoned it up, straightening the collar in the wardrobe mirror but leaving the top couple of buttons undone. I wasn't wearing a tie so there was no point choking to death. Then I pulled off my old jeans and swapped them for the newer ones, grimacing at the stiffness of the material. I breathed in as I zipped them up. I really needed to remember to wear these more often or they were always going to be so tight they'd crush my balls.

I flung the jacket over the end of the bed and attempted to retrieve the Kindle without feeling like my legs were separate from my whole body. Maybe I should just wear the old ones and hope no one noticed they were a little battered.

"Okay, I just need to get changed and I'll be ready," Connor said from behind me. "Oh my fucking God, babe. You look amazing in those jeans."

"Really? They're a little… stiff."

Connor snorted as I turned to look at him. "Nah, they look great. And I love the shirt."

"Er, thanks," I muttered, momentarily distracted by his beauty. His make-up was flawless as usual with perfectly highlighted cheekbones that shimmered in the sunlight. He'd clearly decided not to go for the sunset colours, but instead his eyeshadow was a perfectly blended array of pinks from a soft pastel to almost neon, a touch of glitter catching my eye and the perfect dark line making his beautiful eyes pop. His lips were dual shaded with a softer pink towards the middle that faded into something darker at the edges of his mouth. It made his lips look plump and full and oh-so-fucking kissable. I wanted to take his mouth with mine and kiss him until his lipstick was smeared and stained across me.

"Wow. You… you look incredible."

Connor smiled softly, and if I didn't know better, I'd have said he looked embarrassed. "Thank you. I try."

He sauntered over to the wardrobe, retrieved his suit bag, and quickly threw off his clothes. I finally turned to retrieve the Kindle and switch it off so I wouldn't stare at the perfect expanses of Connor's skin and his slim, toned body. I was bordering on creepy, and I really needed to stop.

Five minutes later, we were both ready, and by the time we got downstairs, most people had already headed across the yard to the barn. I double-checked the cake in passing. It would need a few bits doing to it just before we served it, but I'd sneak out of the party and do those later. It would at least give me fifteen minutes away from everyone. Don't get me wrong, I loved my family, but they did get a little overwhelming at times, and I wasn't really used to being sociable with anyone who wasn't from work or Connor.

That probably said something very sad about my life, but honestly, it didn't bother me.

I took Connor's hand and led him out the back door. The dogs were pottering about in the yard, and I already heard the hum of chatter and music. There was a black van parked outside the barn with a tent in front of it, delicious smells emanating from inside. A couple of catering staff members milled around with drinks on trays. People spilled out of the barn and into the nearby field, which we'd turned into an outdoor seating area. We'd also equipped it with some giant lawn games, and there was plenty of space for the kids to run around without disturbing the horses, who were all in fields away from the party.

I accepted a glass of Pimm's from one of the nearby waiters as we passed, even though it wasn't usually my sort of thing. But right now, I somehow felt the need for liquid courage. Mostly because of the barrage of questions I was going to be subjected to. There was a hideous churning in the pit of my stomach, and I was suddenly regretting dragging Connor into this mess. Not because I thought my family would be rude to him, but because they were now going to want to know everything about us and our "relationship". The last thing I needed was to fend off seventeen questions from Aunt Mary, not to be confused with my sister, about when we were going to get married.

Thank God Connor wasn't my real boyfriend because he'd probably run screaming after this. Although that would give me a reason for us to break up, even if my family might feel guilty for making him feel so over-whelmed that he dumped me. They might even message him to apologise and beg him to take me back. I wouldn't put it past them.

On second thought, we'd need another reason.

"Where do you want to start?" I asked, taking a sip of my drink and trying not to clutch at Connor's hand. They were my family for heaven's sake.

"Um, I don't mind. I think Mary's over there." He pointed with his glass before taking a very elegant sip through the straw he'd procured from the waiter. "Shall we go say hi?"

"Sounds good," I said, pretending it wasn't a giant lie. Mary spotted us and waved so there was no avoiding her now.

"Don't you clean up nicely?" Mary said as we reached

her. "I haven't seen you this dressed up since Orla got married."

"I could say the same." I gestured at the floral dress she was wearing and smiled. I was more used to seeing my sister in jeans and old band T-shirts.

"Ah, that's 'cos you don't come out with me in Plymouth. I can dress fancy then."

"Patrick said your best friend is a drag queen," Connor added. "Who are they?"

"That would be Pink Champagne. She does burlesque and drag. I met her a couple of years ago. She's a hoot. You'd love her. If you're ever down this way again, I'll take you to see her."

"Done. I'm gonna follow her on Insta too," Connor said, pulling his phone out of the pocket of the slim fitting grey trousers he was wearing. "Ooh, you should follow my friend Lola. I think you'd love her."

I let the two of them chat because there wasn't much I could really add to the conversation. I started to realise that maybe I didn't know my sisters, or at least Mary, as well as I thought. Maybe if I'd known more about her personal life, I would have come out to her years ago. She clearly wouldn't have been bothered. Maybe it would be nice for us to get closer after this.

"Hey, Patrick." Mary tapped me on the shoulder and beckoned me slightly away from the others.

"Everything okay?" I asked as I followed her for a few steps.

"Yeah, of course." She smiled at me. "I just wanted to say… I'm so happy you finally felt you could be open with us. I know I've teased you in the past because you're my little brother, and that's my job, but honestly, I want you to know that I'm so fucking proud of you. We all are. You're amazing, Patrick, and I love you so much." She pulled me into a tight hug and pressed a kiss to the side of my head while something inside me exploded like a million fireworks suddenly being set off all at once.

"Thank you. I don't know what to say." Everything I thought of suddenly sounded fake or redundant. But just knowing that I had Mary's support—that I had my whole family's support—was more than I'd ever dreamed off.

"You don't need to say anything!" Mary laughed. "You're my brother, and I love you. Of course I'm going to support you. You should believe in yourself, Patrick. You're fucking awesome."

I wasn't sure about that, but I wasn't going to say anything. We chatted for a bit longer before a couple of other relatives drifted by to say hello. These were all aunts and uncles I hadn't seen in years, so most of the conversation was just general life catching up. I introduced Connor to all of them and he beamed, his vibrant energy bubbling over and lighting up the air around him. He was like a living ball of sunshine; his warmth drew people to him. He'd always been a people person, and right now, he was in his element. If he was nervous, he didn't look it.

And, of course, as soon as the news spread that I was here and had a charming, beautiful boyfriend on my arm, everyone wanted to meet him.

"Isn't he lovely," my Auntie Betty whispered to me

while Connor was chatting to a couple of my cousins. "What does he do?"

"He's a dance teacher and a ballerina."

"I thought so." Betty nodded seriously. "He's got the arse of one." She sighed wistfully. "Reminds me of the man I dated in the seventies. He was an absolute firecracker. I've never met anyone so flexible or with as much stamina." I stared at her, slack-jawed, trying to process the words my elderly aunt had just said. She was seventy-two for Christ's sake. "I hope you're having fun, darling. You're only young once. Enjoy your beautiful man while you can, and make sure you have a solid bed frame."

She patted me on the arm, then changed the subject to ask me about a new cake recipe she'd been trying. I fumbled through the rest of the conversation, extraordinarily glad when it was announced that the food was ready so I could escape.

"Your cousins are nice," Connor said as he took my hand, walking towards the barn entrance. "Did you know your cousin Lou makes wedding cakes? She showed me some of the cakes on her Instagram. She's really good. And your cousin Izzy is a tattoo artist. He's the one with the blue hair. I think he's more like your second cousin, but I'm not sure how these things work. Anyway, he's very funny. Very dry witted."

"Lucky for you." I chuckled. "My elderly aunt just told me you have a dancer's arse, that she dated a very flexible man in her youth, and that I should enjoy you while I can."

Connor threw his head back and laughed. "Well, I guess it's nice to be appreciated. Maybe I should talk to her." He made a playful show of pulling at my hand as if he were drifting away. I laughed and tugged him gently back to my side. He fell against me, grinning cheekily up at me. My chest flooded with warmth, and I squeezed his hand tighter.

CHAPTER SIXTEEN

Patrick

WE JOINED the queue for the buffet, which was laid out on long tables down one side of the barn. It was a huge spread that included platters of fresh pizza from the van, fresh bread, cold meats and fish, huge bowls of salads, little quiches, some sticky chicken kebabs, and a million other things. The caterers had really gone all out, and everything looked amazing.

Except for the coleslaw because I'd always had a deep-seated hatred for things drenched in copious amounts of mayonnaise, and for me, drenched equalled any amount of the stuff.

Connor and I filled our plates, and I nearly had to drag Connor away because he looked like he was two minutes away from trying to shove food into his cheeks like a hamster.

There were several long trestle tables laid out across the

barn with benches running on either side that we'd decorated with some flowers in old jars and colourful knitted pom poms Mum had made. There was no allocated seating, so we found a space at the end of one of the tables with Mary, Lou, Izzy, and Orla and her husband Cian. Their three daughters were seated on the other side of them, chatting with some other kids about their age. The barn was filled with the warm burble of chatter, laughter, and happy eating.

I found myself falling deep into conversation with Lou, who I hadn't seen since we were both in our early teens, about baking and desserts. We ended up swapping recipes, and I gave her a few tips while she talked me through making drip cakes, which I'd never had a chance to try before. There wasn't really much call for elaborate cakes in a restaurant kitchen, but now I was itching to try one out just for fun. I'd experiment on Connor; he wouldn't object to having more cake to eat. And maybe it would be something I could do for the five-year celebration that Ben had been muttering about throwing for the restaurant.

As the meal was starting to wind down, I leant across to Connor. "I'm going to finish the cake," I whispered. "I won't be long."

"Do you want a hand?"

"No, it's fine. You don't have to. I don't want to drag you around." He'd been chatting with Izzy and Mary about make-up, and I didn't want to drag him away when he seemed to be having fun, but he'd already swung his leg over the bench and was standing up.

"What if I want to help? Come on, Chef. Let's go finish a

cake." I smiled, shaking my head and giving in instantly. I wasn't going to win.

As we headed out of the barn, I found the head of the caterers and mentioned to them about the cake. They nodded and said they'd wait to put the puddings out until we got back. There were plenty of people milling around—chatting, getting seconds, or grabbing drinks from the little makeshift bar we'd built in one corner. The barn had turned out to be the perfect venue for a gathering like this. It would be perfect for a wedding reception too if anyone else in my family decided to get married.

When we got back to the kitchen, Connor and I got straight to work. I grabbed us a couple of aprons that I'd packed, directing him to retrieve the cake and chop some more fruit while I melted some chocolate in the microwave to pipe onto the top. No matter what some people said, it was easy to melt chocolate in a microwave. It was a hell of a lot easier than a bain-marie for a small amount. You just had to keep an eye on it. Besides, I wasn't doing anything fancy with it like tempering. I just needed some for decoration.

"How's this?" Connor asked, pointing at the little pile of carefully sliced strawberries, each slit in several places so they could be easily fanned out. "Is that enough?"

"I think you've done enough to feed an army."

"You said to slice the strawberries, but you never said how many." He stuck his tongue out, then popped a strawberry into his mouth. My tongue darted out to wet my lips, remembering the sensation of his fingers on them when he'd pushed the strawberry between my lips last night. He picked up another one, pressing it slowly into his mouth, his eyes locked on mine.

I broke my gaze away and swallowed. I was never going to be able to think of strawberries the same way again.

Quickly filling a little piping bag with the chocolate, I hurried to finish the cake. There was still some whipped cream left over from last night, so I added some little swirls on the top along with the chocolate lettering, the strawberries, and some meringue pieces from a little tin I'd brought with me. The cake was slightly old-fashioned in design, but I knew it was something Mum and Da would love.

And Connor too.

"All set?" Connor asked, putting the last of the bowls and knives into the sink. I'd take care of them later. "It looks fucking amazing, babe. They're gonna love it." He reached up and pressed a kiss to my cheek. "Good job." My fingers automatically reached to touch the place he'd kissed, wanting to cherish the sensation. "Don't worry. I didn't leave a mark. This lipstick is a fucking godsend. Apparently, it's even blowjob proof, but I've never tested it."

I nodded, even though I wasn't worried about that at all. My cheek was tingling, and I wondered if that would always happen when Connor kissed me.

I picked up the cake, carrying it carefully in both hands. Connor had two of the trays of spare cake, which we'd decorated last night, and there was another one in the fridge that someone could grab later if we needed it.

Slowly we made our way back to the barn. Connor quickly handed the trays off to one of the catering team, swapping them for two birthday candles—a seven and a zero—and a lighter. Connor placed the candles carefully into the cake I was holding, then lit them. I raised my hand to shield the tiny, flickering flames. I hoped they wouldn't go out before we reached Mum and Da. The cake was a joint wedding and anniversary one, but my family had always insisted on birthday cakes with candles, no matter how old you were.

Mary had obviously been watching for us because as soon as she spotted me, she began to sing.

"Happy birthday to you. Happy birthday to you..." I joined in and so did Connor, and soon the whole barn was full of singing and cheering voices. I wove my way through the crowded benches to where Mum and Da were sitting. Both of them had huge grins on their faces, and there was even the shimmer of tears in Mum's eyes. I put the cake down in front of them, in a hastily cleared space, while Connor snapped a couple of photos.

One of the caterers appeared with a knife, and once everyone had finished singing, I handed it to Da. "You have to blow out your candles and make a wish first."

"I don't think I need a wish. I've got everything I could ever want." But he dutifully closed his eyes and blew out the candles while a lump rose in my throat. I'd never heard him sound so happy, and it made something churn in my chest. It suddenly struck me how much I loved my family and how much I wanted to treasure each and every one of these memories. I'd missed out on so much by hiding from them, but I wasn't going to do that anymore.

Mum wrapped her hand around the knife handle, and

Da wrapped his fingers around hers as they cut into the cake.

"Thank you, love," Mum said. "It looks gorgeous."

"You're welcome."

"Speech!" someone yelled; I didn't know who. But soon a couple of other people were calling out. I ducked out of the way, taking Connor with me, and weaving back to our seats as Da stood up, glass of wine in hand. Everyone cheered.

"I hadn't planned on giving a speech," he said, his Devonshire burr suddenly stronger. "So you'll have to forgive me for ramblin'. But I do want to say that I'm so happy to be surrounded by so many of my family and friends here today and to see you all enjoying yourselves. I've been married to this amazing woman for fifty years, and why she's still putting up with me is a mystery only God knows, but I'm glad she is because I'd be lost without her." He looked around the room, a wide smile on his face, and when he spoke again, he sounded almost choked up. It made the lump in my throat tighten. "I've been blessed with not only an amazing wife but five amazing children, who I love very much. I know we drive each other crazy sometimes, but I think that's what families are supposed to do." There was a little chuckle from some of the tables and some fond nods from some of the guests. "Cara, Imogen, Orla, Mary, Patrick… I love you all so much. It's been my greatest joy to be your father, and you're all my greatest achievement, although I won't lie and say that having a winner in the National in '96 wasn't a close one." I chuckled and shook my head because I still remembered that day like it was yesterday, even if I had only been five at the time. "I also want to take a second to welcome Connor into our family. Meeting your boyfriend's family is hard enough, but when it's this lot, well, I reckon it's a damn sight more challenging. But we're so happy you could be here today, and we're hoping we haven't scared you off."

Beside me, Connor smiled and shook his head, but I saw his eyes were shining with tears. I felt my own eyes prickling too. God, I wanted this to be real, and with every passing second, I wanted it more and more. It was like an unbearable weight on my chest that I didn't know how to shift.

I reached out and interlaced my fingers with Connor's, squeezing his hand tightly in mine. He looked over at me and smiled as warm and beautiful as ever. And just for a moment, as his eyes met mine, I felt something shift between us as if something had finally slotted into place.

CHAPTER SEVENTEEN

Connor

OKAY, so I probably shouldn't have been getting as emotional as I was listening to John's speech, but in all fairness, I'd never had anyone welcome me into their family the way he had.

Guilt and happiness swirled inside me, and I wasn't quite sure what to do with myself except for clutching at Patrick's hand and trying hard not to cry. Most guys would have said this was downright embarrassing, being singled out in front of their new boyfriend's entire family, but I knew it was a gesture of love, not humiliation. In the past twenty-four hours, I'd felt nothing but welcome, and it was clear Patrick's family utterly adored him. To have them extend that love to me too was… well… it was something I didn't really know how to deal with.

I'd grown up with just my mum, and for so long it had just been her and me. She'd been sixteen when she'd realised she was pregnant with me, and her then boyfriend —aka my sperm donor—had fucked off as soon as she'd told him, like the immature prick that he was. Most of her family had told her to "get rid of the problem"—aka me— but she'd refused, and when she'd done that, they'd kicked her out. Luckily, there was a fairy godmother in this story in the form of my Auntie Linda, who'd taken my mum in. Mum had gotten a job and gone to college for hairdressing, and once I'd been born, she'd kept going. Auntie Linda had never taken any rent, insisting my mum save her money so she could one day get a house of her own.

I don't really have any memories of my auntie, unfortunately. She died of breast cancer when I was three. I have vague memories of blonde hair and smiling eyes, but that's about it. She left everything to my mum though. It wasn't much, but it did include her bungalow in a village on the outskirts of Braintree. And that was where I'd grown up. Just mum and me. Mum's family had never reached out and neither had my dad's. I'd never had anything like the sort of family Patrick had.

And I'd never imagined a situation where I'd be welcomed in some sort of grand gesture in front of my boyfriend's family and friends. I thought that sort of thing only happened in romance novels.

"Are you okay?" Patrick said, his voice quiet but laced with concern.

"I'm fine." I shook my head, gazing down at the floor between the benches. "Actually, that's a downright lie. Fuck!"

"Do you want to go outside?"

"No, no, it's fine. I don't want to make a scene." There was some applause and cheering. I guessed the speech had come to an end. A hum of chatter picked up again. "Do you think your mum will say something?"

"Maybe." I glanced over at Patrick. He gave me a smile. "Come with me."

He pulled me gently to my feet, and I saw him lean in to say something to Mary. Then he tugged my hand again and led me through the benches. I heard him say something about cake and caterers to a couple of people as we passed, the lie falling off his tongue like honey. As soon as we were outside, he pulled me around the corner and into the field by the side of the barn, out of sight of everyone.

I felt like a fucking idiot, but somehow, now that I'd started, I couldn't seem to stop crying. I was going to make a serious mess of my make-up if I kept this up. Waterproof mascara was only waterproof up to a certain point, and I was not willing to test its limits today. Pandas were cute, but that didn't mean I wanted to look like one right now.

"Sorry," I said, trying to sound like a normal human being and actually sounding more like a swamp monster because apparently today's crying came with a side of snotty nose. "I don't know what the fuck is wrong with me."

That was a lie, but I wasn't going to admit it. I hated being vulnerable even around someone I knew as well as Patrick. I'd always been the bouncy, extroverted one. No one was supposed to know I had a vulnerable side. I'd never let anyone see it before. I'd always needed to be the strong one, and my walls were so high you practically needed a trebuchet to scale them. But apparently there were cracks in them somewhere because parts were starting to tumble down, and I didn't like what they were revealing.

"You don't need to be sorry." Patrick's voice was soft again, flowing over me like liquid sunshine. He wrapped his arms around me and pulled me into a tight hug. "I'm sorry my family is a little overwhelming. I didn't know Da was going to single you out like that."

"No, it's not that." I took a deep breath, but Patrick beat me to the punch.

"It's the fact that my family loves you and are being, well, them. It's a bit much when you're not used to it… and sometimes even when you are used to it." He cleared his throat, but I already knew he was just as choked up as I was. When he spoke again, his voice was quieter, and I wasn't sure if he was speaking to me or himself. "Especially when you realise they love you for who you are, and you never had any reason to be scared in the first place."

"They love you, Patrick," I said into his chest. I'd always loved how broad Patrick was, but now I felt more than warm and happy in his arms. I felt safe. Wanted even. Like he could always be my harbour in a storm.

"They love you too." He pressed a kiss to the top of my head. "I wish…" His voice trailed off, but I wasn't stupid enough to miss the note of longing. Hope exploded in my chest. Please, please, fucking God, please let him want the same thing I did.

"What do you wish?" I asked, trying desperately not to let my hope get out of control. It was stupid and ridiculous because there was no way Patrick would ever really want someone like me... not really. I was too *me*. And nobody ever really wanted that. I had twenty-eight years of evidence to prove it.

"Don't worry about it."

I tilted my head up, catching his gaze. "Do you wish it was real?" My words were barely louder than a whisper, but to me they sounded like they'd come from a fucking foghorn. My face flamed, and for a second, I hoped my foundation might work a miracle and stop me from looking like a fucking tomato. God, I was such an idiot. Patrick was never going to want me the way I wanted him.

"Yes..." One word. One single fucking word punctuated the air, and all of a sudden, I forgot how to breathe. I opened my mouth, but no words would come out. So instead I did the only thing I could think of.

I kissed him.

Every kiss we'd had up until that point had been perfect —sweet and soft and so full of the promise of *something*. This one was different. It was heat and desire and pure want all bundled up in one delicious moment. I moaned against Patrick's mouth as my tongue caressed his lips. My fingers fisted into the front of his shirt as his hands gripped my hips, my cock thickening in my briefs as I thought about him gripping my hips while we did other things. Fuck, I needed to get laid. Preferably with Patrick, and preferably about ten minutes ago.

I wondered if he'd be up for sneaking away from the party for twenty minutes or so. I mean, I didn't think it would take that long for me to get Patrick to blow his load down my throat. Oral was one of my absolute favourite things to do, and I considered myself rather talented in that area. Since Patrick was a little lacking in experience, it would probably take a little less time than usual, but that didn't mean I wasn't going to make it perfect for him.

We broke apart, both our chests heaving. I wanted to chuckle at the little pink stain now gracing Patrick's lips. Maybe my lipstick wasn't quite as foolproof as it claimed.

"We, um, we should..." Patrick swallowed, clearly having trouble processing words. I giggled but couldn't help the sudden giddy feeling filling my chest because I'd done that. "We should get back."

So much for sneaking off. Still, he was probably right about this one. I sighed then chuckled, remembering what had happened that morning. "Probably for the best. Unless you want one of your sisters to find us making out."

Patrick huffed a laugh. "Not really. If it's Mary, I'll never hear the end of it."

"You might, um, you might..." I pointed to his mouth, trying to conceal a smile when he wiped his finger across his lips, tinting his skin with the remnants of my lipstick.

"I thought you said this was supposed to survive blowjobs. Shouldn't it be, I don't know, more resilient than this?"

"Honestly, you just can't get the products these days." I laughed. "Although, as I said, I've never tested it on a dick, but I think we can rule out it being 'desperate kiss' proof." I gave him my best teasing smile. "However, I wouldn't be opposed to testing it out more thoroughly." Patrick's mouth dropped open in the most adorable way, and I laughed again. He didn't totally object, so maybe there was a possibility there.

Patrick scrubbed his fingers across his lips, which didn't really help. Yes, it removed the colour, but it also made his lips very pink and almost puffy. Like he'd been thoroughly ravished. Which wasn't totally untrue.

"You're making it worse," I said, reaching for his hand. "Stop rubbing them."

"Sorry." His cheeks tinted. "You might want to top it up, it's uh, er, a little smudged."

"Of course it is." I'd left the lipstick up in our room, relying on the product to do as advertised. C'est la vie, I'd just have to go top it up. Plus, it would give me five minutes to calm myself down and recentre myself after everything that had happened. "I'll be right back. Save me some cake."

I pressed a quick kiss to Patrick's cheek then hurried across the farmyard towards the house in search of my lipstick.

When I got back to the barn, people were milling around the buffet tables again or standing at the barn door and spilling out into the yard. It seemed like the main meal had finished and people were just going to chill until the band started. I had no idea what sort of music the band would play, but I'd assumed it would be something like a wedding band.

When I entered the barn and saw the four musicians setting up and some of the tables being pushed to the sides, I realised it wasn't going to be quite what I'd expected.

"Oh my God. Is it a ceilidh?" I asked Patrick when I reached him. He was perched on the end of a bench with Mary, and as soon as I'd sat down, he handed me a plate piled high with puddings and a large slice of the strawberry and cream cake he'd made. I gasped happily, momentarily distracted, and took the fork he offered so I could take a huge bite of the cake. The sweetness of the cream and the slight tartness of the strawberries were exquisite, especially with the little crunch of the meringue, and I made a happy little sound in the back of my throat.

"Are you okay?" Mary asked with a wry smile. "Do you and the cake need a moment alone?"

"The cake and I are just perfect, thank you!" I smiled and licked my lips before taking another bite, already wondering if there'd be enough for me to have more later. Like everything Patrick made, this cake was perfection. "You didn't answer my question."

"Yeah, it's a ceilidh," Patrick said. "They do them once a month in Ivybridge, and I know Mum and Da always go. It's the same band, right?"

"Yeah," Mary answered. "I've been a few times. They're really fun. They're never pushy if you want to sit out, and they're never strict about who partners with who since these events tend to be unbalanced anyway. Have you done one before?"

"A couple of times when I was at uni," I said. "Someone I danced with knew a steampunk-style group who used to run them in London, and she took me. It was really fun. I had some other friends take me to Edinburgh for Hogmanay once just because they wanted to do the 'Strip the Willow' at the ceilidh there. It was fun but fucking exhausting. I was knackered the next day, although all the drinking might have had something to do with it."

Mary laughed. "You'll be fine then. You can teach Patrick."

"Not a fan?" I asked, turning to face my beloved chef, who already looked slightly nervous.

"Not really. I've got two left feet, and I'm not the most graceful person."

"It's ceilidh, Patrick. You can't really go wrong," Mary said. Patrick nodded, but he didn't look any better.

"Don't worry." I nudged him gently. "You don't have to dance if you don't want to. I'll just make Mary dance with me instead."

"Oh, will you now?"

"Yup. I hope you brought your A game."

"Bring it on." She laughed. "You're definitely going to have to come down again. There are so many people I need you to meet."

"I'd love that," I said because I genuinely would. Mary was so like Patrick. She lit up every space she was in without even realising it. She was definitely more extroverted than Patrick was, but she was warm, generous, and kind. I already knew we were going to be friends for life.

We chatted for a little bit longer while I worked my way through my pudding mountain, occasionally getting Patrick to try things. The catered desserts weren't as good as his, but they were still nice. I was making a list in my head of everything I wanted to get Patrick to try making because I knew his would be even better.

"Good evening, everyone, and welcome to Aoife and John's anniversary party," the caller said from the middle of the little stage they'd built. He was a giant of a man with a bushy ginger beard and looked distinctly like a Viking. Like the rest of the band, he was wearing a white shirt and a black waistcoat. "Are we ready to do some dancing?"

He summoned everyone who wanted to dance onto the floor, saying that since it was a wedding anniversary, we were going to start with one they often used for first dances. I grabbed Mary's hand and pulled her behind me, noticing she'd swapped her heels for a sensible looking pair of sandals. We lined up, me on one side and Mary opposite, as the caller talked us through the steps, giving a bit of a demonstration.

"But don't worry, I'll keep the instructions going, so all you've gotta do is follow me. Are we all good to go?" he asked, hopping back up on the stage. The band itself consisted of a drummer, guitarist, and fiddler, and the caller perched himself on a low stool in front of a mic, picking up an accordion and playing a couple of notes to warm up.

The same calm and tense excitement I always felt before I danced warmed my veins. It didn't matter what I was doing—ballet, pole, or in this case, folk dancing—it was always the same. This was my happy place, and I already knew I'd be dancing every single dance. Hopefully, I'd be able to convince Patrick to join me for at least one. Maybe two.

The music began and off we went. It was an easy dance

with couples winding their way around each other and some simple spins. Even so, it was faster than I'd anticipated. I laughed as I spun Mary around, then passed her off to the next person in the line while I spun the person who'd been next to her around before Mary and I met again in the middle. We continued down the line until we reached the end, happy and gasping. The line was pretty long, but soon we'd made it back to the top and off we went again.

The first dance lead to another and then a third, each with a brief breather in the middle. I threw off my jacket, putting it on the bench next to Patrick and pressing a hurried, happy kiss to his cheek. I wasn't going to pressure him. He'd come to me when he was ready.

And sure enough, he did, two dances later.

"Can I join you?" he asked, holding out his hand.

"Of course!" I was hot and sweaty and probably looked a fucking mess, but I didn't care. I took his hand and we joined one of the little circles we'd been separated into for this dance. I stood on Patrick's left, holding his hand and listening to the instructions. I didn't think it could be more perfect.

Except it was because after the dance he was grinning and squeezing my hand, leading me into place for the next dance, the last one before a break between the sets. This one was bouncier, and when he spun me around, his hands locked in mine, I'd never felt more alive. It was so fast that I knew if he let me go, I'd go flying, but his grip was like iron, holding me steady, and I knew I was safe in his hands. A fierce, wild joy flooded my veins as the music sung through me, Patrick's hands warm against me, anchoring me to him.

As the song ended, he pulled me close to him, our chests heaving and sweat beading on our skin.

There was so much unspoken between us, but I'd never felt closer to him.

CHAPTER EIGHTEEN

Patrick

THERE WAS a wild sparkle in Connor's eyes and a fierce grin on his plush lips as we spun to a stop, our hands clutching on to each other. My chest was heaving, but I wasn't just out of breath from the dancing. Something about Connor made me feel alive. His energy was electric.

I was utterly entranced. My heart pounded, want surging through me. Was it odd to feel this way after dancing together? It wasn't as if we'd done anything particularly sexy, but just the feel of his hand in mine and the look of pure exhilaration and happiness on his face was enough.

That and the kissing.

God, the kissing.

My tips tingled at the ghostly remembrance of his lips against mine and the way his tongue had pressed against the seam of my mouth like he was claiming me for his own.

The dance floor was beginning to clear, the band setting their instruments down for the first of their breaks. Most of the other guests had decided to hit the bar or had grabbed a seat on the nearest benches.

"What do you want to do?" Connor asked, his tongue darting out to wet his lips. His fingers were still entwined with mine.

What did I want? That was the million-pound question.

If I were honest with myself—really, truly honest—I wanted Connor. I wanted to take him upstairs and peel off his shirt and beautifully tight trousers. I wanted to kiss him until there was no breath left in my body. I wanted all the things I'd never shared with another person before. Because if I was going to do them with anyone, I wanted to do them with Connor.

My one fear was that he wouldn't want them with me.

Connor might have kissed me, fallen asleep on me, and pushed up against me in bed, but that didn't necessarily mean he wanted anything more with me. I was sure he preferred his partners with a bit more experience than I had. After all, who really wanted to guide a nearly-thirty-year-old gay virgin through his first blowjob? Or at least his first blowjob on a real dick, not just the dildo he'd finally bought last year. I was never going to be worthy of him, not really. But that didn't mean I couldn't try. Just because I knew I'd fall short didn't mean I couldn't reach for the stars.

"I… I…" My tongue was tied, and I realised I still stood on the dancefloor, probably looking like a first-class idiot. "Shall we go back to the house?"

"The house is good," Connor said, leading me off the floor. He grabbed his jacket off the bench as we passed, carrying it on one arm. The sun was lower in the sky as we emerged this time, a soft breeze ruffling my hair. I had no idea what time it was, but my guess was about half seven. There were a few people milling around with drinks and some kids playing in the field—turning cartwheels, doing handstands, and playing with the giant Jenga set we'd set up.

Nobody paid Connor and I any attention as we walked across the yard, and I let him lead me where he wanted to go.

"You never answered my question." Connor's voice was soft and playful. We reached the house, and Connor paused, waiting to see what I'd do next.

"I, um, I don't really know what my options are."

"Do you want options?"

"They're usually a good idea." I opened the kitchen door, then let go of his hand to open the fridge, checking to see if the caterers had come to get the extra cake. It was a good pretence to give me a moment to breathe and get my thoughts in order.

"Is there still cake?" Connor asked hopefully, his presence looming behind me. I chuckled.

"Yes, there's still a whole one."

"Oh, good. I can have some later!"

"You're not going to eat a whole cake."

"I can try." His hands found my waist, and he gently turned me to face him. "You're hiding from me."

"No…" Connor raised an eyebrow, and I felt my face flush. "Maybe. Just a little."

"Do you want to go back to the party?" he asked. "We can get a drink, maybe some cake, and dance."

I swallowed. "No… not yet… I mean, I… If you want…" I trailed off, not really sure what to say. Apparently, my brain had uninstalled the dictionary because I'd forgotten any words beyond *no, er,* and *um.* I must have sounded like an idiot.

"Or we can stay here? Maybe go upstairs?" Connor's voice was soft with no hint of pressure in it. He was leaving the decision up to me, which was absolutely lovely of him, except I didn't know what to say or do, and I had no idea what he wanted. How could I make a choice without knowing what his opinion was? I didn't want to make the wrong one, and I didn't want to force Connor into something he didn't want. Not that I could make Connor do anything. That was what I loved about him. He knew exactly who he was and what he wanted. His confidence and self-assuredness floored me. If I could have even five percent of his confidence, I'd be lucky.

"What, um, what do you want?" I was almost proud of myself for getting out a full sentence.

"Do you want me to be honest?" Connor asked, looking up at me from under his long lashes.

"Always."

"I want you." My heart leapt into my throat.

"Are you sure?"

"Why wouldn't I be?" He looked confused.

"Well, I'm, um, I'm not exactly, er, experienced…" I fixed my eyes on the door behind Connor. There was a moment of silence.

"And? Do you really think that bothers me?"

"I… No?" It was more of a guess than an actual answer. Connor's hand came up to cup my jaw, tilting it down until I was looking into his beautiful eyes.

"No, it doesn't. Not one bit." He grinned cheekily. "Besides, now I get to teach you, and I'm an excellent teacher."

I snorted, a weight easing off my chest. "So that's how it's going to be?"

"Why don't we go upstairs and find out?" Connor took my hand, leading me through the empty house towards the stairs. I followed without hesitation. When we got to the stairs, he paused, stepping onto the bottom step and looking at me over his shoulder. "Don't worry. We won't do anything more than you're comfortable with. But I do want to find out what you look like when you come." He turned and leant in close, his eyes burning with heat. "I bet you look fucking gorgeous."

Then he turned and started walking again, leaving me speechless behind him. I nearly tripped up the stairs as I followed. My eyes never left his perfect, round ass, which swayed enticingly in front of me. I couldn't think of anything except his last few sentences. God, I wanted this to be good for him.

I wanted to be good for him.

I wanted to kneel down in front of him and worship him from head to toe because Connor was my world and I needed him to know just how much I adored him. Even if I could never tell him, I hoped I could show him so, when all this was over, he'd never forget what had happened between us.

Connor opened the bedroom door and ushered me inside, clicking it shut behind us and sliding the lock into place. I knew nobody would come looking for us, but it was nice to know nobody was going to come barging in on the off chance we were missed. He took my hand, pulling me towards the bed. I swallowed, feeling suddenly too hot in my shirt, like my skin was on fire, and I just needed to jump into a pool to cool off.

"Take off your shirt," Connor said. His voice was soft but firm, and my hands moved before he'd even finished speaking.

His eyes roamed over me appreciatively. Part of me felt like I should be nervous because I looked nothing like the man I thought Connor deserved, but then I remembered he wanted this. He wanted *me*.

"Fuck. You're so sexy, babe." He reached out as I undid the last of my shirt buttons, sliding the white fabric over my shoulders. I pulled it off as his fingers skimmed over my chest and down to my stomach. "Wow. You're perfect."

"I'm really not."

"Yes, Patrick, you are. I love your body." Connor leant in close, his lips tantalisingly close to mine. "I can't wait to see the rest of it."

"D-do you want me to take my jeans off?" I asked, my voice coming out breathier than I'd intended. My cock was already straining at the confines of the tight denim. I reached my hand towards it, desperate for some release.

"No." Connor gently brushed my hand away and smirked. "I'm in charge, and that's mine now. Yes?"

"Yes." I nodded. "I'm yours. All yours."

"Good." He kissed me. His lips were firm against mine, his fingers gripping my hips as his tongue pushed into my mouth. I moaned as he sucked on my tongue then nipped my bottom lip. My mouth chased his as he stepped away. I heard a whine but wasn't sure if I'd made the sound or not.

"Take your jeans off but not your boxers." Connor began to unbutton his shirt, revealing firm, toned, smooth skin that sent my pulse skyrocketing. He shrugged the shirt off and reached for the button on his trousers. It was only then I realised I'd been frozen in place, watching him. Connor raised an eyebrow and his lip curled into a hungry smile. "Jeans, babe. Now."

"Sorry." I moved my hands, my eyes still on him.

"It's okay. I know I'm gorgeous," he said cheekily, sliding his trousers off before doing a little twirl. He was wearing the tiniest pair of baby-blue briefs that clung to his perky, round ass and highlighted the bulge of his erection. My tongue darted out to lick my lips. I was desperate to get my mouth on him. Sure, I didn't have skills, but enthusiasm had to count for something.

I finally got my jeans open, pushing them over my thighs and toeing off my socks at the same time. Connor made an appreciative noise, and I blushed.

"God, you're so fucking sexy." He stepped close to me,

kissing me again and taking the arguments out of my mouth. "Lie on the bed."

Nodding, I turned then squeaked loudly as Connor grabbed my ass. Then I laughed. "Wow, that was a dignified noise. Can we, um, can we forget I made that sound?"

"It was cute," he said. "Besides, laughing during sex is good. It means you're having fun, and sex is supposed to be fun."

"Are... are we going to have sex?" I asked as I climbed onto the bed, settling myself in the middle and quickly adjusting the pillows so my head didn't get lost between them.

"If you're asking if I'm going to fuck you, then no, I'm not." Connor's voice was matter-of-fact. "First, I don't want to rush you into something you're not ready for. And second, I didn't bring any condoms or lube. This wasn't something I'd imagined happening."

"Are... are you..." I trailed off, not really sure what I was asking.

"Are you asking if I'm glad this is happening? Because, yes, I am. Are you?"

I nodded.

"Good." He crawled onto the bed and into my lap, his hands cupping my jaw as his cock rubbed up against mine, the drag of the fabric across the sensitive skin driving me wild. I looked up into his eyes, completely under his spell. "Then no more talking. Well... less talking about mundane things."

He kissed me again, and all my worries fell away. My hands reached for him, caressing the firm muscles of his thighs and sliding up to squeeze his ass, groaning into his mouth as I did. Every single touch sent heat coursing through me. I'd never thought I'd be able to touch Connor like this, and yet here he was. In my lap. In the tiniest pair of underwear I'd ever seen. It was like all my fantasies come true.

My cock throbbed in my boxers. I was already very aware that if Connor touched me, I wasn't going to last long. There was a world of difference between this and my own hand. If I wasn't careful, I was going to come in my underwear like some horny teen making out with their first boyfriend. I mean, the situation wasn't *entirely* different. There was just at least ten to twelve years between mine and most other people's first sexual experiences.

I had no idea when Connor had first done this with someone, and now wasn't the time to ask. Why was I even thinking about this when I had the man of my dreams in my lap?

"Oh God." I groaned as Connor circled his hips, grinding his cock against mine. His fingers slid down my chest and reached for my nipples, teasing the sensitive buds. Fuck. I'd never really played with my nipples much before. It had never really done anything for me. But apparently it did when it was Connor touching them. "Connor…"

"Yeah? You like that?"

"Y-yes." I nodded, another whine sliding from my lips as he pinched a nipple between his thumb and forefinger. "Can I… can I touch you?"

"Of course, baby. I love having my nipples sucked.

They're so fucking sensitive." I took that as an instruction. My hands gripped his hips as I lowered my mouth. I kissed across the smooth skin of his chest before taking one nipple into my mouth. "Fuck yes, baby. A little harder… Shit. Use your tongue. Fuck yes, Patrick. Just like that!"

My body thrummed at his praise. I desperately wanted to please him. I needed him to feel good. I slowly kissed my way across his pecs before sucking his other nipple into my mouth. Connor's fingers twisted in my hair, his words an equal amount of encouragement and pleasure. I flicked my tongue over the hard nub, teased it with my teeth, then groaned as Connor ground down against me. He gently tugged my hair, pulling me back. Connor's face was flushed, his lipstick smeared, and he'd never looked more beautiful.

"Fuck, darling. You're a fast learner." His skin was tinted pink and his chest was heaving. "So fucking good for me."

"Yeah?"

"Oh yes." Connor grinned. It was wicked and hungry and made my body tense with anticipation. Whatever he was planning, I knew he was going to completely undo me. He rose gracefully, his feet still planted on either side of my thighs. His crotch was now directly in my line of vision, and I stared at the straining blue fabric before me. God, I wanted to touch him.

"You can touch me," Connor said as if he could read my mind. "You can even take them off. I think it's about time I get naked."

I nodded and stretched my hands towards him. Surprisingly, they weren't trembling. His thighs were warm and smooth under my palms as I ran them slowly up Connor's toned muscles. Connor had the most perfect legs I'd ever seen on anyone. My brain was happy to supply me with endless fantasies of lying between them while I worshipped Connor with my mouth, his thighs twitching as I swallowed his cock down or tongued his ass. Would it be too soon to suggest that?

I reached for his briefs and skimmed my fingers over the material to reach the waistband. My breath caught in my throat as I slowly pulled them over his erection and dropped them down his legs. His cock bobbed in front of me, the head already red and swollen and wet with precum. I swallowed and licked my lips. I just wanted to lean forward and kiss it. What would it taste like? What would it feel like under my tongue?

Without thinking, I leant forward and pressed a gentle kiss to the engorged head, letting my tongue dart out to lap up the few drops of precum that had gathered there. The skin was softer than I'd imagined… silky even. The precum was almost bitter, not what I'd expected at all, but that wasn't a bad thing. In fact, I wanted to taste it again.

Connor groaned, and I heard a thump as his hands hit the wall, bracing himself. "Fuuuuuck." I tilted my head to find him looking down at me with that wicked smile, his eyes wide. "Do you like my cock?"

"Yeah." I nodded. "Can I… can I suck you?"

"Yes, but only a little. I have plans for you." My face must have fallen because he laughed softly. "Good plans. I promise."

I didn't say anything, even though I was intrigued. I knew Connor would take care of me. Instead, I leant forward again, letting my tongue dart out to lick over the head of Connor's cock again. My hands gripped his thighs, more to steady myself than him, and feeling his solid muscles under my fingers kept me grounded. Connor wasn't expecting miracles. All I had to do was try my best.

"Oh shit. Yes, like that. Just like that. So good for me," Connor said with a deep groan as I wrapped my lips around his shaft and gave a tentative suck, feeling the weight of him on my tongue. I hadn't seen a lot of dicks in my life, and I wasn't convinced the ones in porn really counted, so it wasn't like I had a lot to compare Connor's to, but to me it was perfect. Thick and long enough that it felt good in my mouth but not so large that I wondered how the fuck it was ever going to fit inside me. Monster dicks could stick to porn, thank you very much.

I sucked again, slowly bobbing my head in an attempt to pick up a steady rhythm. I wasn't completely successful, making myself gag a couple of times by going too deep too quickly, but I didn't stop. My cock throbbed in my boxers, leaking against the fabric. I was desperate to touch myself, but I didn't trust taking my hands off Connor's thighs. Saliva dripped out of my mouth as the blowjob got sloppier, but that just seemed to make Connor moan more. I was filing that information away for later. If I could remember it.

"Fuck, Patrick. You… you need to stop." I'd never heard Connor sound like that before—breathless and desperate. But underneath it, I still heard the note of control. He was still in charge here, and that made my chest flutter with excitement. I needed him to tell me exactly what he wanted. The idea was calming in a way. I knew I wouldn't be able to fuck it up because Connor would take care of me and make sure it was good for both of us. I trusted him.

Slowly, I released his dick from my mouth. There were strings of drool connecting us. It was the sexiest thing I'd ever seen.

"Fuck, that's hot!" Clearly Connor felt the same. "Take your boxers off."

He stepped back to watch me, standing in the middle of the bed, slowly stroking himself. I quickly wiggled out of my underwear and threw them off the bed. As soon as I'd resumed my position, Connor folded himself into my lap again, and I gasped as his slick cock bumped against mine. It felt like I'd been struck by lightning, the sensation sending a bolt of pleasure through me. Connor held out his hand and smirked.

"Since we don't have lube, we might need a little help. Suck my fingers."

"Okay." I nodded as the word slipped from my mouth, the rough sound surprising me. I wrapped my fingers around his wrist and lifted his hand, tentatively sucking two digits into my mouth. Connor groaned.

"That's it. Good boy. Get them wet for me." His other hand caressed the side of my face. "I'm going to use them to jack us off together. I want you to come all over me. Will you do that for me, Patrick? Will you come for me?"

I groaned and nodded as best I could. I wanted him to make me come, but more than anything, I wanted to be good for him. I sucked his fingers deeper into my mouth, wrapping my tongue around them and making them slick. Connor tipped his head back, soft expletives dripping from his lips like honey.

Soon he gently pulled his fingers away and wrapped them tightly around my aching cock, pulling it against his. The heat and wetness of his fingers had me gasping, but as he started to move, the friction sent pleasure spiralling through me. This was the most intense thing I'd ever experienced in my life. I was already dangerously close to the edge, and he'd barely started, but all I could focus on was how amazing it felt.

"Oh… oh God… Connor…"

"Yeah? Do you like that, babe? Does it feel good?"

I nodded my head violently, biting my lip to keep from crying out. "I can't… I'm not…" I gasped as he twisted his hand over the head of my cock. My hands gripped his thighs, clutching at them like they were the only connection I had between this world and the next. "I'm so close."

"I know. Me too." He kissed me, his tongue pushing into my mouth. "Don't think about it," he whispered against my lips. "Just feel. Come for me, Patrick." Connor pumped our cocks, twisting his hand again, and that was it. My whole body stiffened, and I cried out as I pumped cum all over his hand, some of it spurting out across my stomach, painting me with wetness. Pleasure, more intense than any I'd felt before, flooded my nerves and set my skin on fire. Connor cried out against me, his mouth brushing mine, and two seconds later I felt the splash of his cum on my skin as he stilled in my lap.

My heart was racing faster than the speed of light, and in the quietness of the room all I could hear was his heart-beat and mine, accompanied by our ragged breathing. Connor kissed me again slowly as if savouring the taste of me. I knew right then that I would never get enough of this man.

CHAPTER NINETEEN

Connor

PATRICK and I didn't go back to the party. Too much had happened, and neither of us were ready to burst our bubble and face reality again.

Instead, we'd cleaned up with the box of tissues on the bedside table, shrugged on our shirts and trousers, and pottered down to the kitchen. Apart from my lipstick, my make-up was still perfectly in place, and the lipstick was easily removable. Anyone who saw us would have guessed in a heartbeat what we'd been doing, but I didn't care. I'd finally had a taste of Patrick, and my entire world had shifted. I knew that no matter what happened, things were never going to go back to the way they'd been before.

We could pretend, sure, but that didn't actually mean shit. I'd always know what Patrick's mouth felt like on my nipples, the way his cock had felt against mine, and the face he made when he came. The possessive part of me revelled in the fact that I'd been the first person to see Patrick like that. That would be mine and mine alone, and I loved it.

I'd always been a bit of a jealous, possessive bitch, but I worked hard to keep a lid on it. I didn't like sharing things that were mine. Maybe it was an only child thing. Maybe it was just a me thing. All I knew was that I was going to have a hard time giving Patrick up, and it was going to hurt like a bitch when I did.

Maybe I should just put a Tesco order in now to stock up on ice cream, tissues, and alcohol for Monday night when we went home. I doubted it was going to be pretty when it finally hit me. I'd always been an ugly crier.

Part of me, the possessive part, was wondering *why* things had to end at all? Why couldn't I keep Patrick all for myself? After all, we were clearly compatible in some ways. I'd always wanted a sweet, soft, submissive man who'd let me take charge, and Patrick ticked so many of those boxes it was unreal. The way he'd craved my praise and tried so hard to please me made me want to spoil him rotten now and forever. He was clearly a fast learner if the way he'd brought me tantalisingly close with his mouth on my nipples was anything to go by. I couldn't wait to see what happened next time.

If there even was a next time. Should there be a next time?

Should there have even been a this time?

"Hey, the cake is still here. Do you want some?" Patrick's soft voice derailed my train of thought, and just in time too. There was absolutely no need for me to go down that path and end up cross with myself for something we'd both wanted. It had happened, and I couldn't change that now.

"Um, sure. Will people mind if we eat it?"

"I don't think so. I mean, our other option is to go back to the party."

"Then give me that cake." I chuckled, and so did Patrick. He pulled the cake out of the fridge and took it into the kitchen, grabbing a knife from the block on the side. He quickly plated up two large pieces and dug forks out of a drawer.

"Let's go sit outside," he said. "There's some garden furniture out there, and it's got a nice view."

"Okay." I followed Patrick through the house into the back garden. I stopped as I stepped outside, the sight taking my breath away. The cottage's back garden sloped downwards and overlooked a rolling expanse of sharp hills decorated with fields and pastures with a brook cutting its way through the grass. There were old stone walls and horses grazing, and in the distance, I saw woodlands off to one side. It was picture perfect but in an imperfect way. This wasn't a cookie-cutter countryside view. There was a wild, rough edge to it. It made me want to start walking, taking Patrick with me as we explored every inch of it.

"Wow." I couldn't think of anything else to say. With all the excitement of the party and the busyness of last night, I hadn't seen this before. Now I was almost upset at Patrick for depriving me. Except that wasn't true because I could never be upset with Patrick. "It's beautiful."

"Yeah, it is." Patrick sounded almost melancholy as if

he'd forgotten what this looked like. When was the last time he'd been back here?

He directed me to some rattan furniture with dark-blue cushions, and I curled up next to him on a two-seater sofa that had the best view. We ate in silence. The cake was delicious, but I was distracted from enjoying it because I suddenly had questions I wanted to ask. I just wasn't sure where to start.

"Why did you leave?" I asked finally. Patrick looked at me, confused. I hadn't phrased that the right way. I nibbled on a bit of strawberry while I tried to put my thoughts in order. "I mean, is there a reason you never moved back here? After you finished training. Like your whole family is here, or like an hour away, and you moved halfway across the country. I mean, I know Aaron and Ben offered you the job, and they picked Nottingham because that's where the pub was, but I just wondered if there was more of a reason?"

Patrick was quiet for a second, his eyes fixed on the skyline. "I thought about it, but I never felt like I fit in here. I was so much younger than everyone else, and I was often by myself. I wasn't interested in horses or following in Da's footsteps, and I just… It felt like there was something missing." He sighed. "I don't know if that makes sense."

"No, I get it." I shifted, nuzzling up against his shoulder. He put his arm around me, and I snuggled into his chest. I loved it when he held me like this. We'd been cuddling like this for years, but now it suddenly felt infinitely more meaningful. "I think a lot of queer people feel that, especially when you haven't really figured it out yet. Like there's a piece of you missing, but you don't know what it is."

He nodded. "Something like that. I know my family loves me, but I wanted to be my own person for a while. And here that's hard."

"I can see that."

"Besides, I wasn't sure how long Mum could manage to go without trying to set me up on dates. Her heart was in the right place, but every time she mentioned dating girls—"

"It felt wrong?"

"Yeah. I mean, girls are lovely but not really for me." Patrick shook his head, smiling wryly. "It still took me a while to figure it out though."

"What was the breaking point?" I asked. "Suddenly realise you were more interested in the dicks in porn? Or did you just see a really hot shirtless guy one day?"

"No, actually. Well, seeing Chris Hemsworth shirtless in *Thor* might have helped, but it was something really silly."

"No such thing." I nudged him and gave him my best encouraging smile. "Seriously. There isn't. You know you can tell me anything."

"It… it was back in 2014 when the first gay weddings were taking place. I saw a picture of these two guys getting married, and I suddenly had this huge rush of relief and this singular thought of 'I can get married now'. And then it all kind of clicked into place. Everything suddenly made a lot of sense." He smiled at me weakly. "See? Silly."

"That's not silly at all, babe. I think that's adorable as fuck."

"Really?"

"Of course! And one day you're going to find someone to have the perfect wedding with, and it'll be beautiful and fabulous and everything you deserve." I tried to make myself sound positive, even if I was dying a little inside at the idea of Patrick marrying someone who wasn't me. A strange expression I couldn't place dashed across Patrick's face, but it was gone too fast for me to read.

"Did you ever have a moment like that?" he asked. He'd put our empty plates on the ground and now his fingers were stroking down my arm.

"The clicking into place thing?"

"Yeah."

"Not really. I mean, I figured it out really early on. My closet door was see-through." I laughed, and Patrick chuckled. "But when I finally told my mum, it all felt a thousand times more real if that makes sense?"

"It does."

We sat in comfortable silence for a while, watching the sun set over the horizon. The sky was splashed with colour —pinks, purples, oranges, and reds bleeding across the sky. It was utterly spectacular. Patrick's hand was still resting on my arm, casually stroking up and down. It felt like an unconscious gesture, something soothing you'd do for the person you cared about without even realising it.

Except Patrick and I did this all the time, and we'd been doing it for years. I couldn't even remember the first time we'd cuddled like this anymore. I doubted there was anything more behind it than habit. Even if I desperately wanted there to be.

I wondered if I should talk to Patrick about how I felt.

That's what the characters in romance novels said you should do—the good friends who always came to rescue the protagonist when they were floundering in their own stupidity. I'd done it myself with Taylor and Simon. Well, sort of. More like I'd accidentally drawn Taylor into confessing his feelings while Simon stood behind him without Taylor realising he was there. I was still taking credit though.

Maybe it would be helpful to get some external perspective on this whole mess or at least another voice of reason who'd tell me to quit while I was ahead and not break Patrick's heart. I couldn't be what he needed. I just needed someone else to tell me that because my own resolve was starting to wear thin.

I knew we'd both hinted that we wished it were real when we'd been outside after John's speech, but I wasn't going to count that. I'd been raw and vulnerable, and I was sure Patrick was just being sweet. Besides, I'd kissed him before we could talk about it, and it hadn't come up since, which was just proof that it was nothing more than a momentary fantasy. One of those moments where dreams drifted into reality but ultimately were nothing more than leaves on the wind.

If I wanted to keep Patrick in my life, I'd have to work out how to let him go. Otherwise we were going to end up in a short, disastrous relationship that utterly destroyed both of us, after which we'd never speak to each other again. And that was everything I didn't want. Because no matter what, I couldn't lose Patrick. I'd never survive the fallout.

Perhaps I was being selfish, and maybe it was stupid to shoot down the idea of a relationship with him before we'd even tried. But I'd had my heart broken enough times by stupid fuckbois to know how relationships went when I was involved. I valued my friendship with Patrick over anything in the world, and I loved him too much to put him through a breakup. And everything with me was always going to involve a breakup. My exes had all made that quite clear—I was the problem in my relationships. My personality was incompatible with anything more.

So I was going to make sure it didn't happen with Patrick and me. I was going to stop it before it had even started.

The only problem was making sure I actually went through with it.

CHAPTER TWENTY

Patrick

CONNOR and I sat in the garden watching the sun set until the sky was almost dark. A cool breeze had picked up, rustling the leaves of the old apple tree at the end of the garden and nudging my hair. I could still hear the sounds of the party from behind the house, the last strands of music floating on the air.

I guessed the ceilidh had finished because it was now just the bouncing notes of pop music, the sort of songs people played at weddings. I had no idea what time it was. My closest guess was about ten. I couldn't remember when we'd left the party, but I assumed we'd been gone for most of the evening. I wondered if we'd been missed.

Nobody had come looking for us, so either my family had decided to give us some space, or they were too busy to care. I was guessing it was probably a mix of both. Mum and Da would be wrapped up with their friends and family, and most of my sisters would be busy with their husbands and kids. Mary had probably noticed since we'd spent most of the afternoon with her. There was a good chance she'd tease me about it tomorrow, but I didn't have it in me to care. Not now anyway.

So much had changed today, and I was still trying to process it all.

There was no doubt in my mind that I loved Connor more than ever, and if he'd have me, I wanted nothing more than to be with him. But I still wasn't convinced Connor wanted me. Not permanently. Why would he? I could write a list as long as my arm of reasons why I wasn't good enough for him. And I didn't want to ruin our friendship by pushing for something he didn't want. Sure, he was happy to fool around with me, but that didn't necessarily mean he wanted a relationship. Plenty of people had sex without dating. Maybe we could do that? Just keep it casual. I mean, that worked for some people, right?

Connor's friends Taylor and Simon popped into my mind, reminding me that they'd tried this exact arrangement and had ended up dating. Okay, but maybe they weren't the best example. I just couldn't think of any others.

I racked my brain trying to think things through but came up short.

The best thing to do would be to talk to Connor and see where his head was at. That would be the grown-up thing to do in this situation. It was also the most terrifying option. What if I poured my heart out to him only to find we weren't on the same page? Would there be any coming back from that? Or would our friendship fall apart when we realised we wanted different things. There was no way to tell whether it would survive the fallout of me saying I wanted so much more than to be friends.

Connor shivered in my arms, and I suddenly realised just how cold the breeze was.

"Do you want to go inside?" I asked.

"Hmm?" Connor's voice was thick with sleep. "Yeah, we can go in. Are you tired?"

"A little." Although whether I'd be able to sleep with my brain going haywire was a different question. Connor sat up and stretched, making an adorable squeaking noise as he did. I smiled, my chest wanting to burst from the swell of love I felt for him. But now wasn't the time. I wasn't going to ruin the last of this weekend by forcing a conversation. I'd wait until we got home. At least that way we'd have some space if we needed it.

Connor swung his legs off the sofa, and I scooped up the plates, carrying them through into the kitchen and placing them in the dishwasher. There was still nobody around, so they'd either gone to bed or were still at the party.

We made our way upstairs, Connor's fingers interlaced with mine. He looked sweet and sleepy, and I wanted nothing more than to wrap him in my arms and fall asleep with his head on my chest. When we reached our room, I began to shrug off my clothes, hoping I could just crawl into bed. But after our earlier explorations and the dancing, I could really do with a shower.

Connor was already half-naked when I turned around. He sat at the dressing table in nothing but his tiny briefs with a packet of make-up wipes and various small bottles and jars in front of him. I swallowed, still not used to the sight of him like this so close to me.

"I'm going to shower," I said, grabbing my pyjamas from the bed where I'd tucked them earlier. Connor turned to look at me, a small but sneaky grin on his face.

"Can I join you? I could really do with one too, and this way, it'll be faster and we'll save water."

Those sounded like paper-thin reasons to me, and I wasn't convinced that showering together would be any faster. I wasn't stupid. Then again, was I really going to pass up the opportunity to see Connor naked, wet, and pressed up against me? If I was, I was more of an idiot than I thought.

"Save water, huh?"

"Of course. I am nothing if not environmentally conscious. David Attenborough would be proud."

I snorted. "Well then, we wouldn't want to disappoint Sir David."

Connor beamed then rummaged in his bag for his toiletries. At least he was taking the premise seriously, even though I doubted we'd get to anything resembling getting clean for a while. He grabbed his shorts and T-shirt, not bothering to put them on. I thought about asking him if he wanted to get dressed, but the bathroom was only two steps down the hall, and nobody was around. If they were, well, Connor could move fast.

When we got to the bathroom, I locked the door behind us before turning the giant, walk-in shower on to warm up while I finished getting undressed. My parents had redone this bathroom a couple of years ago, and I had thought it was a bit extravagant at first, especially as it was mostly for guests, but now I was extremely grateful.

Connor was watching me with hungry eyes. He'd stripped off his briefs, and his cock was already half-hard. "You should really get naked, or I'll have to start without you." He winked at me and stepped into the shower, leaving the door open behind him. The water cascaded over his skin, and he sighed happily, closing his eyes and pulling his lip between his teeth as he ran his hands across his chest. "Mmm, this is perfect."

My fingers snapped into action as Connor's fingers drifted lower. My shirt was only half-buttoned anyway, and it was easy to shrug it off onto the tiled floor. My jeans and boxers quickly followed. Connor grinned at me, cocking his finger and beckoning me towards him.

The water was deliciously warm as I stepped under the spray, and a little sigh of contentment slipped from my lips. Bliss. Connor's hands found my waist and his body pressed up against mine. His skin was silky from the water, and I groaned as his hard cock brushed up against mine.

"I'm so glad I could join you," Connor said teasingly. "I'll help you get clean."

"Really?"

"Of course. I might just get you a tiny bit dirtier first." He winked then stood on tiptoes to ghost his lips over mine. "I do love getting you dirty." Connor's mouth was firm and demanding, and I melted into his touch. Whatever he wanted he could have. I just couldn't promise it would last long. I was really hoping I'd be able to develop some stamina at some point.

"Yes. Whatever you want." My arms wrapped around him, pulling him as close to me as possible.

"Good. I like getting what I want."

"I like… I like giving you that." God, why were words so hard?

"Good boy." Connor's voice was smooth as silk and rich as ganache. How was it that two words could undo me from the inside out? He kissed me again and again, his fingers roaming across my body. I held onto him tightly, convinced I wouldn't be able to stand by myself if I suddenly let go. Connor was the only thing holding me in place.

I gasped into his mouth as his hand slid in between our bodies and wrapped around our cocks. His grip was tight but so fucking perfect, and I moaned loudly as he began to jerk us slowly, the friction driving me insane.

"Shhh, baby. You have to be quiet. You don't want someone to hear, do you?"

"No?" I thought that was the right answer. I wasn't convinced I'd understood the question. Something about being quiet.

"Exactly, so you need to be quiet. You can do that for me, can't you?"

"Yes… I-I-I can be. I can be quiet."

"Good." I bit my lip to muffle the moan that was threatening to escape me as Connor twisted his hand over the slick head of my cock. My body was burning, and I could already feel my orgasm building low in my spine, threatening to overwhelm me at any second.

"Don't come," Connor said, his voice suddenly firmer.

My dick throbbed in his hand. "I want to get my mouth on you first. Would you like that?"

"P-please. Please, Connor. Yes. I... I want that."

"Say it for me, baby. I want to hear you say it."

"Please, Connor. Please will you suck my cock?"

"Of course." Connor kissed me one last time then sank to his knees in front of me. I let out a whimper at the sight. It was everything I'd ever dreamt of and more. He smiled up at me, the ultimate picture of seduction. "You asked so nicely after all."

I gasped as his lips wrapped around the head of my cock, sucking it gently and teasing the slit with his tongue. My hands balled into fists by my side. I wanted to reach out and grab him and tangle my fingers in his wet hair, but I wasn't sure whether that would be rude or not.

"You can touch me," Connor said, once again reading my mind. He pressed kisses down my shaft, wrapping his fingers around the base and squeezing just hard enough to stave off my impending orgasm. "It's okay. I'll tell you if it's too much."

Another groan slipped from my lips as he took me into his mouth again. I tried desperately to register what he was doing with his mouth so I could try it on him later, but it was hopeless. I was never going to remember anything more than the sensation of pure bliss. One hand stretched out, tentatively reaching for his hair. Connor moaned around me as I buried my fingers in the wet strands, tugging them gently. Okay, that was a good thing. I should try to remember that.

Then Connor swallowed around me and any semblance

of thought I'd been clutching vanished. I gripped Connor's hair, trying to keep a foothold in reality as he took me apart with his mouth.

"C-Connor," I moaned. Somewhere in the back of my mind, I had a vague recollection that it was polite to let your partner know you were close, but I couldn't form any other words. All I could manage was Connor's name, chanted over and over like a litany. "Connor…"

Connor's mouth tightened around my cock, his hands reaching around to squeeze my ass. One finger slid down my crack and brushed over my hole. And that was it. My balls tightened, and I slammed my spare hand across my mouth to muffle the sound as I cried out and came down his throat. Connor swallowed my cum, massaging my cock with his tongue and drawing my pleasure out until I felt utterly boneless.

I glanced down and watched as Connor released my softening cock, placing a last kiss to the sensitive tip. He grinned at me and casually rose to his feet. He was still hard, and I clumsily reached for him because I didn't want him to think I was selfish.

"Don't worry, babe," he said, stepping close to me and kissing me. I could taste myself on his tongue. He moaned softly against my lips. "You taste so good. Loved having your cock in my mouth. Did you like it?"

"Y-yeah." I nodded. "Thank you."

"So polite for me, saying thank you." He groaned. "Want me to come all over you again? Paint you with my cum?"

"Please."

"Good boy." Connor groaned again, and I heard his hand moving faster. God, I wanted to touch him, but my mind still felt disconnected from my whole body like it wasn't quite mine. Connor grunted and stilled, and I felt his cum splattering my skin. It felt almost possessive, like he was making me his, even though I knew I was only projecting. I wanted to be his more than anything.

The water continued to fall around us, slowly growing cooler. Eventually we moved, washed ourselves quickly, and exchanged soft, lazy kisses whenever we got even vaguely close to each other. By the time we got back to our room, exhaustion hung heavy in my bones. I climbed into bed and opened my arms to Connor, who buried into my side with a little sigh, and I was asleep before I'd had a chance to even consider what all of this might mean.

CHAPTER TWENTY-ONE

Connor

ACCORDING to every romcom I've ever seen, waking up in bed next to your best friend after you hooked up the night before was supposed to be a terrifying experience. So bad that you both had to scream and then have an awkward conversation where you denied everything and pretended to be just friends.

I wasn't sure if I'd been completely expecting things to play out like that with Patrick since we'd woken up cuddled up together perfectly fine after the night before. However we'd now introduced sex into the equation, and we all knew sex was the problem in situations like this.

Except… it didn't happen. I woke up half on top of Patrick, like yesterday morning, with my face buried in his chest. I'd taken one deep breath, put my arm around his waist, and realised I never wanted to move again. I just wanted to stay there forever like a very large koala. Patrick had eventually stirred and pulled me into a tight hug, and we'd exchanged lazy kisses until we heard other people pottering around and figured it was time to get up.

We'd taken our time, talking quietly as we found clothes, and I debated which top to wear. I eventually settled on a soft, comfortable T-shirt in pale grey. It reminded me of Patrick's eyes. I almost wanted to steal Patrick's hoodie to go with it since it looked so big and snuggly, and I knew it would smell amazing, but I thought that would probably cross a line.

Besides that was the ultimate sign of banging, and I wasn't sure my beloved would appreciate me showing up to breakfast with his family in his clothes. I was ninety-nine-point-nine percent sure they all knew what we'd been doing anyway, especially given Aoife's previous comments, but I didn't want to rub it in their faces.

Plus, Patrick put the hoodie on before I'd even had a chance to grab it.

When we finally got downstairs, we found Aoife, John, and Mary in the kitchen, chatting away over mugs of tea. Aoife was looking at something in the oven while John sat in a chair at the small kitchen table chopping mushrooms and tomatoes while surrounded by three eager looking terriers. I had to admit that Mary looked slightly worse for wear, clutching her mug to her chest and looking like she'd rather be in bed. She looked like I'd felt after my twenty-third birthday when I'd drunk nearly two-thirds of a bottle of vodka. That had been messy. I didn't think Mary had had that much to drink before Patrick and I had sneaked out, but since we'd missed the rest of the party, I had no idea what had happened while we'd been gone.

"Good morning, boys," Aoife said as she stood, shooting us a grin. She looked considerably more awake and alive than her daughter. "Sleep well?"

"Yeah, we did. Thanks," Patrick offered, tucking himself into the corner and putting his arm around my waist. "Did you?"

"Not bad at all, considering I only got about four hours." She shook her head and laughed. "I know I said we weren't going to stay up late, but when you get to talking, sometimes you just can't help it. And I haven't seen your Auntie Lydia in nearly two years. We had a lot to catch up on."

"You talk every week on the phone for at least an hour," John said with a laugh.

"Well, there's some things you just can't talk about on the phone. I didn't see you complaining while you were drinking God knows what with Brian and Smiffy."

"It was just sloe gin, nothing fancy."

"Jesus Christ, John. That sloe gin of yours is flammable. Are you sure you should be drinking it at your age?" Aoife teased, scooping the sliced tomatoes off the board in front of him into a bowl.

"I've been drinking it for forty years. It ain't killed me yet."

"And it better not. I want a card from the Queen for our diamond wedding anniversary. You've gotta do another ten years yet."

"Lord help me," John said with a fond smile. Aoife just

rolled her eyes. They were adorable to watch, and I loved the fact that they were clearly still hopelessly in love with each other even after fifty years.

"Do you want a hand, Mum?" Patrick asked from behind me.

"No thanks, love. I'll be just fine."

"Are you sure? I don't want you to do everything yourself."

"You're a sweet boy," Aoife said, "but this is my kitchen, and it's not like it's a lot of trouble to cook breakfast. I'm sure you wouldn't want me poking around in your kitchen."

"Oh God no," I said with a laugh before I could stop myself. "You should see him at work. He *hates* when someone goes into his kitchen without asking." I tilted my head to look up at Patrick. "Do you remember that time Aaron popped into your kitchen to 'borrow' a pair of scissors and some oranges? I thought you were straight up going to murder him."

"Patrick? Commit murder?" Mary asked, somewhat groggily. "It's gotta have been bad."

"They were my scissors," Patrick grumbled. "He had six pairs of his own. I know because I made Ben buy them for him because he kept losing them. They've never been the same since."

"That doesn't sound like much," Mary said.

"Oh wait, it gets worse." I grinned. "Aaron took a whole tray of oranges that Patrick had bought specifically to use in a chocolate and orange mousse, and in the process of taking them he knocked over two trays of mini pavlova nests and a whole cheesecake. Splat, all over the floor. An hour before service. On a Sunday."

Mary winced. "Yeah, that'll do it."

"Did you know that when Patrick gets mad, like proper apoplectic, he doesn't say anything? Not at first. He just gets this look in his eye that would give even the hardiest serial killer a run for his money, and then it's like watching a volcano explode in slow motion. You almost want to run away, but you can't bring yourself to move, even though you know you might get burned. I don't think I've ever seen Aaron look so contrite in his life."

"You know, I'm almost tempted to see that," Mary said with a wry grin. "When he was little and he got angry, he'd just get very quiet and say he wasn't going to be my friend anymore and then go and sit in his room."

"Awww, that's so cute!" I pressed a kiss to Patrick's cheek. "That sounds adorable, babe."

Patrick huffed, his cheeks tinting. "Thanks? I think."

"I was nowhere near as nice when I got angry. I got petty instead—although that was mostly as a teenager. Once, Kyle Mitchell stole all my make-up and wrote insults all over my bag in Sharpie during PE, and in revenge I pulled a sicky next lesson and casually took all his clothes and put them in the showers with some bright orange dye I'd bought in Wilko." I sighed almost fondly at the memory. "He looked like an Oompa-Loompa from *Charlie and the Chocolate Factory,* and that's saying something considering how much fake tan most of us wore. The month's worth of detention was almost worth it. I mean, his mum wanted me suspended, but when my own mum pointed out Kyle had stolen and destroyed a hundred quids' worth of make-up and written homophobic slurs all over my possessions while the school had done fuck all, they decided against it. Not gonna lie, it wasn't the greatest school ever."

"Remind me never to piss you off," Patrick said.

"Don't worry, babe. You're safe."

"Thanks." I smiled as Patrick leant down and pressed a quick kiss to my lips, my chest filling with warmth.

We spent the rest of the time before breakfast chilling in the kitchen, chatting with Aoife and John. Mary joined in occasionally, but she mostly just clutched her tea. She'd feel better with food inside her. I always did with a hangover. Mind you, I hadn't had one that bad in years.

Eventually, breakfast was ready, and we helped ourselves to bacon, sausages, scrambled eggs, fried tomatoes and mushrooms, and mountains of toast. I carried my heaped plate through to the dining room, suddenly feeling ridiculously hungry. It felt like an alien was about to burst out of my stomach at any moment and eat everything it could get its greedy little mouth on.

I sat next to Patrick on the far side of the table while John and Mary sat opposite us and Aoife took the seat at the end. The conversation flowed easily but sporadically as everyone tucked into their food. I was far more interested in eating than talking.

I wondered if there was any cake left, and whether it was acceptable to have cake for breakfast. Although technically it would be dessert with brunch since it was nearly ten thirty. Since I'd eaten a full meal, having pudding didn't seem like a terrible thing, and it would be rude to leave the cake uneaten. Especially since Patrick had worked so hard on it.

"The barn made a really good venue," Patrick said offhandedly.

"It did," Mary agreed. "There was plenty of space for everyone, and it worked well having the bar in the corner and the long tables."

I nodded. "And there was plenty of room for dancing. It was perfect."

"If you wanted to make some more money, you could offer it as a reception venue for weddings," Mary said. "I bet loads of people would love it, especially because they could hire the cottages on the farm too. You could make some of the features permanent, like building a proper bar in that corner for example."

"It's a thought," John said, nodding his head. "But I'd need someone to run that part of the business. I think your mum'd kill me if we took much more on. We're supposed to be slowing down."

"So unless you're offering," Aoife added with a smile, "it's probably not going to happen. It's a nice idea though."

Mary paused. "I'm not going to say no. I mean, I'm not saying yes either, but if I'm being honest, work is driving me nuts, and I was looking for something new. Besides, it would be nice to work here."

We stared at her. I couldn't quite believe she was willing to jump headfirst into something new like that, but it was glorious to watch. Then John huffed out a laugh and shook his head.

"I guess we'll be holding weddings then. You have a

think and come up with some plans, and we'll take it from there."

"Perfect!" Mary beamed, suddenly looking a lot less hungover. "I might need some test subjects though." She glanced at Patrick and me. "You don't happen to know anyone who wants to get married?"

My heart sank, and I shook my head, my throat suddenly tight. "No... sorry."

"Mary, don't tease them," Aoife said.

"I'm not."

Somebody said something, but I wasn't really listening. My stomach was churning, and it felt like my breakfast was suddenly about to make a reappearance across the table. Shit. I'd never, ever meant to let it get this far. Fucking fuck, fuck, what was I doing? It was one thing to pretend to be Patrick's boyfriend and fool his family, but it was another thing entirely to make them think we were so in love we might want to get married.

That was so wrong on a million different levels.

And yet my heart tugged painfully because I wanted that more than anything else in the world.

I knew Patrick wanted to get married, and the idea of him celebrating here, with some faceless man, smiling and dancing together without a care in the world, surrounded by his family, made me more nauseated than ever.

His family that had welcomed me with open arms and made me feel like I belonged here. Who hadn't cared that I wore make-up or taught pole or that I was cheeky and opinionated.

A family I wanted to be a part of forever.

My imagination took over, flooding me with visions of what it would be like to marry Patrick—a wedding full of our friends, his family and my mum looking on proudly, summer sunlight pouring down on us as we took photographs in the fields, drinking Pimm's and eating a mountain of food, feeding each other cake and pushing it into each other's mouths before kissing. I'd be able to taste the icing on his tongue. Dancing for hours and spinning in circles as the band played until the night sky was dusted with stars before we fell into bed, stripping off our clothes and slowly making love until we were sweaty and sated and I didn't know where his body ended and mine began.

Christmases here on the farm—loud, joyful, and full of food.

Birthdays together at home, celebrating with friends, curling up with The President and boxes of takeout and Netflix's cheesiest romcoms after a long day. Building a life together one day at a time.

I wanted that more than anything else, and it hurt because it was never going to come true. Because I was too scared to ever put myself out there, too afraid to risk it all for the one thing I really wanted. Too afraid of more heartbreak and rejection from the one man I loved more than anyone.

But just for today I could indulge. Today I could pretend it was real.

CHAPTER TWENTY-TWO

Patrick

I LOVED MY FAMILY, but after almost four days, I was ready to go home.

They were amazing, and it had been great to see them again, but I missed the freedom of my own house and my own kitchen. I hadn't been allowed to cook anything, and this was the longest I'd gone without cooking in years. My fingers were starting to get itchy.

Plus, I knew if I stayed much longer it was likely I'd get dragged into Mary's wedding venue schemes, and I knew there would be the inevitable questions of why didn't I move home and run a catering business here. I didn't really want to have to explain that while I loved my family, that wasn't really my dream.

Besides, I knew that if Mary and I ended up working in close quarters we'd probably drive each other nuts. I'd take Aaron's swearing and shouting any day because at least I could tell him where to shove it when he really annoyed me. I knew it sounded selfish, but I loved The Pear Tree and my kitchen there. It was a space I'd carved out for myself, and I couldn't see myself leaving it.

The other reason I'd never move was because Connor's life was in Nottingham. There was no way I was giving up our friendship to move to the wilds of Devon. I don't think I'd be able to do it if I tried. After this weekend, I was going to have trouble giving Connor up at all.

We'd shifted into this weird twilight zone relationship where we weren't really dating but we'd gone beyond friendship. Unless friendship meant giving your friend a blowjob in the shower or a slow, teasing handjob in bed when you'd just woken up, in which case I'd think we were living in a porn world instead of reality. Neither of us had said anything about it. It was like we were just waiting for this weekend to be over and the other shoe to drop.

I wasn't sure what would happen when it did.

I tried not to think about it as I shoved the last of our bags into the boot of the car. Without the cakes there was a lot more room, although my mum had tried to send us home with a mountain of food. I wasn't even sure where half of it had come from since there hadn't been many left-overs from the party. There'd been a little bit of the extra sheet cake leftover by Sunday night, but Connor and Da had happily polished that off.

Connor's logic had been that it was fine to have cake with every meal, but I didn't think I'd have been able to survive the sugar coma.

"Is that it?" I asked over my shoulder, watching Connor

bounce across the yard holding a Tupperware tub. Lord only knew what was in it.

"Yes, we're all good." He pressed a kiss to my cheek as he passed me. "Your mum gave me some slices of barm-brack to keep me going."

"You've only just had breakfast."

"Well, this is for second breakfast. Car breakfast. It's probably better for me than the chocolate twists you get at Costa."

"When were you planning on getting any of those?" I asked in amusement.

"I was hoping you'd be lovely enough to stop at a services so I can get coffee." Connor fluttered his eyelashes and smiled at me. I knew he was being deliberately over the top, but it was still adorable. And I had never been able to say no to him.

"I suppose, but the nearest one isn't for a while."

"That's fine. I can wait. And at least if I get hungry, I already have a snack."

I chuckled and shook my head as he placed the tub on the front seat. He laced his fingers with mine and we headed back towards the house to finish saying goodbye to my parents. Since it was a Monday, Mary had gone home the previous evening but not before giving us both giant hugs and making us promise to come and visit her soon.

Mum and Da had both been up early because even though they were supposed to be taking it easy these days, neither of them seemed to be slowing down. They were both in the kitchen with the dogs, and Mum swooped us both up in huge hugs.

"Don't leave it so long next time, okay?" she said as she pressed a kiss to my cheek. "I know where you live, Patrick. If I have to, I'll come to you. I'd like to visit your restaurant anyway."

"Lord help us if you come to visit," I said with a chuckle. Mum would definitely give Aaron a run for his money if they met. The first thing she'd probably ask him was why he swore so much. And why he'd ruined my cheesecake. She'd never let him forget that.

Mum muttered something to Connor I didn't catch and gave him a kiss. It was sweet to see how my family had pretty much adopted him over the weekend. I knew he found it a little overwhelming, but I hoped he knew it came from a place of love. I'd have to keep my promise to Cara and bring him and his mum down for Christmas.

Da gave me a hug and told me to drive safe. "I'm proud of you, Patrick. I hope you know that."

"Yeah, I do." I tried not to let my voice get thick.

"You keep hold of that man. He's perfect for you. I've never seen you as happy as I have these past four days." Da smiled and squeezed my shoulder, and something inside my chest tightened.

"Thanks."

"You take care now. Give us a call when you get home, or your mother'll be in the car before I can stop her."

"Will do." I knew it was worth more than my life not to let mum know we'd gotten back safe. Da smiled and turned to Connor, giving him a hug and saying something while Mum asked me again if I wanted anything to eat or drink before I left.

We finally extracted ourselves from the kitchen and headed for the car. When we drove past the house, my parents were stood by the back door, waving at us.

"Your family are so nice," Connor said as I turned the car down the driveaway and headed towards the winding road that would lead us back to the motorway.

"Yeah, they are. I love them even if they drive me crazy."

Connor nodded. "I think families are supposed to do that. In a good way though."

We settled into the drive, Connor flicking through Spotify and singing along happily as we made our way through Devon and back towards the motorway to head North. I was glad we'd waited until Monday to leave because now it was mid-morning and there wasn't much traffic. At this rate, we'd be home by mid-afternoon at the latest. Then I'd be able to spend the rest of the day freaking out and trying to figure out what the hell I did next.

I wondered if I'd get any sleep before I had to go back to work tomorrow.

"Oh shit!" Connor exclaimed. He sat bolt upright in the passenger seat suddenly looking at his phone like it had bitten him.

"Something wrong?" I asked, trying not to take my eyes off the road.

"Yeah. Maybe?" He laughed nervously. "I just got a Facebook notification from the East Midlands Pole Championships that they're going to be sending out emails about whether we've made the finals in the next hour."

"It's going to be fine. I promise." I tried to keep my

voice as reassuring as possible. "You're an awesome dancer, you put together an amazing routine, and they're going to love it. And you're going to go there and win and blow everyone's minds."

"Thanks, babe." Connor sighed. Out of the corner of my eye I saw him fiddling with his phone. "I mean, I know the routine is great. Maybe not my best ever, but still really fucking good. But the competition got lots of entries this year and there were some really fucking talented people submitting, and there are only six places in the final."

"I'm sure it's going to be great." I glanced at a nearby road sign. "There's a services with a Costa a couple of miles away, want to stop and get coffee?"

"Honestly, Patrick, you are a literal angel!"

"So that's a yes then?

"Obviously."

The services wasn't busy, so we didn't have to queue long to get drinks. Connor got another salted caramel coffee monstrosity topped with whipped cream. There was even caramel sauce drizzled around the side of the cup. It made him happy, and I wasn't going to complain as long as he didn't make me drink it. I wasn't a huge coffee drinker, so instead I settled on a frozen mango and passionfruit drink that was sweet and refreshing without melting my teeth.

We sat on some benches outside to drink them, enjoying the morning sunshine. It was nice to stretch my legs and switch off for a few minutes before we had to get back on the motorway. I hadn't done this much driving in years, and I'd forgotten how knackering it was. Maybe next time I went to visit my parents I'd take the train, even though the route was a pain in the ass and took forever, at least I wouldn't have to concentrate.

"Oh!" Connor let out a sharp intake of breath from next to me. "I got an email."

"And?" I held my breath, crossing my fingers on the hand Connor couldn't see. I watched him carefully as he clicked on the notification and scanned the email. I saw his face fall, and I knew what the answer was before he opened his mouth.

Bollocks.

"I… I didn't get in." Connor's voice was soft and laced with shock. I knew he'd said he was worried, but saying you might not get in and then actually not making it were two different things.

"I'm so sorry, babe," I said, putting my arm around his shoulder and pulling him against me. I pressed a kiss to the top of his hair, breathing in the scent of the honey and macadamia shampoo he'd used. "Did they say why?"

"No, they don't give individual feedback. They just said they got a lot of entries, all very high quality, blah blah blah." Connor sighed. "Fuck, this sucks ass. I've never had this happen before."

"I know," I said quietly.

"God, that makes me sound like such a huge fucking asshole, but I've always made the finals for competitions. I mean, if it was Chrome Stars then I'd have expected it because that competition is fucking huge! But this is just the East Mids championships… I just… Ugh, whatever I say is just going to make me look like a salty bitch."

"It's okay. You can be as salty as you want with me."

"Thanks, babe. You're the best." Connor stared down at his phone, looking utterly miserable. I squeezed him tighter, wishing there was a way I could make him feel better. I couldn't imagine how much it sucked not to get in, especially when he'd wanted it so much.

"Oh God," Connor said. "Levi's asking if I got in. Would it be terrible if I ignored him?"

"No, of course not."

"Good, then I'm not even going to open it. I'm just going to wallow in my misery a little longer." He sucked on the straw of his drink, slurping up the last dregs of cream and coffee. My eyes were suddenly transfixed on the way his lips were wrapped around the paper. Maybe there was one way I could make it up to him... but we'd have to get home first.

CHAPTER TWENTY-THREE

Connor

I SULKED ALL the way home.

I was probably acting like a brat, but in my defence—actually, I didn't really have a defence. I was just being a sulky child. It hurt though. I knew the routine hadn't been my best ever, but I'd still put in a hundred percent because I always did. And to add insult to injury, Levi had made the cut. Not that I thought Levi was a worse dancer than I was, he wasn't, but it still sucked because we were pretty much at the same level. I didn't get why he'd made it and I hadn't. I'd made it before. I'd even won a couple of years ago. But apparently it wasn't going to be me this year. It was going to be Levi instead.

I'd known Levi for five years. I'd first met him backstage at a pole competition in Leeds. We'd sat next to each other in the green room because we were both in the same category, and we'd started chatting. It had been mostly polite small talk at first, but after we'd both performed, we'd kept going. We had to sit backstage until everyone in our section had performed, and it was a *big* section. We'd just clicked. We liked similar styles of dance and had similar backgrounds, although his was in ballroom while mine was in ballet. Plus, we'd been the only two male competitors, so it had been nice to find someone who understood what that was like. I'd won that section, and Levi had come in second.

We'd kept in touch after that, and when he'd floated the idea of setting up his own dance school past me, I'd encouraged him and ultimately ended up moving to help him. We trained together, bitched together, and always supported each other.

But this one stung.

I knew I shouldn't feel jealous because Levi had worked really hard on his routine, but a little insidious voice in my head had started whispering that if I couldn't even get into the East Midlands Championships, there was no way in hell I was making it into Chrome Stars. I should just give up now.

I pushed the voice away. I had no room for those thoughts, and they weren't productive at all.

There was always room for improvement, no matter how good you were. If the judges didn't think my routine was good enough, then it wasn't good enough. I needed to get back some of the toughness from my teenage ballet days. Things had been cutthroat at times, and there'd been numerous occasions when I hadn't gotten the roles I'd wanted. Although sometimes that might have been because I'd slightly overestimated my abilities. And sometimes it was never going to work because the principal girl was half a foot taller than me, and it didn't matter how strong I was.

Being short sucked ass sometimes, but I'd never let it get me down. I'd just kept working. My teachers had been tough but fair. Well, most of them anyway.

But this had never happened in pole, and it caught me off guard. I strongly suspected everything from this weekend had me feeling all sorts of vulnerable, and that was probably making me feel worse. I'd get over it by tomorrow. Maybe Wednesday. After all, if I acted like a brat for too long, then Levi was bound to notice, and I didn't want him feeling guilty for something that wasn't his fault.

For now though, poor Patrick had drawn the short straw and had to put up with my salty, mardy ass all the way back home. He was very good about it though, leaving me to my own devices or occasionally chatting about random things like whether we thought President Whiskers would forgive him for going away for the weekend.

By the time we got back to Nottingham, it was early afternoon, and as we drove towards the city, I suddenly had a gnawing feeling in the pit of my stomach. I assumed Patrick was going to drop me off at my flat before going home, but I didn't really feel like being alone. I knew it was selfish, but I wasn't ready for the weekend to end, and with everything that had happened, including this morning's shitty news, I just wanted to stay with him for a little while longer. I wanted to keep one good thing going.

"Can I... Are you... Were you...?" No matter how I tried to start the sentence I couldn't find the words I wanted.

"Do you want to come back to mine for a bit?" Patrick

asked. Apparently he'd suddenly become a mind reader. "I could make us some late lunch, and we could just chill for the afternoon. I can take you home later."

"That sounds perfect. Thank you, babe." I loved how he knew what I needed without me having to ask for it. Patrick seemed to know that I hated being vulnerable, and that I was useless at asking for things for myself. So he didn't make me.

"I know I've got some cheese, and there's bread in the freezer. Are you okay with cheese and beans on toast?"

"Honestly, that sounds like the best plan right now." Comfort food for the win. There was still some of the barm-brack left. And if all else failed, I'd order some ice cream on Deliveroo. I was going to end my long weekend of indulgence with yet more indulgence. I deserved it.

We pulled up outside Patrick's house. I left my suitcase in the car and helped Patrick unload his bag and the stuff from Aoife into the house. As soon as I stepped into the kitchen, I heard the jet-engine purring of Whiskey, who sauntered straight past Patrick to wind himself around my legs.

"Hey, baby. Are you pleased to see me?" I reached down to rub him gently behind the ears. He meowed loudly at me before resuming his purring. "I'll take that as a yes then. You're a smart boy."

Behind me, I heard Patrick chuckling. "You'd think he hadn't been fed in four days. You're lying, Mr. President. I know Cathy from next door came in to feed you twice a day. I have proof."

"Awww, but he's starved and sad. Just like me."

"Is that a hint?"

"Maaaaybe." I smiled at him, and Patrick raised an eyebrow. "Okay, yes. It's a humongous hint, but I am hungry and heartbroken, so please feed me."

"Let me just put this case upstairs then I'll make something."

"You spoil me."

"I know." As he walked past me, he pulled me close and pressed a quick kiss to my mouth. It was a sudden, sweet gesture that left me reeling. I ran my fingers across my lips like I wasn't sure what had just happened, staring at the door to the living room where Patrick had suddenly vanished. I thought we'd stop that now that we were home, but maybe I was wrong.

There'd been a gentle casualness to the kiss, almost like it was an everyday thing that he hadn't even thought of. It was almost relationshipy. But not new relationshipy. Established, comfortable relationshipy. The sort I'd always craved but had never seemed to find.

Patrick was back before I could get too lost in my thoughts, and I perched on the side while he made lunch. We ate at the kitchen table with Whiskey staring at us, hoping one of us would slip him something. I wasn't even sure he'd want beans on toast, but that didn't stop him from trying.

Afterwards, Patrick and I retreated to the sofa. I pulled up Netflix, flicking through the endless selection of movies and TV shows until I found something that would hold my attention. I ended up selecting a Christmas movie, *The Knight Before Christmas*, which I'd watched countless times last year when it had been released. Even though it was the middle of summer, there was something endlessly comforting about the marshmallow warmth of a Christmas film. Especially one as sweet as this.

Watching it gave me the strangest craving for hot chocolate and snuggles. At least I could easily have the second one.

I snuggled into Patrick, the rest of me curled up on the cushion next to him. His arm came down around my shoulder, pulling me close to him as I rested my head on his chest. It was perfect, and I soon got lost in the film. I didn't notice Patrick was slowly stroking my arm until we were at least halfway through. Had he been doing that this whole time, or had he only just started? Either way it felt lovely. My skin tingled under his touch, heat blossoming under my skin. I wanted more but simultaneously was completely content to lie here and drag it out. If this was leading where I thought it was, then I wanted it to last.

After all, some of the best orgasms I'd ever had were ones where we hadn't rushed things.

Sure, a quick fuck or suck was fun. Sometimes it was exactly what was needed in the moment. But I loved being able to take it slow, laying my partner out and teasing them until they couldn't do more than beg, kissing every inch of their skin and discovering the little spots that broke them apart, bringing them to the edge but not letting them come because the end release would be so much sweeter with a little patience, fucking them slow and deep until sweat dripped down our skin, and right at the end, finally letting them come and watching pleasure overtake their body. It was a heady experience, bringing someone that much bliss.

I wanted to do that to Patrick, in his own bed, where we had time and privacy. Where I could make love to him gently and slowly until I couldn't tell where his body ended and mine began.

"Do you want to take this upstairs?" I asked, not looking away from the TV but not really paying attention to what Vanessa Hudgens was saying either.

Patrick was quiet for a moment. "Would you like to?"

"You can't answer my question with another question, babe. That's not how this works." I chuckled and tilted my head up to look at him. Patrick smiled softly at me, a faint trace of worry around his eyes. "And if you're worried because you're not sure I want to, well, I wouldn't have asked if I didn't."

"Okay." He nodded. "Yeah… let's go upstairs." He flicked off the TV. A thought suddenly popped into my head, and I realised it was a question I had to ask before we went any further. I sat up and looked at Patrick carefully.

"Honey, do you have anything here? Lube? Condoms? Anything like that? I mean, I don't know how far you want to go, but I thought I'd ask the question." I put my hand on his thigh. "And this isn't me pressuring you. This is me trying to cover all our bases. If you want to just cuddle, make out a little, maybe more handjobs, then we can totally just do that. 'Kay?"

"Okay." Patrick nodded, then he took my hand and interlaced our fingers. "And what if I want more? What will you give me?"

Oh, that was a dangerous question. It was a question I didn't have the answer to. If he'd let me, I'd give him everything. My heart, my mind, my body, my soul. Patrick could have all of them without a second thought.

"Anything," I said. It was all I could say. I didn't want to lie to him.

"Will you make love to me, Connor?" Patrick's fingers cupped my jaw, drawing my mouth to his. He tasted like strawberries, but I didn't know why. Maybe he'd always taste of strawberries to me. "I want to feel you inside me."

"Are you sure?"

"More than I've ever been about anything."

I wanted to tell him he was being ridiculous, that he shouldn't want this with me because we were both only hurting ourselves and that I had no idea what would happen tomorrow. But the objecting voice in my head was getting smaller and smaller with every nanosecond that passed because I wanted this. I wanted him.

"Okay then. You'd better get your pretty ass upstairs, Patrick." I kissed him again, deeper this time. With tongue. Then I pulled back to whisper quietly. "I am going to make you feel so good, baby. I promise."

"I know. I trust you." His face went pink. "And don't worry. You won't be the first thing I've had in my ass."

"Whatever are you trying to tell me, darling Patrick?" I teased.

"I, er, I may have bought a dildo last year. To experiment with."

"There's absolutely nothing wrong with that at all! Did you like it?"

He nodded, the blush staining his cheeks deep pink. "I did, but I think your cock is going to feel even better."

"Oh, I know it will." I winked cheekily, hoping to take some of his nerves away with a cheeky bit of flirting. It couldn't hurt, and I wanted to put him at ease. "You still never answered my question by the way. Are we good to go, or do I need to make a mad dash to Tesco?"

Patrick chuckled. "I, um, I have lube. And condoms too, although I've never... Well, I've never done anything with anyone except you, so it's up to you if you want to use them, I guess. I don't think you're gonna get me pregnant. That's all I can remember from sex ed at school—use condoms or you'll all get pregnant. That and the really graphic pictures of infected penises from STIs." He shuddered. "No wonder I didn't want to look at dicks for years."

I snorted and shook my head, trying to school my face into a serious expression and failing miserably. "Oh my God, babe. Seriously. I did not need to remember that."

"You got the visit from the school nurse too?"

"Worst hour of my life. I did not need to see any of that. And it was all such heteronormative bullshit too." I sighed and Patrick giggled. I'd never heard him do that before. It was adorable as fuck. "Anyway, circling back to the point. I actually got tested when I broke up with whats-his-face. That guy I was seeing for a while before I discovered he'd cheated on me with half his gym."

"Tom?"

"Ah yes, that douche. Anyway, the tests came back fine, so if you don't want to use condoms, we don't have to." I was putting on an air of calm, but inside my brain was currently at war. I'd never gone bare with a guy. Ever. I'd never trusted anyone enough, and it wasn't like my relationships had ever lasted that long. And now I was just going to disregard all of that because it was Patrick?

But it was Patrick.

And I trusted him with my life. So that was that.

Besides, I couldn't deny that I was buzzing with excitement at the idea of filling Patrick with my cum. It stirred a little primal desire deep in my chest, something hungry and possessive. I was going to make Patrick mine, and afterwards, he'd never be able to forget me. Like I'd never be able to forget him.

"I trust you." Then he added the five prettiest words I'd ever heard. "Please, Connor, I want you."

CHAPTER TWENTY-FOUR

Connor

THAT SETTLED IT, nothing was stopping me now. I untucked my legs from underneath me and slid off the sofa, stretching out a hand to Patrick. "Let's go upstairs then."

Patrick nodded and took my hand. I checked his expression for any hint of nerves or uncertainty, expecting to find at least a little, but there was nothing. I'd keep checking, of course, because I knew people could change their mind at a moment's notice, and I didn't ever want Patrick to feel uncomfortable. Still I trusted him to be open with me and to tell me if something changed.

We made our way towards the stairs hand in hand, and I gestured at Patrick to go up the narrow stairs first, mostly because I was a selfish man and I wanted to watch his beautiful ass as we climbed. It was so round and juicy, like the most perfect peach. And it was going to be all mine. When I'd first touched his hole in the shower while I was blowing him, I'd noticed the instantaneous effect it'd had, and I'd neatly stored the information away for later. Patrick said he'd been playing with a dildo, which I was going to get him to do while I watched one day because I wanted to know exactly how he touched himself, but that was leagues away from having an experienced and thoughtful partner who was pretty damn good at using what he'd been given.

And if it sounded like I was bragging, I was. Just a little.

I knew I was good with my fingers, my tongue, and my cock, and I'd had enough sex over the years, from the fantastic to the extremely mediocre, to know how to make it good for my partner. Since this was the first time Patrick was considering putting something in his ass that wasn't made of silicone, I was going to make sure it was fucking amazing for him.

Patrick closed the bedroom door behind us just in case Whiskey decided to suddenly make an appearance. Although I didn't think it was likely because Patrick had said he only liked lying on the bed first thing in the morning when the sun shone through the window. Silly furball.

I pulled Patrick into my arms at the end of the bed, kissing him slowly and sliding my fingers under his T-shirt to tug it off over his head. I loved Patrick's body—broad and soft with wide shoulders and arms that made me feel so snug every time I was wrapped in them. His chest was dusted with dark blond hair that ran down his torso and into his jeans. I'd never been a fan of waxed chests, which was slightly hypocritical of me since I'd been doing mine for years. Although that was mostly because it was easier to do pole shirtless without the added friction of chest hair.

I reached for my own T-shirt as Patrick's fell to the floor, then dropped it alongside his before reaching for my jeans. I debated leaving my briefs on and drawing this out, but I was horny and wanted to get to the more exciting part of the afternoon, so I slid them off and toed off the little pink trainer socks I'd been wearing. Patrick had slid his jeans and underwear off too, and I sighed happily as the rest of his body was exposed. The man had amazing thighs and a nice dick of his own. One day I was going to slide down onto it and ride it until we were both dripping with sweat and absolutely exhausted. But not today.

"On the bed," I said, giving him a final sweet kiss. "On your back. Make yourself comfy." I gave him a little smile. "Is the lube in the drawer?" I pointed to the bedside table which had a reading lamp, a stack of well-thumbed books, and a box of tissues on it. That reminded me that I should ask him whether he'd enjoyed the romance novel I'd given him. He'd not said anything, but I'd noticed that he'd been seventy percent through when I'd last opened my Kindle. I'd ask him later. Now wasn't really the time.

Patrick nodded as he pulled the duvet back and settled himself in the middle of the bed, stacking the pillows up behind him. I walked quickly over to the table and pulled out a bottle of organic lube from the drawer, which was tucked in next to a flesh-coloured dildo. I smiled to myself because it was so utterly Patrick to get the good stuff, not just the cheap shit you could get at Tesco or Boots. The last cheap lube I had tried to use had been flavoured, and as soon as the guy had smeared it on my ass, it had started burning. That had ended that pretty quickly.

I placed the bottle on the bed within easy reach before climbing onto the mattress. Patrick was smiling at me, and I couldn't resist leaning over to kiss him gently. We had all the time in the world, and I was going to make the most of it. I moved between his thighs, kissing him again before slowly making my way along his jaw and down his neck, cataloguing the little hitches in Patrick's breath and the soft moans when I found a particularly sensitive spot on his collarbone. His hands skimmed over my shoulders and down my back as I moved lower, pressing kisses down his chest. Patrick gasped, his fingers tangling in my hair as I sucked one of his nipples into my mouth and swirled my tongue around the hardening nub.

"Do you like that?" I asked as I kissed across his chest, looking up at him through my lashes. Patrick nodded and I smiled. "Words, honey. Tell me."

"Y-yeah, that feels so good." He gasped again as I gently nipped the other nipple and then soothed it with my tongue.

"Good." I slowly trailed my mouth lower, taking my time to explore every inch of Patrick's torso. And if I drove him slightly mad in the process, then that was all the better. I wanted him to want me, need me, more than anything. I wanted to make this experience so memorable that nothing and nobody else would ever come close. In the back of my mind, I was still convinced that whatever this was between us would have to end, and if it did, I wanted to ensure that Patrick remembered me forever.

My own cock was maddeningly hard as I slid farther down the bed, feeling the delicious touch of friction from the sheets against the sensitive head. But today I wasn't going to be selfish, and my own needs would have to wait, at least for a little bit. It would be utterly worth it in the end when I was buried inside Patrick.

I kissed down Patrick's hip, laving my tongue over the hot skin. His cock was hard against his stomach, the head beaded with precum. I kissed across his abdomen and sucked the tip of his cock into my mouth, loving the way he gasped and swore. It was so tempting to swallow him down and suck him until he was a babbling mess again, but that would have to wait for another time. I pulled off with a soft pop and reached for the lube.

"I'm going to prep you now." I looked up at him, studying his face for any sign of discomfort. That was the thing about knowing Patrick so well—every twitch of his face, every small expression was familiar to me. I'd understand if he was nervous, but if he looked uncomfortable in any way, I would put the brakes on here and now.

"Okay." Patrick nodded. "Do it, please. I need you." He spread his legs a little farther, bending his legs and pulling his knees up, giving me perfect access to him. I sat up on my knees, so I could watch all of him because this was a sight I didn't want to miss. What had I done to deserve someone so wonderful? The lube opened with a little snick, and I poured some onto my fingers. Patrick gasped as I ran my slick fingers across his sensitive rim, teasing him, then groaned as I slowly pushed one finger into him.

"Fuck!"

"Does my finger feel better than yours?" I asked teasingly as I gently began to pump it in and out of him. I wasn't sure how much Patrick had used the dildo, but given that the bottle of lube looked to be about half-full, I was going to guess it got a fair bit of use. A little possessive feeling curled around my heart. This might not be the first time, or tenth, that Patrick had had something inside him, but it was the first time he wasn't alone. I was the one who got to touch him, and I loved that I was the only person who'd seen him like this. I wasn't quite sure I'd ever be able to give up the feeling.

One finger slowly became two, and Patrick moaned as I gently rubbed his prostate, driving him a little insane with my touches. I wanted him desperate and on edge when I finally sank into him. I wanted him to be thinking about nothing but me and my cock. By the time two fingers became three, Patrick was gasping and moaning, his hands gripping the sheets.

"P-please, Connor. Please. Stop teasing, just give it to me."

"Give you what?" I asked, grinning at him like the little bastard I was. I knew I was teasing him, my touches aimed at driving him wild but not getting him off. I wrapped my other hand around his cock, stroking it slowly as I pumped three fingers in and out of his hole. "My fingers? Did you want four?" I rubbed my thumb across his slit. "My tongue?"

"I want you to fuck me," Patrick said, already sounding perfectly desperate. "With your cock. Please, give me your cock."

"Of course, babe. Anything you want." I leant over him to kiss him softly, licking my tongue into his mouth. I slowly eased my fingers out of him and reached for the lube, adding a little more to his ass and then slicking my cock. A tiny part of me wondered whether fucking him like this was too personal, but I pushed that thought away immediately. I wanted to watch Patrick's face as he took my cock for the first time, wanted to see the way he fell apart underneath me. And I wanted to be able to kiss him, touch him... love him. I didn't want some impersonal hookup where the focus was just on getting off. I wanted to make love to the man I loved and bring him pleasure.

"I'm going to go slowly," I said, kissing him again. "If you want to stop at any point, just tell me."

"You're not going to break me," Patrick said, a dry, wry smile spreading across his lips. "Just fuck me already."

I was utterly tempted to come back with some snarky comment, but instead I gripped my cock and slowly pressed it into him, watching the way Patrick's eyes widened and his mouth fell slightly open, his plush lips slick and perfect as a deep groan slid out of them. I took my time because no matter what Patrick's opinion was on the subject, taking a real dick was different than taking a dildo. Mostly because he'd been using the dildo on himself and thus was well aware of his body and his reactions, but I knew none of that. So I was going slowly. This time.

I kissed him as I bottomed out, letting him adjust around me. His channel was hot and tight, and I was already ridiculously on edge just from the situation alone.

I'd hardly touched myself, and I was ready to blow my load just from sinking into Patrick's perfect ass.

"God. Fuck, that feels so good." Patrick's voice was breathless. He laughed softly, grinning up at me. "You feel amazing. Shit, why did we wait?"

"Because I wasn't fucking you without lube where your parents could hear." I ground my hips forward and Patrick groaned. "You like my cock?"

"I think I'm in love with it," Patrick said, his fingers snaking into my hair to draw me closer to him. He kissed me again, soft and deep. Then he looked up at me with wide, grey eyes full of lust and emotion. "Fuck me. Please."

Well, I wasn't going to say no to that.

But that didn't mean I was going to rush.

I began to move, thrusting into him deep and slow, taking him apart until there was nothing left of us but atoms. The kisses, the smiles, the push and pull of our bodies and the words on my tongue that I choked back over and over because I couldn't say them, no matter how much I wanted to. Instead, I used my body to tell Patrick exactly how I felt because that was all I could do. Pleasure burned inside me, white hot, and I used it to fuel me on. Patrick's legs were wrapped around me, pulling me ever closer to him, and it felt like we were one.

"Connor, I'm so close," Patrick murmured as he kissed me again and again, sliding his hand between our bodies to tip himself over the edge. I wanted to sit back and watch him, but I couldn't bring myself to put even an inch between us because what if whatever was happening between us disappeared as soon as I moved.

"Come for me," I whispered into his mouth.

And underneath me, Patrick shattered.

Sometime later, when we were snuggled together underneath Patrick's duvet half dozing and not really doing anything more than indulging in each other's company, a lazy thought began to circle in my brain.

Patrick had asked why we'd waited, and I'd automatically assumed that he'd meant why hadn't we done this at an earlier point during the weekend. But what if he hadn't meant that at all. What if he'd actually meant we should have done this *earlier* earlier, as in, before this whole fake relationship thing. Maybe I was reading too much into it, which wouldn't surprise me, but if Patrick had meant that, then maybe he wouldn't want to give this up, and maybe we could keep it going for a little while longer. Perhaps it also meant that I meant more to Patrick than just a meaningless fling between friends.

I grinned as I snuggled deeper into Patrick's arms.

CHAPTER TWENTY-FIVE

Patrick

THERE WAS STILL a smile on my face when Aaron found me in the kitchen on Friday morning.

I'd hardly seen him all week, both of us working different services and being rushed off our feet when we were at The Pear Tree together, so we hadn't had a chance to chat. But I was pleased when he stuck his head around the wall of the pastry kitchen, an easy smile on his face.

"Long time no see, stranger."

"It's only been a week," I said with a smile as I rolled out some dough for scones. The afternoon tea booking was full, and I was going to need at least a hundred.

"That's a long time for us. I missed you."

"Did you really?"

"Well, I missed having someone to vent at." Aaron grinned and leant against the wall.

"I see the swear jar is gone." I raised an eyebrow at him.

Unsurprisingly, the jar had been conspicuously absent when I'd turned up on Tuesday morning. "How long did it last?"

"Sadly, the jar was broken beyond repair on Friday evening," Aaron said, attempting to fake some sort of sincerity. "So it had to go into the bin."

"And you didn't get another one?"

"An attempt was made."

"Did that one break beyond repair too?" I asked as I grabbed my cutters from the plastic tub on the shelf above my head. They were old metal ones I'd had for years, but they were the absolute perfect size for scones, and I refused to replace them.

"Yuuup." Aaron tried to look contrite, but like the sincerity, it was a poor imitation. "So, how was your weekend? Did you and Connor have fun?"

"It was nice." I didn't look up at him, but it was hard to hide the smile on my face. "It was good to see my family again, and Mum and Da loved the cake. There wasn't any left by Monday, although that was because Da and Connor polished off the leftovers."

"Good. And they liked Connor?"

"Yeah, they did. They think he's good for me." As soon as the words left my mouth, I realised how deeply I'd suddenly put my foot in it. I hadn't told Aaron we were dating, fake or otherwise. But apparently my brain hadn't thought about any of that before I opened my mouth. I looked up at Aaron, expecting to see a smirk or for something snarky to come out of his mouth, but instead his smile was soft.

"So, you're dating then? I thought you might be. I'm so fucking happy for you, Pads."

"Thanks, but we're, um, we're not really…" I trailed off because I wasn't really sure where to go from there or how much to admit to. Connor and I had never talked about what we'd say if anyone else—outside my family—found out. The obvious answer was just to come clean and tell Aaron everything, or I could laugh it off and say we were just friends.

The second option didn't feel true anymore though. Connor and I had crossed a line over the past week and were now so far over it, I didn't know where the line was anymore. It would have been one thing if we'd acted as just friends while we were away, at least in private, but we hadn't.

It would have been another thing if we'd stopped doing whatever the hell we were doing as soon as we'd come home. But we hadn't. Not only had we had sex on Monday night, but Connor had ended up at my house every night since then and each evening had ended with some kissing at minimum. Most of the kissing had been accompanied by Connor's hands, or mouth, down my trousers.

The fact that we'd been doing all of that had not helped my emotions. Especially because a small part of me wondered if this was what a relationship might be like. I couldn't imagine how it would be any different. And that was making me even more confused because my heart and head were now at war—one convinced Connor could never want me, and one telling me to look at the evidence in front of me.

Perhaps I wouldn't have felt so confused if we'd talked about it, but both of us had firmly refused to initiate that conversation. We'd just stubbornly continued on as "best friends", which apparently now came with benefits.

"Are you two just banging then?" Much as I loved Aaron, he was not a subtle man. "Like a friends-with-bene-fits kinda thing?"

"Um, maybe?"

"How is this a maybe?" He laughed. "Are you fucking?"

"Well, er, yes," I mumbled.

"But you're not dating?"

"Not technically." I sighed. "It's complicated."

"How?" Aaron asked. He was like a dog with a bone, and I wished he'd just let it go. I put scones onto a tray and chewed my lip wondering what to say. Apparently, I wondered a little too long. "Pads, you know you can talk to me, right? Like, we're friends, and we've known each other for fucking years. I'm never gonna fucking judge you if that's what you're worried about. I'm not exactly one to talk."

"If I tell you, you promise not to laugh?"

"Never." Aaron's voice was soft, and he sounded genuinely concerned. Behind him I heard the sounds of more people arriving to prep for lunch. "Wanna go outside?"

"Shouldn't you be prepping for service?"

"Eh, they'll manage without me for ten minutes. If not, then they're all fuckwits." He grinned, and I shook my head. "Come on. Your scones'll survive."

Reluctantly, I put the cutter down and followed Aaron

down the corridor and out into the sunshine. He led me around the corner of the building where there was a little patio area for staff tucked away. Technically, it was a smoking area, but Ben had put some tables and chairs out in case people wanted to chill there between services so we didn't have to be inside all the time in the oppressive heat of the kitchens. Aaron planted himself in one of the metal chairs, resting his elbows on his knees and looking at me as I seated myself next to him. I twisted the hem of my apron in my hands, wondering where to begin.

"Tell me what's going on," Aaron said.

"So, well. Um." I took a deep breath. "I'm gay."

"Congratulations. I'm assuming this is a new thing?"

"Sort of. Not new to me, but new to everyone else."

"Okay."

"Before the party, I finally told my parents and they, well, they put two and two together and made five. They thought because I spend so much time with Connor and because I came out, that we were dating. So they asked me to bring Connor with me to the party so they could meet him. I wasn't sure what to do, and somehow I managed to convince Connor to be my boyfriend for the weekend, but now everything's a mess, and I don't know what to do."

Aaron was quiet for a second, but I could see him putting everything together and filling in the blanks. "So you went as just friends and came back as fuck buddies?"

"I suppose. If you want to put it that way."

"I'm gonna because it's clearly what's happening." He laughed. "So, what's wrong? 'Cos clearly something's bothering you." He paused and then grinned. "You like him, don't you? You don't wanna just be fuck buddies. You wanna be boyfriends for real!"

"Are you twelve?"

"Don't dodge the fucking question, Pads."

"Fine. Okay, yes. I love him, Aaron. I've loved him since I first met him, and I thought I'd be fine with us just being friends forever, but now we're doing whatever this is, and I don't know what to do. I'm scared as hell because I have no idea what I'm doing. I know I can't lose him, but I know I'll never be good enough for him because he's the most amazing man in the universe, and I'm just some bloke." I'd said all of that very fast. I was staring at Aaron because I'd given a voice to all my fears, and they all felt a lot more real.

Aaron put his hand out and patted my knee, giving me a fond smile. "Have you told him any of this?"

His question caught me off guard because he made it sound like such a simple thing. "No."

"Maybe you should start there then."

"You make it sound so easy," I said, unable to keep a wistful, sad note from lingering in my voice. "What if he doesn't feel the same way? What if he doesn't want to be friends anymore?"

"Well, then he's an asshole 'cos you're fucking brilliant, Patrick." He gave me a firm look. "I'm fucking serious. I've never met anyone as wonderful as you, and if he doesn't want you, then he doesn't fucking deserve you."

"Thanks." I felt oddly more at ease. Aaron wasn't the most eloquent man I'd ever met, but I always knew where I stood with him. If he said something about you, that was genuinely what he thought and how he felt. A little smile curled the corners of my lips.

"I know it's bloody hard, talking to someone you like and putting yourself out there, but I can guarantee you if you don't do it, you're gonna regret it for the rest of your fucking life." He patted my knee again. "I know Connor, and honest to fucking God that boy looks at you like you've hung the fucking moon. It's sickening."

"Really? I've never…"

"Of course you've never noticed. He don't exactly moon over you while you're looking." Aaron smiled. "Talk to him, Pads. Promise me."

"Okay. I will," I said, then laughed as Aaron sternly raised an eyebrow. "I promise."

"Good." He patted his knees and groaned as he stood up. "C'mon. We'd better get back before they send out a fucking search party."

"Is Josh in today?" I asked.

"No…" Aaron sounded like I'd caught him off guard, which was odd because, well, he'd never reacted that way. "He's in later, but I've hardly seen him this week."

That was… odd. I frowned as Aaron turned away. Had something happened while I'd been at my parents'? I shook my head and followed him back towards the kitchen. Whatever was going on, I wasn't going to get in the middle of it. Not until I had to.

I settled into my routine, finishing off my scones for the afternoon before getting the last few puddings sorted. The easy flow of work gave me something to focus on, allowing my mind to settle and my worries to drift away. Cooking was almost like a form of meditation for me. I could easily get lost in work and not think about whatever was bothering me.

By the time the lunch service had finished, and I'd thrown myself into the prep for afternoon tea, I'd hardly given my situation with Connor a second thought.

It wasn't until much later, when I finally found ten minutes to myself and flopped into an old chair in the break room, that I finally checked my phone. There were a couple of messages from Connor, mostly just complaining about teaching or being hungry. Except for the last two messages he'd sent ten minutes before.

CONNOR *It sucks you're working a double today and I don't get to see you =(*
CONNOR *I really miss you <3*

I stared at them, warmth and worry swirling in my heart.

CHAPTER TWENTY-SIX

Connor

I HAD an hour between two classes, and instead of working on my own routines like I'd usually do with the time, I had flopped on the floor of the studio and was staring up at the ceiling, questioning my life choices.

For not the first time today, I asked myself what the ever-loving fuck I was doing.

Back in Devon, I'd promised myself that I would shoot down a relationship with Patrick before we tried, failed, and cried miserably. Except that since we'd been back, I'd done absolutely nothing of the sort. Instead, I'd done the opposite and had spent every moment I could with him. We'd made dinner together, watched movies—well, started them at least—and then fallen into bed together. It had been perfect every time, and it felt like I was living in a fantasy.

The only concession I'd made was that I went home to my own bed every night. According to my ridiculous brain, we couldn't be dating if we weren't spending the night together, regardless of what we did beforehand. I tried not to think too hard about it, despite the fact that I was basically the living definition of an eye-roll emoji. Or maybe a facepalm.

The other line of reasoning my brain had come up with was that if I didn't acknowledge what was going on or talk to Patrick about it, then *technically* I wasn't breaking my promise. If we didn't talk about it, we couldn't start a relationship, and if we didn't start a relationship, then we wouldn't fail at having one. Simple.

Except it wasn't simple at all. It was stupidly, ridiculously over-fucking-complicated, yet I still couldn't bring myself to do anything about it.

I was a giant class-A idiot.

I sighed and threw my arm over my eyes, wondering if it would be possible to sleep for the next fifty minutes and escape my self-inflicted idiocy. Maybe I should talk to someone. Someone who wouldn't be afraid to call me out on my bullshit and who'd tell me whether I was being a dick or whether my fears were genuine. There was only one man I knew who fit that description. My best friend since the age of twelve. Taylor.

Grabbing my phone from the table where it had been resting, I shot him a message to see if he was free. I had no idea whether he was in his office today or working from home. It was Friday afternoon, so I assumed he'd be at home.

My suspicions were confirmed two minutes later when Taylor's face appeared on my screen.

"I'm going to assume something is really fucking wrong," Taylor said as soon as I swiped the green icon.

"How do you know?" I asked, staring up at the ceiling.

"Well, it's Friday afternoon. You teach a class at four, then at six, then quarter past seven, and in the middle, you do your own practice. Except today you're asking me if I'm free during your hallowed practice time, so I'm going with something's wrong."

"I feel like I should be worried that you know my schedule so well."

"Babe, it's been two years. It's not hard to remember."

"Fine."

"So, what's up?"

I sighed, wondering where to start. "Do you remember last year when I came to see you, and I told you I didn't think Patrick would ever like me romantically." I'd gone to visit Taylor in London, and we'd gone out with his not-quite-boyfriend-at-the-time, Simon. A couple of cocktails in, which had been stronger than I'd anticipated, I'd told Taylor that I didn't think anything was ever going to happen with Patrick. At the time, I'd been convinced nothing was going to. I'd always told myself I'd put my feelings for Patrick in a box, and I had. Mostly. Except when I was drunk. Which was why I never drank around Patrick.

"Yeeees," Taylor said suspiciously. "What happened?"

"It's kind of a long story."

"I've got time. Talk." Taylor's voice was firm, and I wanted to giggle.

"I'm not Simon. You can't use your Dom voice on me."

"Trust me, I'm not," Taylor said, and I could hear the

smirk in his tone. I knew exactly what expression was on his face, and I was hit with a wave of longing. All I wanted to do was curl up on the sofa with him, a bottle of wine, and an enormous pizza and pour my heart out to him. Taylor had always been there for me, throughout all the highs and lows of my dating life. He knew all my secrets, and I trusted him with my life. "C'mon, babe. Stop stalling and talk to me. You wanted my advice, and I can't give it to you if you don't tell me what the fuck is going on."

"Ugh, fine." I rolled my eyes, more at myself than at Taylor, then I told him everything, starting with the moment Patrick had told me he was gay and ending with last night when we'd spent the evening curled up on the sofa, and I'd blown Patrick while we watched some movie on Netflix. I left out a couple of minor details, like the fact that Patrick had been a virgin, because they weren't my details to share. But I told Taylor everything else, including my ridiculous emotional back-and-forth. If anyone stood a chance of unpicking this tangled mess it was him.

"Okay, let me get this straight," Taylor said.

"I feel like there's a joke in there," I interjected, smiling up at the ceiling and twirling my foot in a circle where it was rested on my opposite knee. I felt a little lighter after telling him everything. Just getting it out in the open seemed to have relieved some of the pressure building up in my chest.

"Don't start."

"Spoilsport."

"Anyway," Taylor continued, ignoring my attempts to derail the conversation again. "You love Patrick, you're pretty much dating Patrick—and don't say you're not because you practically admitted it. Now you're afraid of telling him how you feel because you've convinced yourself that your friendship will never be the same if you actually start dating. And you've convinced yourself it's all going to go horribly, horribly wrong and burn down in *the* most dramatic fashion possible, and you'll have lost one of your best friends in the process, all because you wanted to get some."

"Yes?"

Taylor sighed. It was the sigh of a man who had reached the end of his rope. I could see the pained expression on his face from a hundred miles away. "Babe, I love you, but oh my fucking God, you are an idiot."

"I'm not that bad," I protested.

"Yes, you are. Look, because I love you, I'm going to be honest with you. You are being a dickhead, and you know it. You and Patrick are dating, whether you say you are or not. You two have already added feelings to the fucking mix, and not talking about it is only going to make things a million times worse. You said you don't want things to burn down, then open your fucking mouth and use your fucking words. Stop being a knob and start talking. Otherwise you're gonna be in trouble. Like more trouble than you're already in." There was a pause, then Taylor added. "Am I wrong?"

"No," I said with a sigh. "You're not." As much as I wanted to tell him he'd missed the mark, he hadn't. Taylor had just confirmed everything I already knew. But instead of feeling relieved, this huge bubble of fear started to rise inside me.

"What... what if I talk to him, and he doesn't want me? What if I tell him all of this and he tells me it was just a fling? That I'm cute but not dateable. That I'm fuckable but nothing more. That it was fun while it lasted, but we can't ever be anything more than friends or fuck buddies." The words vomited out of me, leaving a sour taste on my tongue. They were all my deepest fears, forcing their way out of me like last night's tequila. I hadn't realised how violently these thoughts had been simmering away, not just for the past two weeks, but for years. These were the excuses men gave me when they decided I wasn't worth it anymore. For years I'd just brushed them off because, hey, it wasn't like I wanted any of those assholes anyway. But maybe, deep inside me, I'd desperately wanted someone to want me. Not to see me as just a cute piece of ass but as something more.

For my whole life, I'd only ever been wanted by three people: my mum, Taylor, and Patrick.

My mum had always told me the right man was out there if I wanted him and encouraged me not to let her terrible luck with relationships get me down. She'd said it as a joke on more than one occasion, but now I wondered whether she had really been joking or if deep down she was hurting the same way I was. She'd poured all her energy into giving me the best life she could, and that hadn't left a lot of time for her. Maybe she wanted to be loved as much as I did. I made a mental note to bring it up to her the next time we spoke.

Taylor and I were never in a million years going to be compatible—there was too much fire and similarity there. We both wanted the same things from our partners, and ultimately, we'd never be what the other needed. Besides, I kinda viewed him as the brother I'd never had, and that wasn't really my thing. And after seeing him with Simon, I wanted what they had more than anything, no matter how much I'd tried to tell myself otherwise.

That just left Patrick... sweet, perfect, beautiful Patrick who'd welcomed me into his life with a smile, a kind heart, and more love than I'd ever experienced even if it was just as friends. I'd always felt wanted by Patrick, and for the past two weeks the knowledge that I could have more had frightened me as much as it had delighted me.

"Babe? Babe? Are you still there?" Taylor's voice snapped through the speaker.

"Yeah, I'm still here. Sorry, I zoned out for a second."

"I thought so." There was an added note of softness in his tone, and somehow it just made me feel worse. Like I wanted to curl up into a ball and cry. I sniffed.

"Hey, it's okay," Taylor continued. "Sorry, I was probably being hard on you."

"No, you were right. I'm being a dick. I'm just so fucking scared that it'll go wrong, and I'll lose one of the only people who's ever cared about me."

"I don't think that's going to happen."

"How can you be sure?"

"Because of everything you've just told me and everything you've said about Patrick over the past three years. I don't think Patrick's the sort of man who's just in this for the sex because otherwise you wouldn't have been friends for three years and he wouldn't have just told you he was gay. If he just wanted your dick, he'd have told you years ago, and we'd have dealt with this already."

"Okay," I said slowly. Taylor's logic was pretty solid there. I couldn't really argue with him.

"Secondly, like I said, you're already dating. Just without the confirmation. And trust me, it's not gonna happen without talking to each other. You can't magically hope that it'll all become clear without that." Taylor sighed, then laughed. "Simon and I hooked up for ages as 'just friends' and even early on I knew it was different, but I kept trying to convince myself otherwise because I didn't think he'd want me. Turns out, I was wrong. He'd been in love with me all along."

"Can you not steal my issues please?" I said with a chuckle.

"Since I dealt with them first, they are my issues. You're just copying me," Taylor said. "But please, for once just take my advice. I do actually know what the fuck I'm talking about. You need to talk to him even though it's hard as fuck and you just wanna pretend your feelings don't exist."

"Technically, you didn't talk to Simon; you word vomited at me, and he heard you."

"It still counts, especially because we did actually talk afterwards."

"Okay." I wasn't completely convinced, and that was the closest I could get to committing to a conversation without actually committing.

"By the way, don't think you're getting out of this. I'm

gonna fucking check in on you, and if you don't talk to him, I will. Or worse, I'll make Simon talk to you, and you'll never be able to turn him down."

"I will! I'm not you. I don't fall over every time he smiles," I said with as much snark as I could manage. Which, let's be honest, wasn't much.

"I can't help it. It's a nice smile."

"You two are sickeningly adorable, and I love it. I miss you so much."

"I miss you too. You'll have to come stay again soon. You can bring Patrick. I think he and Simon would get on great."

"Yeah," I said, "I think they would too." I could imagine the four of us in London, chilling out in a restaurant or a bar or a park together. It would be fun. "As long as we don't have to listen to a repeat performance of last time." Last time I'd had to listen to a live porno from the other side of the wall and had spent the entire night remembering what Taylor looked like chucking his guts up after his twenty-fifth birthday to convince my dick to go down.

Taylor chuckled. "I can't make any promises. Simon's too sexy. I mean, have you seen his ass?"

"I do try not to look at my best friend's boyfriend's butt. I'm not a complete perv." A buzzer sounded, indicating my time was up and my students were starting to arrive. "Okay, babe, I've gotta go. But thanks. I needed this."

"Always. I love you. Talk to him soon, or I'll come visit you and nag you until you do."

"Ugh, you're so mean, but I love you too." We rounded

off the conversation and I took a couple of deep breaths to centre myself.

Taylor was right, but it still hadn't been easy to hear. And now I needed to think about what to do next.

If I was going to do this, I was going to do it my way.

With style.

CHAPTER TWENTY-SEVEN

Patrick

I STARED down at the list of bullet points I'd written in my notebook and sighed. I was supposed to be making an order list and figuring out a pudding menu for the next week, but instead I'd found myself jotting down ideas of things to say when I finally plucked up the confidence to talk to Connor about how I felt.

I'd promised Aaron I'd do it, but I hadn't said *when* I'd do it.

Tapping my pen on the page, I crossed out one of the points that read, "mention how long we've been friends". I wasn't sure that was relevant. At least, not in the way I'd written it. So far, my points were: we're already very good friends so we know we get on well and have similar interests. We're sexually compatible (which I thought we were from our brief period of sexual interaction). We spend a lot of time together. You don't mind that I work weird hours.

My family likes you and you like them. You love President Whiskers as much as I do. I love you.

They sounded like good points, but I wasn't sure what order to bring them up. Was I supposed to start by telling him that I loved him? Or was I supposed to start slowly and list all the reasons out? My love of romcoms had given me a skewed sense of perspective. In the movies, the guy made some sort of grand gesture and declared his love, then the girl said yes, and they lived happily ever after. But it couldn't be that simple in real life, could it?

How did you even do a grand gesture? Was I supposed to get a hundred roses or a million pink balloons and make an idiot of myself in the hope Connor would say he loved me too? That sounded more like a bad marriage proposal than a grand gesture. I was only asking him if he wanted to date me.

I groaned and tore the piece of paper off the pad, scrunching it up and throwing it in the nearby bin. This was getting me nowhere, and it was just making me more confused. Putting the notepad on the shelf above me, where I kept an assortment of notepads, recipe files, pens, cutters, piping nozzles, and old storage tubs, I tried to focus on what I needed to do. Maybe instead of making a list, it would be better if I just got on with the baking. My subconscious would figure it out while the rest of me got lost in pastry.

I headed for the chillers, tray in hand. There were several tubs of soft fruit that really needed to be used. They'd make a nice compote. There was plenty of soft cheese, so cheesecakes were a given. I spotted a box of lemons I hadn't noticed before. I wondered if one of the main kitchen sous-chefs had put them in here. Maybe they'd had extra or maybe Darcie had ordered them. To my left, I saw a carton of pasteurised egg whites that I used for making meringues because it was easier than separating several trays of eggs by hand. Lemons and egg whites screamed lemon meringue pie to me. It wouldn't be hard to knock up some pastry shells if I didn't have any already. And any leftover meringues could be easily broken up to go in something like Eton Mess. That was always a popular summer option.

We had quite a lot of cream, and there were several large blocks of chocolate in the kitchen. I could easily make a ganache, and having something chocolate on the menu would give it a nice balance. Plus, I could make a nice white chocolate and raspberry crème brûlée too.

The tray was full by this point, and I'd even wedged a few things under my arms. It was a bit of a balancing act to get everything back to the kitchen, but I got there eventually. Setting everything on the side, I divided everything up and began.

Time seemed to slow, and everything slipped away as I focused on cooking. I heard someone walking up and down the corridor outside the kitchen, and at some point, it registered that they might be calling my name, but I wasn't really listening. Instead, I chopped and sliced and mixed and measured, heating fruit, sugar, and the tiniest bit of vanilla slowly on the two little burners I had until the kitchen was bursting with sweetness and I had the perfect compote cooling in a pan. I emptied huge tubs of cream cheese into the mixer, blending it until it was smooth before combining it with icing sugar and lime zest and juice, until it was just the right amount of sharp before spreading it out onto a base of crushed ginger biscuits and butter that I'd had in the fridge. I'd had enough to make two huge cheese-cakes, and I carried them on a tray back to the chiller to set, retrieving the pastry I'd set aside to cool. I could roll that out and make shells now, blind baking them before I filled them with a tart lemon filling and topped them with perfectly piped meringue.

I was halfway through whisking egg whites into stiff peaks when a hand on my shoulder jolted me out of my calm reverie. I spun around to see a concerned-looking Aaron standing behind me in the doorway of the kitchen. He wasn't wearing whites, just an old T-shirt and jeans. I wondered why he was here. He wasn't scheduled today. Nobody came in on Mondays, unless they had something they needed or were prepping new menu items. That was about the only time I saw Aaron on a Monday, and then it was best to steer clear while he worked his food magic. I wasn't even supposed to be here today, but it had seemed like the better option than sitting at home and worrying.

"Jesus Christ, Aaron. You gave me a heart attack," I said, turning down the stand mixer and examining the egg whites. I'd be able to add the sugar soon, it just needed another minute.

"Sorry. I tried calling your name, but I don't think you could hear me." He looked down at the mixer. "That thing's louder than a cement mixer."

I shrugged. I couldn't disagree with him. Flicking the

mixer back on, I leant closer to him so he could hear me. "Everything okay?"

"Yeah. I was coming to ask you the same question." There was a deep wrinkle of concern on Aaron's forehead, and he raised an eyebrow at me. "It's a Monday, and you've been here for hours, Pads. Your timecard says you started at six this morning."

"What time is it now?" I asked. I didn't think it was that late.

"Nearly four."

"Well, that's not that bad," I said as I walked over to the giant bin of caster sugar on the other side of the kitchen, taking the scoop out of it and quickly measuring some into a bowl. Then I used the scoop to slowly trickle the sugar into the stiff egg whites, transforming them into a perfect, glossy meringue. "That's a standard day."

"Yeah." Aaron didn't sound convinced. He gestured to the counters and the large trays of lemon-filled pastry shells. "But you're not done, are you?"

"Not quite, but I won't be much longer. Besides, why are you concerned about me working so much? You're hardly one to talk."

"True, but I'm an asshole with no life outside my kitchen." He chuckled, but it sounded hollow. "I thought you were going to talk to Connor?"

"I am. Or at least, I will. I just haven't had time yet."

"Didn't you see him at the weekend?"

I shook my head. "No, we were both busy. He had some extra classes to teach and he said something about Levi suddenly wanting to do a summer showcase, so he was going to spend the evenings with him to plan it."

"It sounds like you're avoiding each other."

"We're not." Despite my denial, it was something that had crossed my mind. I hadn't seen Connor since Thursday night, and although we'd texted all weekend it had been strange not to see him. I did wonder whether something was going on, but I hadn't given myself time to think about it. Darcie had asked for the weekend off, and I'd happily covered for her. It had given me a chance to keep busy, and if I'd happened to stay late last night to deep clean parts of the kitchen so I wouldn't have to go home by myself, well, that was something nobody else needed to know.

Connor had still been in contact, so it wasn't like he'd dropped off the map, and he'd even rang me yesterday morning to complain about Levi having too many ideas and not enough actual plans. I'd mentioned working all weekend, and we'd promised to catch up as soon as possible, so were we really avoiding each other?

Aaron huffed. He clearly didn't believe me. "Sure you're not."

"Did you actually want something?" I asked, switching off the mixer and lifting the arm to remove the giant balloon whisk. The meringue was perfect. Grabbing my piping bag off the side, I began to spoon the meringue mix into it. I'd have to work quickly because meringue had a nasty habit of deflating if left out in the heat for too long, and the kitchen wasn't exactly cold. Luckily, I'd be able to fit all the lemon meringue pies in the oven to cook at once.

That was the one benefit of having something industrial sized.

"I just wanted to check on you," Aaron said. He grabbed an empty piping bag off the side. "Can I help?"

I paused for a second then nodded. Usually I wouldn't let anyone apart from Darcie help me, but I trusted Aaron. He washed his hands in the sink at the back of my kitchen before filling a piping bag and starting at the other end of the counter, carefully piping meringue on top of the lemon filling in exactly the same pattern as me.

"After Friday, I just wanted to check everything was okay. I didn't know if you'd said anything to him," Aaron continued.

"No. I will though." I sighed and went to refill the piping bag. "I just have no idea how to say it or what to say. I may, um, I may have made a list earlier. I binned it though." The admission made my skin heat, and I couldn't bring myself to look at Aaron in case he laughed at me.

"I don't know. A list sounds like a good idea to me. Everyone always says speak from the heart, but I think that's bollocks. How the fuck are you supposed to know what your heart thinks? If it were me, I'd fuck it up as soon as I opened my bloody mouth if I hadn't thought about it."

I nodded, a small smile creeping onto my lips. "I'll make another list then."

"Good."

"Why are you here, Aaron?" It was the question that had been circling my mind ever since I'd seen him. "Did you need something?"

"No, nothing like that." He wasn't looking at me, and

that was suspicious. "I was at home, but I got a message from someone who said they were worried about you. So I thought I'd come down and see what was going on."

"Who?" I asked, feeling my face wrinkle. "Connor?"

"Why the fuck would Connor have my number?"

"I don't know." I was genuinely bemused. I hadn't seen anyone else... except Ben. I was sure I'd heard him pottering around earlier. "Was it Ben?"

"Nope. It doesn't matter who it was. They were just worried about you." He chuckled wryly. "They said they'd never seen you stress bake this badly."

"I'm not—" I tried to argue, but Aaron raised an eyebrow. "Fine. But it helps."

"You know what would help more?" Aaron said, finishing off the last of the piping with a flourish. "Actually fucking talking to him."

"You're an asshole, you know that?" I grinned and Aaron returned it.

"It's been said, Pads. It's been said."

CHAPTER TWENTY-EIGHT

Connor

I STARED around at the bomb site that was my tiny kitchen and sighed exasperatedly. How the fuck had it gotten to this point?

There were two burnt tins of cake on the side, cake mix dripping onto the floor from a beater perched near the sink, flour everywhere, and a sticky patch of egg crusting itself onto the counter. The window was wide open, letting in a soft, summer breeze, which was lovely but not enough to dispel the God-awful smell of burnt cake. Baking wasn't supposed to be this hard.

I was a reasonable cook, everyone I knew would attest to that, but apparently my skills did not stretch to cake. Baking seemed to be a magical art in which I had exactly zero power. I didn't think it would be that difficult. The BBC website where I'd gotten the recipe hadn't made it sound like I'd be attempting alchemy, but that's what it had felt like. I hadn't even been trying to do anything hard. I just wanted to make a fucking sponge cake.

"Jesus Christ, what the fuck happened in here?" The front door banged open, and I heard Levi's voice coming down the corridor towards me. "It smells awful."

"Thank you for stating the fucking obvious, babe," I said, turning to look at him. Levi grinned from the doorway and brandished a yellow bag for life. It always surprised me how much Levi looked like his older brother, Ben, except Ben was a literal giant while Levi was more of a regular-sized human. He had bronzed skin and light brown hair and these deep soulful eyes that reminded me of a Labrador puppy, except they were accompanied by a square jaw and full lips that seem permanently set in a wry smile.

We were ridiculously similar in personality, and on paper, we should have clashed, but somehow things just worked. Out of the two of us, he was probably the more measured. But only just. He was a horrible enabler, but he was also the one who knew when I needed to take a step back, and I trusted him.

"Why the fuck are you still trying to make it from scratch?" Levi asked, staring around at the chaos in front of me. "I know you wanted to surprise Patrick, but at this rate you're just gonna give him food poisoning, and nobody wants that."

"They're not that bad," I protested. "Just a bit… crispy."

"Yeah, no. I'm not letting you declare your undying love for him with burnt cake. It's just fucking rude." Levi put the bag on the floor and pulled out two red and blue boxes with pictures of a cake on the front. "We're gonna use Betty Crocker because at least that way you can't really fuck it up. I got devil's food cake or vanilla, take your pick. And I got icing to go with them too."

"You didn't… This is…" I sighed, my dream of presenting Patrick with the perfect homemade sponge cake that even Mary Berry couldn't fault dissolving in front of me. I grabbed the box of devil's food cake mix. "Ugh, this is so much easier in movies."

"At least if you fuck this one up you have a spare," Levi said with a grin. I shot him a look that I hoped expressed my displeasure. "Come on, it's not that hard. Even I can make these!"

"Since when do you bake?"

"Since I was like fourteen. Mum got stuck working extra shifts at the hospital, and I didn't want Ben to have a seventeenth birthday without a cake, so I got a box mix and made it. It wasn't hard." Levi shrugged and began to look for a clean mixing bowl. The joke was on him though because there wasn't one. I hadn't done the washing up.

"You're very sweet." I took pity on him and moved over to the sink to begin rinsing a bowl. Maybe I'd let Levi make the cake while I washed up, then it might end up being edible. Behind me, I heard Levi flicking the oven on and making a slightly disgusted sound at the burnt cake bits still littering the hob.

"It's a good thing your soon-to-be boyfriend is a pastry chef because I'm never eating anything you attempt to bake."

"That's a bit harsh."

"Have you even tried it?" I looked over my shoulder to see Levi raising an eyebrow in challenge.

"No, but it can't be that bad." I'd followed the recipe *exactly*. It wasn't my fault it was burnt and flat as a pancake. Levi grabbed one of the bits of cake and tapped it suspiciously on the side. The fact that he could even do that wasn't the best sign. He broke off a piece and passed it to me. Wiping my damp hands on the old T-shirt I was wearing, which was already covered in various baking-induced stains, I took it from him. The cake was suspiciously solid. Fuck, this did not bode well for my poor intestines. Did I actually have to swallow it? Couldn't I just taste it and spit it out?

"You film this and I will fucking murder you," I said to Levi, whose grin had widened gleefully.

"I thought you said it wasn't that bad."

"I changed my mind." Suddenly the box cake was looking like a much better idea. I opened my mouth and took the tiniest bite.

For about half a millionth of a second, everything was fine. Then the sour taste of salt and burnt cake and something powdery hit my tongue, and I gagged. I spat the cake into the sink, coughing violently and forgetting everything about looking like a dignified human being.

"Fuck my life," I said when I could finally speak again. I grabbed the glass of water I'd been drinking when Levi arrived and downed the whole thing. It made me feel marginally more human, but my tongue still felt fuzzy, and I could still taste salt. Where the fuck had the salt come from? "That was disgusting."

Levi's smug expression was the epitome of "I told you so". He didn't say it though. He took the bowl off the drainer and opened the box mix. "Let's not poison Patrick before you get to the good stuff," he said. "I don't think he'd be up for anything if your reaction was anything to go by."

For once I had to agree.

An hour later, and under Levi's slightly bossy but well-meaning instruction, two large chocolate cakes sat cooling on my kitchen counter, ready to be sandwiched together with chocolate fudge icing. The kitchen smelled a hell of a lot better, and this time I'd managed not to burn anything, spill anything, or accidentally swap sugar for salt. The washing up was done, and my counters didn't look like a bomb site either. I was surprisingly pleased with myself, and I had to admit, painful as it was, that Levi had been right.

"So," Levi asked from his position on the sofa, his long legs stretched out along the cushions. "When are you going to give it to him?" I snorted. "Get your mind out of the fucking gutter for a minute. When are you gonna tell him?"

"Tomorrow," I said, curling myself up into the armchair opposite him. Usually the chair was a dumping ground for clean laundry, shoes, bags, and whatever else I happened to throw there, but it was surprisingly clean at the moment because I'd ended up blitzing my flat over the weekend while trying to work out how to talk to Patrick and simulta-neously trying to help Levi plan for his last-minute summer showcase. A suspicious nugget of my brain wondered if the showcase was just a distraction concocted by Levi to distract me from thinking about the fact I hadn't gotten into the East Midland championships.

He'd found me in the studio on Saturday morning, lying on the floor again as I tried to think about how to put Taylor's demands into action. I wanted to tell Patrick in a spectacular, slightly over the top but not cringeworthy way —a grand gesture straight out of the cheesiest, sweetest romcom or romance novel. The only problem was I didn't have a team of writers to design this shit for me. I just had my brain, which was failing miserably by suggesting the highly normal "make him dinner" and the probably too far in the opposite direction "give him a lap dance".

Levi had arrived, taken one look at me and promptly opened his mouth to say, "I was thinking of doing a summer showcase at the end of August. Can you help me plan?" Whether he'd been considering it up until he'd voiced the idea was another matter entirely.

"Are you still thinking dinner?" Levi asked. He'd managed to get the full story out of me over the weekend, not that I'd taken much convincing to spill. He'd voted for the dinner, but in his words I should "make it extra". Extra was definitely something I could do.

"Yeah, I asked him what time he finishes work tomorrow, and he's just doing lunch service, so he'll be home by three since it's Tuesday, and there's no afternoon tea. So I was thinking I'd text him and ask him to come over about six."

"Sounds perfect, babe." Levi grinned. "I'm guessing you won't be in the studio Wednesday morning for your usual practice?"

"Nope. If I'm very lucky, I'll be in bed with a beautiful man, and I don't plan on getting up until noon."

"Just as long as you're in Wednesday afternoon to teach and not covered in hickeys," Levi said.

"That's what foundation is for, babe." I laughed. "And if all else fails, I'll just tell people I've been working on shoulder mounts."

Levi nodded. Shoulder mounts were notorious for leaving the worst bruises on your neck and shoulders if you practised them too much. In fact, all of pole left hideous bruises. The worst ones I'd ever had had been in my early days when I was practising for my first competition. I'd been bruised up and down my inner thighs. My boyfriend at the time hadn't been impressed, and it had taken me an hour to convince him they weren't hickeys from someone else. Well, it had taken an hour before I'd lost my patience and booted him out of bed. Seriously, why would someone suck hickeys onto the backs of my knees?

We chatted for a little longer, and then Levi helped me assemble and ice the cake. Apparently his mistrust of my baking went as far as not believing I could spread icing out of a tub without fucking it up somehow. After that he left me alone with my thoughts, saying he had a date to get to.

I opened the fridge and stared at the finished cake. It was like an omen of my impending doom. But as much as it frightened me, it also gave me tangible hope for the first time.

Now I just had to put the rest of my plan into action.

CHAPTER TWENTY-NINE

Patrick

CONNOR *Fancy dinner at mine tonight? You don't need to bring anything just come over about six <3 <3 xxx*

I STARED at the message for the fifth time in ten minutes, a nervous lump rising in my throat. Sure, it was just a dinner invitation, nothing Connor and I hadn't done a thousand times, but somehow it felt like more. This was the opportunity I'd been waiting for. Now I just had to take it. And that was more terrifying than I'd imagined.

Aaron and I had talked about it at length, and I'd rewritten my list—on my phone this time so nobody would find it—and I'd thought over and over about what I wanted to say. I just had to say it.

A tiny part of me wanted to back out and tell Connor I was busy, but that would be cowardly of me, and Connor would immediately know something was wrong. I wouldn't put it past him to bring dinner to my house, so I sent back an affirmative and focused on getting through the next few hours. I needed to shower and feed The President, and I should probably do a load of washing while I thought about it. I looked at the clock on my phone, which said 3:27. I could fill the time. I just needed not to think about what might happen later.

That proved to be impossible.

Connor was on my mind from the second I stepped onto the stairs to go and shower. I thought about the way his fingers brushed against my skin when he stripped me naked, the way he always made me feel safe and needed, and the cheeky, wanting smile he always wore when he seduced me. I wondered if that would happen later tonight. If everything went well, would we end up tangled together in Connor's bed while he made love to me. It was what I wanted more than anything. Even just a few days without his touch was driving me insane.

As soon as I walked into the bathroom and pulled off my grotty T-shirt and joggers, my dick started to perk up. My mind was supplying fantasy after fantasy, each one more delicious than the last. My skin felt like it was burning as I climbed into the bath and flicked the shower on, hoping a sharp blast of cold water would help. It did, but I wasn't sure my neighbours were going to thank me for screaming.

By sheer force of will, I managed to get through the rest of the afternoon without thinking about Connor. I did washing; I read some recipe books; I fed the cat, who grumbled at me loudly for daring to let his bowl get even half-empty; and I even convinced myself to dig the duster out and do some housework, even though it was a task I absolutely loathed. By the time it got to half five, I was practically bouncing with nerves. I threw on the nicest T-shirt I had and my fancy jeans, the ones I'd worn at the party that Connor had loved, and asked Whiskey to wish me luck as I headed out the door. I got a rather sarcastic meow in response.

The drive seemed to take an eon, rather than the normal fifteen minutes. Traffic seemed to have slowed to a crawl, even when it was moving, and every set of traffic lights hit red when I approached. It was almost like the universe was trying to keep me from Connor. Or maybe it was trying to drag out the anticipation so it would be all the sweeter at the end. Either way I wasn't impressed. I had the air conditioning turned all the way up, even though it was cloudy and overcast, because my body seemed to be burning up from the inside out. I just had to hope I wasn't too sweaty and disgusting when I reached Connor's. I'd never been so nervous in my entire life.

When I finally pulled the car into a visitor's spot, I turned off the engine with shaking hands and took a deep breath. "You can do this," I muttered to myself. "You just have to tell him how you feel. Be honest." I snorted derisively. "Sounds easy enough, but it's really fucking hard. Okay, okay, I can do this."

I hoped none of the building's other residents were watching me as I muttered my way up to the front door of the building and pulled out my key for the inner door. Connor had given it to me because the buzzer in his flat was unreliable, and it was easier than me calling him every time I arrived so he could come down and let me in. At the time, I hadn't thought of it as a serious gesture, just something to make his life easier, but now, as I looked down at the little bronze-coloured key in my hand, I saw more: trust, openness, friendship, affection, and maybe even love. Whether that was platonic love or romantic love was another question, but it was love all the same. You didn't just give someone the key to your building and a separate one to your flat without reason. And it wasn't as if Connor had pets for me to take care of or plants for me to water while he was away. He'd given me these keys because he wanted me in his life and because he loved me.

It was the smallest of gestures, and it had taken me years to fully realise what it meant, but now I had, and all I could do was marvel at the significance.

Maybe it was just a set of keys. Or maybe it was a sign of something much larger than either of us had ever realised.

I opened the inner door and headed straight for the stairs, climbing them as fast as I could. Connor lived on the third floor, in number eleven, which was on the left side of the building, off by itself. When I reached his front door, I paused, wondering whether I should knock. But Connor always hated that. Every time I knocked, he told me to walk straight in.

I took a deep breath and opened the door.

"Hello? It's me."

"Come in. I'm in the living room," Connor called. His voice was slightly muffled, and when I stepped into the flat, I realised why. At the end of the short corridor, past the two tiny bedrooms and the bathroom on the left, the door to the living room was pushed almost closed. I closed the front door behind me, slipped my shoes off, and walked towards the other door. My heart was pounding so loudly it sounded like a steam train. I felt like it was about to burst out of my chest.

I pushed the door and it swung open gently with a soft creak. I took a step forward and then gasped. "Holy shit."

The living room curtains were closed, and the furniture was pushed back to clear a space on the floor in the middle of the room. The gentle glow of early evening sunlight filtered through the curtains and mixed with the light of what seemed to be thousands of fairy lights strung across the curtain rail and hanging from the top of shelving units by the little hooks Connor used to hand garlands of baubles at Christmas. Connor sat on an old fleecy blanket in the middle of the floor, looking up at me with a nervous smile. He was wearing ripped skinny jeans and a loose, white, off-the-shoulder top, and his make-up was almost understated. The shimmer of highlighter on his cheeks caught the light, making his skin glow. He looked stunning—like some celestial deity gracing me with its presence.

Around him on the blanket was a huge selection of food —everything from bags of the Thai Sweet Chilli Sensations we both loved, to little pots and picky bits from Marks and Spencer's antipasti section, to a fresh baguette and some cheese. And on the left-hand side, in a clear space, was a large chocolate cake with artfully sliced strawberries arranged on top.

"Surprise!" Connor said, waving his hands and giving

me a nervous chuckle. "I, er, may have gone a bit over-board." He took a deep breath and rearranged himself, kneeling up and putting his hands in his lap. He looked so earnest and adorable that I just wanted to sweep him into my arms and kiss him senseless. But he clearly had some-thing he wanted to say, and so did I.

"Patrick, I..." he paused. "Wait, do you want to sit down? Shit," Connor laughed then pointed at a space on the floor that was clearly meant for me. "Sit down. It feels weird talking to you all the way over there."

I laughed, feeling the tension in my chest ease. "Sure." Taking a couple of steps, I lowered myself into the space just opposite Connor. This felt so much more like us. Even if it still felt more like a dream than a real situation. This was a grand gesture straight out of Hollywood, and I couldn't believe it was happening to someone like me.

I wasn't anybody special. I was just some bloke.

Except maybe to Connor. Maybe to him I was someone else, that special someone so many romance novels promised us was out there.

"Okay, so... Shit, this was so much easier in my head," Connor said.

"If it helps, it was easier in mine too." I reached out, and he interlaced our fingers together in mid-air.

"Shit... Okay... Patrick Evans, I have been in love with you since about thirty minutes after I first laid eyes on you, when you handed me a plate of panna cotta and told me you thought my make-up looked pretty. You sounded so sincere, like you actually meant it, instead of teasing me. Then you gave me this smile, and God, you just... you melted my heart, and for the first time in my life, I felt seen."

"I remember that," I said, my voice catching in my throat. It was clear as day in my head. I'd never seen anyone as beautiful as Connor before, and I'd hardly known what to do, let alone say. "You looked amazing. Like you do every day."

"Flatterer. I don't look good every day."

"Yes, you do. You look gorgeous whether you're chilling in those ratty old shorts you still have from when you were seventeen or whether you're fully made-up and going out. Every time I see you, you take my breath away." I was still trying to process what Connor had said. I couldn't believe what he'd said was true. He *loved* me? "Did you... Have you really been in love with me all this time?"

"Yes. Sorry."

"You don't need to be sorry because I've been in love with you since two days after that first shift. You came into the kitchen and said good morning to me, then you asked about my evening and told me about a film you'd watched with Levi. You seemed interested in me, not in a flirtatious way, but like you actually wanted to talk to me and were interested in what I had to say."

"I was. I mean everyone said you were so nice and helpful and to just wait outside your kitchen, but that was all they knew. Nobody could tell me anything more about you, and I thought there had to be more than just 'nice and helpful', so I decided I wanted to get to know you," Connor said, giving me a smile. "It was the best decision of my life."

"Was it just because I was nice that you wanted to get to know me?" I asked with a grin, teasing him slightly because that was just who we were together.

"Well, you were super cute too. That didn't hurt." I laughed, and Connor continued. "But then I thought you were straight or uninterested, and I thought we'd stick to being friends."

"I'm sorry I never told you I was gay. I wanted to, but I was scared you wouldn't want to spend time with me if you knew. It's stupid, but I thought… I'm never going to be like any of the guys you've dated before, and I thought if I didn't tell you, I could pretend that it might happen one day instead of knowing you'd reject me. And I don't want you to think I was only hanging out with you because I was hoping you'd date me. I've always loved spending time with you because you're the most amazing person I've ever known."

"Okay…" Connor's voice was shaky as he exhaled the word. "First of all, those other guys were all douchebags, and I'm so completely over gym gays who only know how to talk about their leg days and protein intake. Honestly, it's boring. And secondly, I never would have run. I've always thought of you as my best friend."

"You're my best friend too. And I'm sorry if I fucked everything up with the whole fake boyfriend thing."

"You didn't." Connor squeezed my hand tightly. "I just think you finally made us do something about our feelings."

"Like admit they were real?"

"Yeah. How could you do that to me?" He grinned

impishly and then the pair of us broke down laughing. "Seriously," he said, voice breathless from laughter. "I was quite happy pining. I didn't want to deal with this whole angsty feels nonsense."

"I mean, you could have just said something."

"So could you."

"Fair enough," I said. "Maybe we both should have said something."

"Maybe we're both idiots," Connor added. "Ginormous, pining idiots. Taylor is gonna be so all over this when he finds out." He squeezed my hand again. "Not that I care. I'm happy I'm such an idiot because it means I get you. I mean, it would have been better without all the worrying I've been doing over the past week, but I think I kinda deserved that. I should have just told you when you first asked me about pretending to be your boyfriend. Or maybe before we'd first had sex. I was just scared I'd ruin our friendship. That we'd get into a relationship, and it would end up like all my others, and we'd have this horrible breakup, and I'd lose you."

"Don't worry. I'm not going anywhere. I promise." I leant forward, moving my hand to cup his jaw. Connor tilted forwards on his knees towards me. "You're my best friend, Connor, and I love you. We can make this work."

"Are you sure?"

"I am. More than anything."

"Good, because I don't think I could go another day without you. I love you more than… more than cake."

I chuckled and closed the gap between us. "Then you must love me a lot."

"I do." Our lips met in a gentle kiss, and all at once it felt like everything was right in the universe again. It had only been a few days since we'd last kissed, but it felt like forever. How had I gone for so many years without this in my life? I'd been so worried Connor wouldn't want me that I'd ignored all the evidence right under my nose. I wasn't the only one though, so maybe one day we'd look back and laugh at how stupid we'd been.

Right now though, I didn't want to think about our mistakes. I wanted to think about our future.

We broke the kiss and Connor adjusted his position, moving things across the blanket so he could snuggle up against me where he should always be.

"This is adorable by the way," I said, gesturing at the picnic.

"I tried."

"Did you make the cake?"

He snorted. "No, and believe me, that's a good thing. Levi made it using a Betty Crocker box mix after I tried and failed to make you one from scratch. He made me try some of my disastrous cake, and trust me, your mouth should thank him for stepping in."

"That bad?"

"Whatever you're thinking, it was worse."

"It's the thought that counts," I said and drew him in for another kiss. "And I love that you tried. Besides, those Betty Crocker mixes are good."

"I feel like we should just eat the cake first. Cake for dinner," Connor murmured against my lips. He kissed me again, his tongue dipping into my mouth, and I moaned.

"Or we could skip dinner for now? My bedroom is literally three feet away. We can eat later. Or rather, we can eat *food* later. I really want to get my mouth on your body."

"O-okay. Let's do that." Connor unfolded himself and stood gracefully, then reached for my hand.

CHAPTER THIRTY

Connor

I'D THOUGHT NOW that everything was out in the open between us, the sex would be slow and sweet—full of whispered "I love yous" and tender touches—but it was anything but. It was like now that we knew exactly how we felt, something had been unleashed inside us, and a tidal wave of intense desire and heat had swept over both of us.

As soon as we set foot in the bedroom, we were on each other, our mouths meeting in frantic kisses as we desperately tried to strip off. I'd deliberately made an effort with my appearance, but now I was cursing my skinny jeans. At least my top came off quickly.

"I want to ride you," Patrick said, his hands gripping my waist and pulling me closer, the heat of his skin burning against mine. "Please. Let me ride your cock."

God, that was a visual and a half—Patrick bouncing up and down on my dick, his entire body right there in front of me to touch and tease and watch. Yeah, we were definitely doing that.

"Yes, fuck yes. I want that. I want to watch you use my cock, and I want to watch you come."

We ended up on the bed, Patrick on top of me as we kissed endlessly, our hands exploring whatever skin we could reach. I gasped as Patrick's fingers circled my nipples, quickly followed by his talented tongue. God, he really was a fast learner. My hands ran down his back and squeezed his ass, teasing his crack, and he moaned against me. His cock was hard against mine, and I slipped my hand in between our bodies to grip them, jacking them slowly and drawing more beautiful noises from Patrick's mouth. Every moan and gasp added more fuel to the fire inside me.

"Get the lube. I want to watch you open yourself for me," I said. "It's on my bedside table." Patrick nodded, and with one final kiss, he pulled away to retrieve the bottle. I'd been a fancy bitch and splashed out for the same organic brand Patrick had after I'd experienced first-hand how nice it was. I propped myself up on a mountain of pillows, slowly stroking my cock while Patrick knelt in front of me, facing away from me so I had the perfect view of his ass. He tilted forward, resting on one hand while the other slid between his perfect, thick thighs. It would be a little awkward for him, but I already knew I wasn't going to be able to resist getting involved. I was too possessive, and I liked being the one to take Patrick apart. Besides how could I just sit here and look at something so delicious without touching it? I was seriously tempted to just spread his cheeks open and fuck his pucker with my tongue, opening him up with it until he was dripping and desperate.

Patrick swore and moaned as he slid a finger inside himself, pumping it in and out before quickly moving up to two. He pressed his shoulders lower to the bed, raising his perfect ass. I was so fucking tempted to fuck him like this instead. It would give me the perfect view of his ass as it worked my cock. But I also wanted to watch his face and feel his cum splattering across my chest. Decisions, decisions. All of them delicious and none of them wrong.

Fuck it, I wanted him like this but with just one adjustment.

"Fuck, you look so sexy, my love," I said, twisting onto my knees and scooting forward to run my hands down Patrick's spine. I pressed a kiss to the top of his ass as he slid a third finger into his hole, then pressed more kisses over each vertebra, whispering words between each touch of my lips. "Can I have you like this? Please. You can ride me later."

"O-okay," Patrick said. He sounded so desperate to be fucked, I wasn't sure he cared how he got my dick. "Give it to me. Please."

"Always, but I just want to do one thing. Turn slightly for me." Patrick twisted to look at me, confusion mixed with pleasure on his face. "I want you to watch me fuck you in the mirror." I pointed at the large, full-length mirror that was built into my wardrobe. From our position on the bed, with just a slight turn, we'd be able to see everything. I'd get to watch Patrick's face as he came, and he'd get to see just how fucking sexy he was. I wanted him to know that, to me, he was the most beautiful man in the universe, and his body was perfect. I'd never found anyone as sexy as I found Patrick.

Patrick paused for a second, then nodded. I smiled and pressed another kiss to the top of his ass, whispering praise under my breath. It took us a moment to readjust our positions, but soon I knelt behind him with Patrick spread out beneath me. His ass was pushed up into the air and looked so delicious I just wanted to stay there and worship it for hours. I gripped my cock and lined up, pushing into his tight, slick ass and watching him fall apart underneath me.

"Oh God, Connor. Give it to me!" Patrick was practically begging as I seated myself inside him. He gripped the sheets and pushed back against me until I was balls deep. I wanted to go slowly, but it was no use. As soon as Patrick pushed back on me, I needed more. My hands found his hips, and I began to move, taking him hard and fast, all the while watching his face in the mirror. His skin glistened with sweat, his eyes wide and almost glassy with pleasure, his mouth hanging open. I'd never seen anything so gorgeous in my life.

"Look at you. So fucking sexy for me, so beautiful. I love you, Patrick," I said as more endearments dripped from my lips. I wanted him to know just how gorgeous he was with every syllable I spoke and each move of my hips. Patrick cried out as I drove into him, nailing his prostate over and over, his body starting to shake underneath me, and I knew he was close. Pleasure danced across my skin, lighting up each and every one of my nerves like a beacon, and I knew it wouldn't be long before I was shooting deep inside him.

Patrick reached for his cock, pumping it hard and fast as I matched his strokes. I watched our bodies in the mirror, moving perfectly together, our faces reflecting everything we felt. It felt like we were one and the same as we chased our release.

"C-Connor, I'm going to… I'm…"

"Yes. Come for me. I'm right there with you." My hands tightened on Patrick's hips as he cried out, and I stared at our reflections, watching his face contort with pleasure as his cock painted the sheets with thick streaks of cum. His channel tightened around me, pulling my own orgasm out of me with so much force it left me feeling more than a little lightheaded as my cock pulsed inside him. My body was shaking, and my breath was coming in ragged pants. I leant forward and pressed another kiss to the middle of Patrick's spine and smiled against his skin.

Slowly, I pulled out of Patrick, watching with possessive pleasure as my cum trickled out of his hole. Fuck, that was a beautiful sight. I slid my fingers over the furled muscle, collected cum on my fingers and then slowly pushed it back inside as Patrick groaned.

My cock throbbed between my legs, and I looked down at Patrick, who'd twisted his head to look at me. His mouth was slack and his eyes wide, and little moans fell from his lips. I grinned.

"Are you ready, darling? We're not finished yet."

"I feel like we should get food now," I said after another round of orgasms. I looked up at Patrick from where I was sprawled on the pillow beside him. "I've been energetic. I need feeding."

"Do you want to go next door, or do I need to bring you food here?" he asked with a wry smile.

"I'll move, mostly because I created the most perfect indoor picnic aesthetic, and I don't want to waste it. Plus, I really don't want to get chocolate icing all over the sheets because that just looks bad." I sighed and sat up slightly, propping myself up on my elbows. I wanted to get up because I'd hardly eaten all day since I'd been so nervous, but I also wanted to stay in bed with this perfect man forever. He was mine now, and I never wanted to let him out of my sight.

That sounded creepier than I'd intended.

Patrick grinned and leant over to kiss me. "You'd better get up then."

"Fine. But only because I want chocolate cake." I pressed another quick kiss to Patrick's mouth and slid my feet off the bed. I didn't fancy putting my jeans on again, especially because they were tighter than necessary and would severely impact my ability to eat three-quarters of a cake alongside all the bread and cheese I planned on consuming. Instead, I grabbed a pair of loose, pink shorts off the floor and slid them on, not bothering with under-wear. I was *well* aware of the fact that they barely grazed my ass cheeks, and if I bent over even slightly, they would show off my butt. They would be very fun to tease Patrick with for the rest of the evening.

I grabbed an old T-shirt, which was one of Patrick's that I'd stolen at some point previously, off the floor. It was a soft grey colour and had lost its Patrick smell some time ago. I didn't want to admit I'd worn it to bed every night until it had finally reached that point. I was tempted to ask him to wear it again and then steal it back. It hung loosely on me, not quite reaching the end of my shorts but almost.

"Is that mine?" Patrick asked from the bed.

"It might have been." I gave him my best charming smile. "You leant it to me after I spilt something on my T-shirt once, and I just… forgot to give it back."

"I see." He raised an eyebrow but grinned. "It looks good on you. I like seeing you in my clothes."

"Good, because this is perfect for lounging in, and I have no intention of giving it back. Unless you really want me to."

"Nah, you keep it." He swung his legs out of bed and stood, giving me the perfect view of his ass and then his dick as he turned to face me. God, he was delicious. I just wanted to eat him all up. It was almost heartbreaking watching him get dressed. Patrick pulled on his jeans, and I suddenly wished I had some more comfortable clothes to offer him. Although he looked utterly fabulous in them, they weren't going to be the most comfortable thing to sit on the floor and eat in. I was going to rectify the not having some clothes of Patrick's in my wardrobe situation as soon as possible.

Maybe we should just move in together. That would make things so much easier.

I shook my head and chuckled to myself. Dating for less than two hours and deciding to move in together would have to be a world record. Except we'd already known each other for three years... and we constantly lived in each other's pockets... I'd thought of it as a joke but maybe... maybe it wouldn't be the stupidest idea I'd ever had.

It would save a lot of hassle in going backwards and forwards. Plus it would save us money on rent and petrol. I wasn't fussed about giving this place up because Patrick's house was nicer than my flat. Then again, maybe we could look for a place together. Something that would be ours.

"You okay?" Patrick asked. "You're staring into space."

"We should move in together," I blurted out. Shit. I hadn't meant to actually say it.

"Do... do you mean it?" Patrick stared at me like he wasn't sure whether I was joking. It had sounded insane when I'd said it out loud.

"Yeah, I do." Because now that it was out there, I realised I wanted that more than anything in the world. It just made sense.

"Okay. Let's do it." He reached for my hand, and when I took it, he pulled me across the room and into his arms, almost sweeping me off my feet. "I don't want to spend another second without you beside me. I love you, Connor."

His words filled my heart to the brim. All my fears and doubts had been washed away, and now I was wondering why I'd ever had them to begin with. "I love you too."

CHAPTER THIRTY-ONE

Patrick

THE FOLD-OUT CHAIR underneath me squeaked as I shifted position slightly. It wasn't exactly the most comfortable seat, but that didn't matter. I was here to watch Connor, and I knew I was going to be easily distracted.

He and Levi had managed to pull a showcase together for the end of August, getting loads of their pole students to sign up and have a go as well as putting routines together themselves. It was more a fun, casual event than a competition Connor had said, and they'd designed it so anyone could take part if they wanted—whether they'd performed before or not. Connor had said it was much easier to get up and perform in front of a small, supportive crowd that you knew, especially for the first time, than stepping on stage at a competition.

Connor and Levi had worked really hard over the past eight weeks to pull it together, and the event had completely sold out. The lights of the second studio had been dimmed at one end, leaving a warmly lit performance space at the other end. There was a black curtain covered in fairy lights behind it, with plain black curtains hung on the side walls, hiding the floor-to-ceiling mirrors that stretched along the length of the room. There were two chrome poles in the performance space, about six feet apart. Connor had mentioned something about one of them being on static and one being set to spin so the pole itself would spin in place when the dancer touched it. Just the idea of clutching onto something spinning at high speed made me feel a little travel sick.

A friend of Levi's had set up a long table covered in a sparkling tablecloth with large speakers on either side of it to provide the music, and Connor had booked a local drag queen, Miss Fortune, as compare. Miss Fortune was brilliant, funny, encouraging, and self-deprecating, and she kept gently ribbing Levi and Connor, which was a hilarious bonus.

The audience of family members, partners, and other students was squeezed into the other end of the room on a random collection of fold-out chairs they'd procured, a couple of low sofas from the reception area that parents usually sat on during the kids classes, and even a couple of mats at the front—although that was mostly for the performers. I was sandwiched between Ben, who'd come to play supportive brother to Levi, and Taylor and Simon, who Connor had invited up for the weekend. It was the first time I'd really met them, but already I could see why Taylor and Connor were so close. They were so funny to watch together. The best way to describe it was almost lovingly snarky.

The first section of performers had already been, which had been mostly people who weren't too far into their pole journey. They were all still ridiculously impressive to me, and I'd clapped and cheered for everyone. I'd never be brave enough to do something like this, and to me they all deserved a standing ovation just for getting up there. We'd also had an interval where the audience had been able to help themselves to cake and donate to charity. I'd provided the cake after a panicked kitchen visit from Levi who was terrified that Connor was going to try baking again. I had no idea how his cake had been so bad the first time he'd tried, but I was almost tempted to get Connor to try again one day so I could see the resulting horror for myself.

I'd hardly seen Connor for most of the evening since he'd been helping Levi with the organisation. But now as I looked around for him, he'd disappeared from sight.

"He's probably gone to get changed," Taylor murmured from beside me before clapping and cheering for the young woman currently performing. She was in some form of inverted position on the spinning pole which looked virtually impossible for any normal human to achieve. I hadn't realised I'd spoken out loud, but when I glanced at Taylor, he just grinned.

"You were looking for him," he added.

"I didn't realise I was so obvious." I chuckled and then gasped as the performer dropped down the pole and into a ball around it.

"You are, but it's cute. Have you seen Connor perform before?"

"Sort of. I've watched lots of his Instagram videos." I'd watched more of them over the past couple of weeks after I'd finally come clean to Connor about only liking them without watching because I'd felt guilty getting turned on by videos of my best friend. He'd pulled them all up on his phone, and we'd watched some of them together. Then he'd offered to show me some of his floor work in person. We hadn't made it far into the incredibly sexy routine he'd started, and then we'd never made it beyond the sofa. "Have you?"

"A couple of times. I used to go and watch him compete sometimes. He's even better in person," Taylor turned to look at me, a wry smile on his lips. "But I'm not his boyfriend, so you might find it a little more... intense than I do."

Something inside my chest fluttered with nerves and excitement. Connor had told me that he loved doing sexy routines, and I was never going to stop him from doing them. Watching him on video had been intense enough, so I had no idea what this was going to do to me. God, it was going to be so embarrassing if I got hard in public. I just had to hope it wouldn't be visible through my jeans in the dark, and that I could get it under control by the end of the night.

The performer onstage finished with a dramatic flair and we all applauded wildly. She gave a breathless bow and then ran into the arms of some friends, who pulled her into giant hugs on the mats. Miss Fortune rose from her chair on the edge of the stage area and reached for her microphone and her clipboard, which had everyone's bios on it, and stepped onto the floor with a flare.

"Oh my God, Ellie. That was amazing! Wasn't she amazing, everyone?" We all cheered. "You definitely need to perform more often, although maybe less of those drops, okay? I thought my heart was going to come out through my throat and that would've just been messy!" The audience laughed, and Ellie beamed from her seat. It looked like she was breathing for the first time in five minutes. "Are you ready for our next performer? Since we're getting towards the end of the evening, it's time for our instructors to get on the stage and put their money where their mouths are. Are you excited?"

We cheered, and my heart leapt into my throat. I couldn't see Levi or Connor, but I knew Levi was closing out the show since he owned the studio.

"Okay, so next up we have Connor. Connor has been poling for eleven years, starting when he was only seventeen alongside his ballet and dance training..." Miss Fortune grinned. "I won't tell you what I was doing at seventeen because it's embarrassing compared to this. Drinking WKD in the park is not comparable in any way."

Taylor snorted from beside me. "No, we just drank it in my room instead."

"Connor started doing competitions as soon as he turned eighteen, and credits pole with helping him embrace his queerness and sexuality—I love that so much, like so fucking much—He's been an instructor at Above the Barre since it opened and is so proud of every single one of his students. Tonight's routine is something he put together for fun—because he wanted to be very gay and extra. He wants to dedicate the performance to his boyfriend, Patrick, who is a continued source of love and encouragement."

I felt my face heating, and I was glad nobody apart from Taylor, Simon, and Ben would be able to see the colour of my face. But I couldn't focus on my embarrassment because I was too fixed on the stage. The first few beats of Connor's music kicked in, and I recognised it instantly, "I Like Boys" by Todrick Hall.

The back curtains parted, Connor stepped onto the studio floor, and my jaw dropped. He was wearing tiny black shorts that just covered his ass, black knee pads, and black patent-leather, knee-high boots with a platform wedge and stiletto heels that must have been at least eight inches high. His skin shimmered with body glitter and his face was perfectly made-up, complete with smoky eyes and dark red lipstick that just made me melt. I wanted him to smear it all over my skin.

He strode over to the static pole, eyes locking onto the audience as he began to move. I was transfixed. Connor moved like water—completely fluid and effortless. Every roll of his hips and bend of his body was entrancing and sensuous. He oozed pure sex appeal as he slid down the pole and onto the floor, spreading his legs then lifting them over his head to crack the platform of his boots on the floor and then together. The sound sent shivers running through me.

Connor's muscles rippled as he flipped onto his stomach and his eyes found mine as he lifted his hips and began to slowly roll them, humping the floor. All I could think of was how he'd moved his hips like that when he'd fucked me three days ago, slow and deep and perfect until I'd painted our skin with my cum. I bit my lip, trying hard not to let it show how much his performance was affecting me. Luckily, everyone's eyes were on him as he slid across the floor and wrapped his knee around the spinning pole, using the momentum to swing himself onto his feet before he began to climb it. I stared at him, watching as the pole almost became an extension of his body. Connor made it look so graceful and easy, even though I'd heard him complain about the pain and the bruises. The sheer strength involved was incredible, and I gasped as he held himself perpendicular to the pole. Then with a simple twist, he was suddenly descending as the pole spun, walking on the air until he reached the floor where he began to dip and spin, dropping down into a bouncing squat before pushing his perfect ass out.

There was a huge grin on Connor's face, and it was easy to tell he was having a fabulous time grinding, bouncing, and spinning while Todrick Hall sung about dick prints and bubble butts and sexy boys. His enthusiasm was infectious, and the whole room was whooping, cheering, and clapping with every move he made. At one point, Taylor had even whistled and then laughed. I didn't know if Connor had heard him, but the way his face had twitched suggested he had.

Connor finished the routine with a final clack of his heels and a spectacular drop to the floor. There was a split second of silence and then the audience erupted with cheers and waves of applause. Connor gracefully climbed to his feet, his chest heaving. He was wearing the most enormous smile and was immediately jumped on by a couple of students who dragged him into giant hugs. He returned them quickly, then sauntered across the room, wriggling through the audience until he reached us.

"Excuse me, darling," he said to Simon and Taylor, his voice hoarse and breathless. He squeezed past them and collapsed onto my lap, stretching his boots out over Taylor who laughed. "Hello, my love. Did you enjoy that?"

"I... er... I..."

"Babe, you've rendered him speechless," said Taylor. "So I think that's a yes."

"Good." Connor burrowed into my chest. "You're very comfy. I think I'll sit here and watch Levi."

Miss Fortune was saying something, and the audience laughed, but I wasn't really listening. I was just staring in awe at the man in my lap, who could command the attention of an entire room with a roll of his hips and the clack of his heels. Who oozed pure sexuality and perfection and could probably have any man he wanted. And whose first thought after his performance was to come and find me.

"You were incredible," I whispered as Miss Fortune began introducing Levi, who had appeared from the back and taken a starting position between the poles. "Truly. I've never seen anything so amazing."

"Thank you, darling," he said. "I'm glad." Then Connor leant in closer as Levi's music kicked in. "Are your jeans a little uncomfortable? Because it feels like they might be."

I felt my face heating because, of course, Connor had

noticed that despite my best intentions, I'd gotten hard during his performance. It had been difficult not to. I wasn't a saint, and watching my boyfriend grinding against the floor in the tiniest shorts I'd ever seen was bound to have an effect on me. I gave the tiniest of nods, trying not to give myself away to the others.

"Good," Connor said, his voice dripping with satisfaction. "I can't wait to take you home and show you exactly how grateful I am that you came to support me tonight."

"Thank you. And, um, perhaps..." I trailed off suddenly wondering whether the request that had popped into my head was weird and ridiculous. It probably wasn't something I should be asking here even if no one was paying us any attention. Connor shifted in my lap, his ass grinding against my erection, and I bit back a moan.

"Tell me, Patrick. What do you want? There are no stupid requests or stupid questions." I wasn't so sure about that, but I knew Connor wouldn't judge.

"Would you..." I dropped my voice until the words were barely there and Connor virtually had to press his ear to my mouth. "Will you wear your boots when you fuck me?" My skin burned as I forced the words out. Connor turned his head, and even in the dim light I could see his hungry grin.

"Oh, darling. Yes, yes I will." He kissed me, deep and hard. "I'm going to make you feel incredible."

There was a small cough from beside us and we both turned to see Taylor giving us a raised eyebrow. I didn't think he'd heard me, thank God, but he'd definitely noticed that something was going on.

"Can you not fuck in public please?" he asked in a withering tone. "Please keep it in your pants until you get home."

"That reminds me," Connor said. "You and Simon can have my flat to yourselves tonight. I put fresh sheets on my bed and the sofa bed in the guest room so you can choose. I'll go stay with Patrick, then we can meet at Annie's for breakfast tomorrow."

Taylor sighed, then laughed. "Well, at least I won't have to listen to you."

"See?" Connor said with a grin. "Aren't I nice to you?"

"Sure, let's go with that."

CHAPTER THIRTY-TWO

Connor

As I STARED at the mountains of boxes in my half-empty bedroom, I was suddenly wondering whether there was such a thing as owning too many clothes and shoes. I'd done a bit of clear out and had filled up the local charity shops, but maybe I should have gotten rid of more. Oh well. I could always have a good sort out of things when I unpacked at Patrick's house. Which was about to be *our* house as soon as I got my butt in gear and got the rest of my stuff loaded into the van we'd hired.

We'd debated trying to put everything into our cars at first, but that was never going to work, considering I had furniture. Some of my stuff was being donated to charity and so was some of Patrick's. We were going for a true blend of furniture and style. My bed was going into Patrick's tiny spare room since his bed was more comfortable, but we were adding my armchair and sofa to fill out the living room a little more. It was going to be a bit of a squish, and maybe at some point we'd look at getting a bigger place, but for now, it would be perfect.

Maybe our next house would be one we bought rather than rented.

I heard footsteps on the landing and a couple of voices laughing. Levi had roped Ben in to help as soon as he found out we were moving, and Patrick had magically gotten both Aaron and Josh to volunteer as well. I'd been expecting fireworks, and not the good kind, from the two chefs as soon as they'd arrived, but they seemed to be avoiding each other instead.

"How're you going in here?" Aaron asked, sticking his head around the door. "You all packed up?"

"Just about." I grabbed a roll of tape and finished sealing the last of the boxes. "I think I have too much stuff."

"Nah, this is nothing." Aaron grabbed an enormous box of shoes and hefted it as if it was made of paper. "You shoulda seen the amount of stuff I had when I last moved house."

"Oh?" I grinned. "A big fashion fan?"

"Nah, cookbooks. And they're a lot fucking heavier than this." That didn't surprise me since Patrick also had shelves and shelves of recipe books and files he'd collected over the years. It was as much a part of being a chef as my shoes were to my dancing. It came with the territory.

I grabbed another box and followed Aaron out onto the landing, squeezing past Levi and Ben who were bickering about something I couldn't catch while picking up the last few boxes that had been stacked on the landing. We passed

Patrick on the stairs, and he leant in to give me a quick kiss. Fuck, I loved him so much. We'd only been "officially" together for two months, but it felt like it had been longer… like years. Which made sense if you thought about how long we'd been friends. Except I wasn't sure that our friendship had ever been just a friendship.

The more I thought about it, the less convinced I was. I mean, Levi and I were great friends, but I wouldn't have done half the stuff I'd done with Patrick with him. Taylor was my best friend in the world, second only to Patrick, but I wouldn't have snuggled up under a blanket with him to watch films with my head on his chest, and I wouldn't have made him dinner most nights or spent more time at his house than my own. It was clear to me now that Patrick and I had let our love for each other bleed into our friendship, no matter how hard we'd tried to pretend it wasn't. We'd basically been dating for three years without realising it.

Hindsight was a wonderful thing, but it was a total pain in the ass.

We hadn't told Patrick's family that we'd only just started dating because we'd both felt that was probably something we should either never tell them or should do in person. I was personally in the "let's take this secret to our graves and bribe-slash-blackmail all our friends into keeping quiet" camp, but I had a feeling Patrick would rather come clean one day. We had told them we were moving in together though, and we'd already had several long phone calls with Aoife offering to send us things ranging from furniture to cake. I didn't know if cake would post, which sucked. I'd also reiterated my promise to drag

Patrick away from The Pear Tree at Christmas for a couple
of days, and Aoife had already extended the invitation to
my mum too, just as Cara had said she would. The way
they'd just opened up their hearts and their home for me
was something I never thought I'd experience. Their love
for me was incredible, and I knew I'd have to make sure my
mascara was stuck like glue for when I inevitably bawled
my eyes out again.

My mum's reaction had been equally loving, although
I'd had to come clean to her about the whole thing because
she'd been hearing about my pining over Patrick for years.
She'd never told me to move on or to give up, and instead
she'd always said it would work itself out. Somehow, I had
to wonder if she'd known what Patrick and I had been
unable to see. I wouldn't have been surprised. When I'd
confessed the whole thing to her and then mentioned in the
same breath that we were looking to move in together, the
smile in her voice was evident. I couldn't wait for her to
come stay again so I could formally introduce her to
Patrick. My boyfriend.

Which in my opinion were the two best words in the
world.

When Aaron and I got down to the van in the car park,
Josh stood in the cargo bed waiting for us. His face tightened when he saw Aaron, but he took the box without
complaint, stacking it on top of some others. I watched the
pair of them with interest—the way Aaron looked like he
wanted to say something but wasn't going to out of sheer
stubbornness, and the way Josh was blatantly refusing to
speak to him. There was definitely something going on

there, but I was not getting involved. I would tell Patrick, then he could find out why the idiots were acting so strangely. My immediate money was on sex, but maybe Josh had finally had enough and quit. Although I was sure Patrick would've mentioned something if that were the case.

"How much more have we got?" Josh asked as he took the box I was holding. "We've still got a bit of room in here."

"Not much. A few more boxes I think."

"I knew wasting my youth playing Tetris would come in handy someday." Josh grinned, but it looked slightly forced. He slotted the box into a space then turned back to look at me, pointedly ignoring Aaron. Whatever. I really wasn't getting involved. They could sort this shit out themselves.

I walked back up to the flat and found Patrick in the kitchen, doing a last-minute wipe down. I'd already paid for a cleaning service to come in tomorrow to deep clean the place before I gave my keys back so the letting agency wouldn't charge me an extortionate fee for cleaning. I was going to give them the receipt and everything. I'd been burnt before, and it was not happening again. I wanted my deposit back so I could put it towards a holiday for Patrick and me because I thought we deserved a break. I'd already found a nice Airbnb in Rome and a website for a walking food tour. It would be the perfect Autumn getaway.

"You don't have to do that you know," I said, putting my arms around his waist and kissing between his shoulder blades. "They're coming to clean it tomorrow."

"I know, but I can't help it. Messy kitchens are my weakness."

"It wasn't that bad!" I laughed with a note of mock offence in my tone.

"When was the last time you cleaned under the cooker hood?"

"Babe, I don't even think the last tenants cleaned under the cooker hood."

"I think you're right." Patrick turned in my arms, and I rested my head against his chest. "Sorry, I might be going a bit overboard. I should probably help the guys load the rest of the stuff."

"Eh, leave them. Levi and Ben are bickering about something, and Josh and Aaron are being hella fucking weird." I rolled my eyes, and Patrick pursed his lips, suddenly looking pensive.

"It's not just me then? You think they're being weird too?"

"Eh, hell yeah. They're not even fighting." I tilted my head up to kiss him because it had simply been far too long since I'd had Patrick's mouth on mine, and I was suffering.

"Yeah, I thought something was going on last week when they were on shift together. Apparently they didn't speak to each other all service. Everyone was talking about it." Patrick finally noticed I wanted a kiss and brought his mouth down to mine. I sighed happily against him. I couldn't wait to get back to our house and relax. We could snuggle up on the sofa, get a takeaway, and chill.

"I wonder who'll crack and tell you first," I said teasingly, knowing poor Patrick had been in the middle of their fighting for years. If they were going to spill the beans to anyone, it would be Patrick.

"Is that a hint for me to tell you when I find out?"

"I mean... Please?"

"You're not very subtle, you know that?" Patrick's lips twitched into a smile, and I scoffed.

"Subtle is boring. I'd much rather be wonderfully exuberant."

"I wouldn't have you any other way." He kissed me again as warmth flooded my chest. Why had I fought so hard to deny myself this when every moment was perfection? If I had a time machine, past Connor and I would be having words.

"There you are," Levi said from behind me. "Come on, slackers. We've finished loading the van while you two are in here skiving off."

"That's what I'm paying you for," I teased, and Levi rolled his eyes so hard they practically disappeared into the back of his head.

"You're not paying me at all, asshole." He was grinning though, so I knew he didn't mind. He still kinda owed me for helping him pull the showcase together so quickly. This, plus the whole cake incident, would pretty much make us even again.

"You're doing it because you love me," I said. "And because we'll give you food."

"As long as it's not your cake, then we're good."

"Ugh, fine. I suppose I can give you actual food." I smiled and stepped out of Patrick's arms, looking up at him. "Do you wanna go ahead in the van and I'll follow in my car? I can just do a final sweep and make sure we've got everything and then you can supervise this lot."

"Hey, we're not totally incompetent," Ben called from the living room.

"That's debatable," Levi added.

I could feel an argument brewing because apparently Aaron and Josh had passed on their penchant for bickering to Ben and Levi. I looked at Patrick and he nodded, clearly thinking exactly the same thing.

"Okay, let's get going then," Patrick said, motioning for Levi to head out the door. He turned and looked over his shoulder at me before he turned the corner. "See you soon."

"I can't wait." Because honestly, I couldn't. Even though we'd decided to move in together as soon as we'd started dating, it had taken ages for us to find a free day to get everyone together. It hadn't come fast enough in my opinion.

I finished wiping down the kitchen and gathered the last of the cleaning products, shoving them into an old bag for life. I did a final sweep around, double-checking all the wardrobes just in case I'd forgotten anything before making my way out the front door, locking it behind me. I didn't really feel any sadness at leaving the flat behind because I was too excited about what was happening next.

I made my way to my little car and jumped in to set off for the new house, making a quick stop at the Co-op to grab a ton of sandwich meal deals for everyone before making my way across town. By the time I got to the house, the van was half-unpacked, and after a quick break for food, it didn't take us long to get everything else unloaded. Soon

Patrick and I were alone in our house with President Whiskers, of course, who'd watched the entire affair from the back of the sofa wearing an air of indifference. Although he had tried to trip Aaron up at one point by winding around his ankles while Aaron was carrying a box through the living room.

"So," I said as we made our way into the living room and collapsed onto the sofa together. It was only four o'clock, but I was fucking exhausted. "What do you want to do now?"

"How about we just chill here for a bit?" Patrick opened his arms so I could snuggle into his side, my favourite place in the world. "Watch a movie, nap, and then later we can order some food? Maybe get a curry?"

"With extra garlic naan?"

"Of course. I'll even kiss you afterwards." Patrick handed me the remote and gave me a fond smile. A smile that told me so many things—that he cared for me, that he thought I was cute, that he was glad I was here, and that he loved me. It was the smile that I'd only ever seen him wear for me. "Cheesy romcom?"

"You read my mind."

I flicked on the TV and scrolled through Netflix, choosing an old romcom that we'd seen a million times. Then I snuggled deeper into Patrick while his arm came down to rest around my shoulders. It was the same thing we'd been doing for years. Only this time I had no doubt in my mind about Patrick's feelings for me.

We were in love. And nothing was going to change that.

EPILOGUE

Patrick

A SOFT SUMMER breeze caressed my skin as I walked hand-in-hand with my new husband across the yard of my parents' farm.

The field next to the barn was filled with people drinking, laughing, chatting, and playing with the lawn games we'd set up, including a ridiculously large game of Jenga, while children ran and played around them, turning cartwheels on the soft grass. I smiled and squeezed Connor's hand, suddenly struck by déjà vu, remembering this scene from two years earlier when we'd been friends pretending to be more, and I'd been desperately wishing it was real.

So much had changed since then, and yet really only one thing had. Connor and I had made the leap from friends to boyfriends, then from boyfriends to fiancés, and now to husbands. I liked that word: husband. It made

everything feel so solid and real, like the shimmering plat-
inum band on my finger was proof of how far we'd come
from that nervous weekend.

"Where do you want to start?" asked Connor, looking
up and grinning, his perfectly highlighted cheekbones
shimmering in the summer sun. We'd spent the last hour
taking photos across the farm, making use of the beautiful
landscape and the sunshine, and I almost wished I could
keep Connor to myself for just a few more minutes before
we had to make the rounds and greet our guests. Although
I'd get him back later for food and dancing, and tonight
when we locked ourselves in the gorgeous bedroom of the
cottage we were staying in. Mum and Da, with Mary's help
and encouragement, had made one of the little cottages into
a wedding suite for couples who held their receptions on
the farm. I'd been a little hesitant to stay there, but the
cottage had been too beautiful to resist. Our own little slice
of secluded paradise for the night. Plus, it had an enormous
bed and a hot tub, and I really wasn't going to turn that
down. I got the feeling I'd be exhausted by the end of the
night and not just at the hands of my husband. Dealing
with two hundred people was hard, especially when they
were my family.

"Divide and conquer?" I suggested. "Or do you want to
stay together for protection? I'm slightly scared several of
my elderly aunts will try and give me advice about my
wedding night and sigh over how flexible you are. Even
though at least one of them has told me over the past two
years to enjoy 'my handsome man as often as possible' so

I'm not sure what they think will be happening tonight. Unless they're going to give me instructions on working the hot tub. Did you see how many buttons that thing has?"

Connor laughed, the sound like music to my ears. "Oh my God, I'd forgotten your aunts. Don't worry. I'll fend them off. Should I just tell them I popped your cherry years ago or should I just distract them with my booty?"

"Careful, or you'll end up hearing stories about that man they dated in the seventies who could do that thing with his tongue." I shuddered. Thanks, Aunt Betty, for that visual.

"Oh, you never know, I might enjoy that!"

"That's what I'm afraid of." I stopped walking and pulled Connor into me, kissing him gently. I wondered if anyone would notice if we disappeared into the garden for half an hour just so I could keep my husband to myself for a little longer.

"Come on," he said, squeezing my hand. "I'm getting hungry, and I see the caterers have started with the canapes. I want at least three cones of mini fish and chips since we're paying for them."

"You know if you ask nicely, I'm sure they'd bring you a little tray of them to carry around for yourself."

"Oh my God, yes! That's the best idea." Connor grinned at me, practically bouncing on the spot. "You have the most wonderful ideas, babe. Come on. I'll ask that gentlemen near Mary. I'm sure he can procure what I want."

I laughed and let Connor tow me across the yard in search of mini fish and chip cones.

We ended up splitting up to cover more ground, and although it was nice to chat with everyone, I was glad when we were whisked away by the photographer for some group shots and then a few more on our own while the guests were seated.

"You two doing okay?" Mary asked, giving me a once-over as we waited. Technically she wasn't supposed to be working this event, and everything was in the capable hands of her assistant, Dylan, but Mary didn't know how to switch off. Ever since she'd had the idea to do wedding receptions at the barn, she'd thrown herself into making it work. Mary had taken all her organisational skills and her local knowledge and produced something spectacular. She'd dragged Aaron and I down one weekend to inspect the plans for the kitchen she was having installed for the caterers in a small building behind the barn that had mostly been used for spare tack and storage. From there she'd found preferred local caterers, florists, decorators, bands, and everything and anything else a couple might need. She'd also looked at the cottage plans and worked out how to turn the entire farm into a package for both accommodations and the reception.

After a couple of guinea pig events, the barn had held its first wedding nine months after she'd first suggested the idea, and it had been a wild success. Even though it had only been a little over a year since then, they were already three-quarters booked up for the next year, and they'd started getting some great recognition, even being nominated for a couple of local wedding awards.

When Connor and I had started planning, his first

suggestion had been that we hold the reception here. "It's special to us," he'd said. "In more ways than one. And I can't think of anywhere more perfect." So that had been that. Mum had been thrilled when we'd told her, and I think she'd nearly driven Mary up the wall trying to be helpful. I was glad we'd had the pair of them, plus Connor's mum, to help out because our lives were ridiculously busy, and it wasn't as if we could just pop to Devon every weekend.

The Pear Tree was doing extremely well. Aaron had gotten his wish for awards, and as a result we were busier than ever. Luckily, Ben had conceded that we needed more staff, and we now had two additional pastry chefs, meaning there were always two of us on a service. It was a bit of a squish in the kitchen, but it meant that I felt less like a headless chicken, so I was happy to deal with it. Aaron had quietly whispered to me that his next goal was a Michelin star, and we'd started having meetings about how we could refine the menus. It was tricky because we didn't want to alienate some of our customers by refining the food too much, but we also wanted to make sure everything sung. I was enjoying the challenge, and more than once Connor had been forced to come and dig me out of the pastry kitchen because I was busy experimenting. Not that he usually minded because he always ended up being fed whatever I was working on. It had become this odd little routine and ritual that we'd settled into—talking about our days over random bits of puddings at midnight on Tuesdays, long after the dinner service had finished.

Connor's days were getting longer too. The studio was

flourishing, and his pole career was taking off. He may not have gotten into the East Midlands Championships or Chrome Stars that first year we were together, but the year after he'd taken them by storm with a sensuous routine that combined ballet and pole with his signature sexy style. He'd spent months perfecting it until his body was bruised and sore and his feet were battered. I'd been a little concerned, but he'd told me it would be worth it when I saw the finished routine. I'd been sceptical, but then I'd seen him perform. It had been incredible, and had left both myself and the rest of the audience utterly speechless. He'd been the runaway winner at both competitions, and it had put him on the map as both a performer and a teacher. These days, he focused on teaching ballet and pole as well as workshops that combined both. He'd even been invited to teach a four-day workshop in Greece earlier this year, and they'd already asked him to come back in the autumn. I was so proud of him that it permanently felt like my heart was going to burst out of my chest.

"I'm starving," Connor said from beside me. "But yes, apart from that I'm having the most wonderful day."

"I thought you ate four cones of fish and chips?" I asked with a grin.

"They don't count, babe. They were just a snack. Besides, that was like an hour ago." Connor looked up at me, a cheeky grin on his perfect, pink mouth. His lipstick hadn't moved an inch, which I knew he'd be pleased about. He'd conducted very thorough testing over the past six months to find the perfect one, attempting to find one that wouldn't move after food, drink, and very thorough kissing. I hadn't minded being subjected to his experimentation, especially the kissing part, because nine times out of ten it had escalated into something more. Connor had been determined to make sure the testing was rigorous.

"Don't worry. Five more minutes and they'll feed you," Mary teased. "Then we just have to keep you away from the cake."

"Oh God, I'd forgotten about the cake. Does it look pretty? I've still not seen it."

"It's gorgeous. You'll love it," Mary assured him. The cake came courtesy of our cousin Lou, who'd happily become one of Mary's preferred cake suppliers and had been more than happy to make ours. She and Connor had several very long and in-depth phone discussions about flavours, and I'd been happy to leave them to it. I knew it would be amazing.

And it was.

I didn't get a chance to have a look at it properly until after the meal and the speeches, when people were wandering around, getting drinks and waiting for the ceilidh to begin. It was three tiers, each one a different flavour, lightly smeared with buttercream icing so although it was covered, you could still see hints of the cake underneath. Semi-naked, Lou had called it. It was decorated with little meringue kisses with colours swirling through them, creating a rainbow effect around the cake, and little piles of strawberries. It was completely and utterly perfect.

"Do you think anyone would notice if I stole a meringue

off it?" Connor asked, leaning in close to me. "I don't think I can wait another hour to cut it."

"You just ate a three-course meal, including half my pudding!" I'd been completely stuffed by the time we'd gotten to pudding, whereas Connor seemed to be nothing but a bottomless pit. When he'd seen half the chocolate and caramel tart on my plate, he'd batted his eyelashes sweetly until I'd slid it across to him. How he could even think about eating something else was beyond me.

"Yes, but this is cake, and there's always room for cake."

I laughed and kissed him. "I'll ask Mary if we can bring it forward. Anything for you, beloved husband."

"I'm going to make you say that so many times later," Connor whispered. "I love the way it sounds coming from your mouth."

I bit my lip, trying not to make a sound, and keeping my face as neutral as possible, even though the grin on his face told me Connor knew exactly what he was doing to me. "Don't be rude."

"That sounds like a challenge," Connor said and raised an eyebrow. "For later though."

"You're incorrigible."

"But in the best way." He slid his fingers into mine and brought my knuckles up to his lips. "Come on. Distract me until we get to the cake, or I am literally just going to shove my face in it."

I threw my head back and laughed, dragging him away to find Aaron, Josh, Ben, Levi, Darcie, and the rest of the restaurant staff. I'd issued an open invitation to the reception and Ben and Aaron had closed The Pear Tree so everyone could come. They were all drinking and chatting with some of the people from the dance studio, and it was nice to see everyone getting on so well. Connor and I sat with them for a bit before we were kidnapped by some of my smaller nieces and nephews, and by the time Mary came to find us to cut the cake, I didn't even realise an hour had passed.

"There you are," she said, giving us a smile. "Do you want to come and cut the cake?"

"Um, does the Pope wear a silly hat?" Connor asked with a grin, grabbing my hand and towing me towards the barn. "Are we doing that thing where we shove cake into each other's faces or is that just something they do in films? If so, please just put it in my mouth. Don't waste good cake."

"I think that's just a romcom thing," I said.

"Thank fuck."

A crowd had gathered around the cake by the time we arrived, and the photographer took a moment or two to place us and check the lighting before Mary handed me a silver knife. Connor wrapped his hands around mine and we sank the blade into the bottom tier, red velvet with a berry filling, while everyone cheered. I grinned and plucked a piece of fruit off the cake, gently pushing it into Connor's mouth. His lips brushed against my fingers. He reached for the front of my jacket and pulled me into a kiss, and I could taste strawberries on his tongue, wild and sweet. It was the taste I always associated with him, ever since that time in the kitchen.

I thought about how far we'd come in the last two years,

and how much of life we still had to live. I wondered if it would always be the same.

I wondered if whenever he kissed me, he'd always taste like strawberries.

THE END

ACKNOWLEDGMENTS

Connor and Patrick had been floating around in my head for eighteen months before I finally managed to put them on paper, and I hope you've enjoyed reading their story as I much as I enjoyed writing it. As always, I have many people to thank for this book's existence. Nothing I create exists in a vacuum and is always the result of the input and support of some wonderful people.

Firstly, I have to thank Ceri for teaching me pole dance for the past two years. I'm well aware I'm as graceful as Bambi on ice, but you make me feel like I can actually do it! You've given me so much confidence in myself and I love you. And to everyone who's ever been part of the Thursday Night Improvers Crew—you're all fucking amazing and you all inspire me.

To my husband for continuing to put up with my mad writing dream and letting me ramble at you about all sorts of ideas and characters. And to Rosie and Ros for the same.

To all my friends in the writing community: Toby, Alie,

Carly, Gwen—thanks for cheering me on throughout the summer while I wrote this.

To Susie, who listens to me ramble, cleans up my terrible grammar and asks me all the questions about my characters that I forget to ask myself.

To Natasha for yet another wonderful cover. Seriously, they're all so pretty and you continually take my breath away.

To Abbie, for the last-minute proof and all your support. And to Stacy for making my life so much easier each day.

And finally, to my readers. Thank you for reading and for all your support, I couldn't do this without you. I said this was a standalone... and it really was meant to be one... but I'm not sure it will be.

ALSO BY CHARLIE NOVAK

Off the Pitch

Breakaway

Extra Time

Final Score

Roll for Love

Natural Twenty

Charisma Check (Coming 2021)

Standalone

Screens Apart

Short Stories

One More Night

For a regularly updated list, please visit:

charlienovak.com/books

CHARLIE NOVAK

Charlie lives in England with her husband and a dachshund named Biscuit. She spends most of her days wrangling other people's words in her day job and then trying to force her own onto the page in the evening.

She loves cute stories with a healthy dollop of fluff, plenty of delicious sex, and happily ever afters – because the world needs more of them.

Charlie has very little spare time, but what she does have she fills with cooking, pole-dancing, reading and ice-hockey. She also thinks that everyone should have at least one favourite dinosaur…

Website charlienovak.com
Facebook Group Charlie's Angels
For day-to-day-musings, giveaways and teasers.

Plus sign up for her newsletter at charlienovak.com for bonus scenes, new releases and extras.

facebook.com/charlienovakauthor

twitter.com/charlienwrites

instagram.com/charlienwrites

bookbub.com/profile/charlie-novak

amazon.com/author/charlienovak

Printed in Poland
by Amazon Fulfillment
Poland Sp. z o.o., Wrocław

21550568R00179